FOR A VIKING'S HEART

ANCIENT SONGS
BOOK 4

LAURA STRICKLAND

ARE YOU SIGNED UP FOR DRAGONBLADE'S BLOG?

You'll get the latest news and information on exclusive giveaways, exclusive excerpts, coming releases, sales, free books, cover reveals and more.

Check out our complete list of authors, too!

No spam, no junk. That's a promise!

Sign Up Here

www.dragonbladepublishing.com

Dearest Reader;

Thank you for your support of a small press. At Dragonblade Publishing, we strive to bring you the highest quality Historical Romance from some of the best authors in the business. Without your support, there is no 'us', so we sincerely hope you adore these stories and find some new favorite authors along the way.

Happy Reading!

CEO, Dragonblade Publishing

Additional Dragonblade Books by Author Laura Strickland

Ancient Songs Series
For a Warrior's Heart (Book 1)
For an Exile's Heart (Book 2)
For a Wild Woman's Heart (Book 3)
For a Viking's Heart (Book 4)

The Three Sisters MacBeith Series
Keeper of the Gate (Book 1)
Keeper of the Hearth (Book 2)
Keeper of the Light (Book 3)

*Do our ancestors travel with us
In the strengths that we possess?
In the lessons learned from past failures
And the longings born of far-off losses.
In the sudden knowing that draws heart to heart
And life to life,
Is there a surer way for spirit to travel
Than in the trading of what is, for what has been?*

—Finlay the Bard

*A*T THE HALL *of a Scottish chief deep in the western Highlands, a bard entertains those gathered, singing and telling tales while accompanying himself on the harp. He weaves his tales in praise of his host's ancestors, with a rare talent that keeps his listeners enthralled from the highest to the lowest. Amid the leaping torches and the flickering candles, there is magic encircling the great chamber this night.*

Now the hour grows late. Already the bard has told three stories to great effect, holding his audience captive with a combination of bright notes from his harp and singing words from his throat. He glances at the chief at the head of the hall, seeking a sign that he should draw this entertainment to an end.

The chief makes a gesture. More, he signals. The audience has not tired of the bard's phrases, and the spell he has woven still holds strong.

A gleam of green flickers in the bard's eyes as he returns his gaze to the face of one young woman in the hall, she to whom, above all others, his heart speaks.

Has she heard what he had to tell her? Has she understood?

He smiles, smiles only for her, and his fingers wring beauty from the strings of his harp. Once long ago, he tells them, when danger did come from the sea, there was a woman so strong she would let no man do for her...save one. List again while I sing for you now a song for a viking's heart.

CHAPTER ONE

Western Scotland, the eleventh century AD

A S HE DID every morning, Quarrie MacMurtray climbed the foot-worn stone steps to the walls that defended the keep, and gazed out to sea.

Last night had been a rough one here on the western Scottish coast, a storm not external like they had so often, but within the keep itself. Quarrie had managed to snatch very little sleep, and he felt now as if he emerged from some dark cave of suffering into the light. For the sun rose behind him, the salt-laden air smelled sweet, and the world held a soft calm.

Deceptive, that calm. As he knew very well, danger lay everywhere. That knowledge had brought him up here at first light, moving like an old man rather than one just past a score and five years, to search and search the horizon. For whatever other troubles beset the clan he loved so well, his first duty must be defense.

Summer fast approached. They would be coming.

This keep where he lived was strong, wedded to the rock. It had been here a long time perched above the stony shingle, enlarged by successive generations. It overlooked both the sea and the passing of time, one coming and going like the other in an endless circle. On a morning such as this, it all looked so peaceful. But a man could not be careful enough, for out among the sleeping green islands, death might wait.

Death, so his ma always told him, just started another cycle.

She was a bit fey, was Ma, and believed in the old ways, the ones of which folk rarely spoke anymore. She it was who had taught him that those who went from them were not truly gone. They could expect to meet again—not in this life, perhaps, but in the next.

Preparing him for Da's death, she might have been. Or remembering all the partings they'd had. Da had been dying a long time. Other partings had been far more sudden, like his best friend—

Someone stepped up next to him with a rattle of light armor. "How fares the chief?"

Borald, the head of the guard and also a good friend to Quarrie, took the place beside him at the wall. Borald had five or more years on Quarrie, a good, steady man and one for whom Quarrie was daily grateful.

Choosing not to answer the query—for it would be far too painful—Quarrie said instead, "Wha' are ye doing here? I thought ye'd be longin' for yer bed."

"Aye." Borald's steady, dark eyes gazed out to sea just as Quarrie's had, and he gave a funny shake to his broad shoulders. "I lingered for the light. I wanted to see—Och, I had this feeling."

"As do I," Quarrie agreed unhappily. It could not be good that the both of them felt it. "See anything?"

"Nay. Though in among the isles…"

Quarrie narrowed his weary, gritty eyes and looked again. The ocean shone silver, as might a sheet of beaten metal. Surely it would be easy to see a dark sail, often the first harbinger of danger.

"How is the chief?" Borald asked again. "I would no' push, but—well, we could all hear him last night. Raving."

To be sure, they would have. Even though Quarrie and Ma both had done all they could to quiet the man, from beseeching to physical restraint.

Attempted physical restraint. Da was still a strong man, and one driven by the impetus of pain both of the body and the spirit.

Quarrie sighed. "'Twas no' an easy night."

"I could hear that."

"The chief is—" Quarrie possessed no words for it.

"Ill?" Borald suggested.

"Aye." The word came out like a groan. Quarrie dropped his head, removing his gaze from the sea for just a moment. He could not give in to despair. If he did, his ma might, though she had more faith than anyone he'd ever known. If she lost faith, the clansfolk would also.

Then they'd all be lost.

Borald's hand settled heavy on Quarrie's shoulder in a gesture of comfort. He said nothing.

"I believe he will grow well," Quarrie said doggedly, to Borald or himself. "I still believe so."

"His wound—"

"'Tis no' healed completely, nay." After the better part of a year. Da had taken the slash, a deep cut to the thigh, while fighting late last summer. It had poisoned and refused to close over. Old Drachan, who looked after them all, had recommended removing the leg.

Da had refused. "Wha' sort o' chief would that mak' o' me, eh?" he had demanded. "How would I go about my duties then?"

For months, he had tried to go about his duties. The pain had been paralyzing and had gradually prevented it. Since last winter, he'd been off his feet.

The wound stubbornly refused to heal. In the back of his mind, Quarrie feared if it would not, his father would indeed perish slowly.

That was not the worst of it. Something had turned the man's mind. All the losses, mayhap. The constant pain and uncertainty. The same things that had Quarrie climbing the stone steps up to the wall this morning.

"Aye, well," Borald said without conviction, "I am sure it will. He will grow well. He is a strong man, and a strong chief. Ye ken, Quarrie, if ye ever need a hand wi' him in the night…"

To hold him down, Borald meant. To hold him down when he raved. Did all the clan know Da was slowly going mad?

"Thank ye," Quarrie said.

With deep sincerity, Borald told him, "There is none here who would no' gi' his life for Chief Airlee, and ye need no' think ye maun keep it hidden."

And could not, following a night like the one just past.

"He grieves," Quarrie choked out. "For those lost, for his own inability to defend the place as once he did."

"Aye, so he has stood between us and those northern bastards many a time. Kept us free."

"Aye." Quarrie lifted his gaze to the sea again.

"Now he has ye. That should comfort him."

It should. It did not always, at least not when the fever beset Da and the pain grew sharp teeth.

"Would ye like to hear somewhat funny, Borald?"

Borald cocked an inquiring eyebrow at him.

"When I was young, I wanted to be a harper. A musician and no' a warrior. Naught more than that. I would listen to the traveling bards who came to stay with us on their yearly rounds. And I thought, wha' higher calling could there be in the world than to spread such beauty? Such laughter.

"Then I learned that as well as beauty, the world was filled wi' treachery and danger. Wi' duty. And I learned wha' my role would be. Since my father put my first sword in my hand, I ha' known it would hold naught else."

"Ye will be chief one day. I suppose there is nay choice in it."

"I will be chief some day." If he survived.

"Ye will mak' a fine one. And we will stand behind ye even as we ha' stood behind—" Borald broke off when Quarrie stiffened. "Wha' is it?"

"There. On the horizon. Is that...?"

"Where?" Borald leaned out dangerously far over the rampart and stared. "I see naught."

It is a shadow, only, Quarrie told himself. The shadow cast by a cloud. Only there were no clouds. All right then, it was a dark ripple of current or—

"There," he said despite himself. "Just alongside *Oileán Iur.* Ducking behind the island."

Many of the islands just offshore, little more than small lumps of rock, were uninhabited. Attackers liked to use them for cover.

Like any canny hunter.

Please, God, nay, Quarrie beseeched silently. Heartfelt. *Nay.*

Borald caught his breath. "Could be a flock o' sea birds."

Or a sail. One barely glimpsed for the glare of sunrise on the water. A peaceful morning after a tortuous night. It should be peaceful. He had earned that, not more blood, more killing, more death.

He blinked and the sail was…gone. What he'd thought was a sail.

The sickness remained in his gut.

"They are bound to come raiding," Borald said like a man trying to reason with himself. "They always come raiding as soon as they can get their damned longboats out o' the northern slips. Why should they hit us, though? They hit the monasteries, mostly. Or the isolated settlements. We ha' always put up a strong defense. Just like last time."

When Quarrie's da took his injury.

"They will no' want to throw themsel's at us again." When Quarrie said nothing, Borald added, "Why would they?"

Quarrie knew why. The Norse came, aye, in search of wealth. Valuables stolen from the churches. Gold and weapons from settlements. Slaves. They did not waste their time or resources killing for the sake of it.

But for revenge?

Last summer, in the act of taking his dire wound, Da had killed the leader of the Norse attackers. Quarrie had himself witnessed that battle—a vicious one, it had been. Fought right down there on the rocks of the shore.

Airlee MacMurtray had generations of good warriors behind

him. He had taken the attacker's head. It had seemed to affect the whole of the attacking force powerfully.

They had called off the raid, taken the body of their leader and their numerous other dead. They had not returned.

That did not mean they would not. They'd had a winter and a spring to lick their wounds. To nurse their grievances.

Who was to say those northern warriors with their strong blades and their cold eyes would not come seeking revenge against those who had killed their leader?

If so, they would come here.

"Tell the men to keep a close watch," Quarrie told Borald. "No' ye," he added when the man looked at him. "Ye go to yer bed."

"I think no'. I will stay a while yet."

"As will I." Quarrie narrowed his eyes on Oileán Iur again. He would stay to be sure, just until this feeling inside him consented to lie down.

CHAPTER TWO

QUARRIE'S BONE-DEEP WEARINESS did not fade, but he had to retreat from the walls eventually, leaving other men, all severely cautioned, in his place. He had more tasks to which he must attend.

By the time he entered the keep, the sun had risen high and strong. It would be a beautiful day, and any sails playing at hiding among the offshore islands would be clearly seen.

He wondered why that knowledge did not reassure him as it should.

His mind ran through a list of possible catastrophes and solutions as he went looking for breakfast. The settlement, large and thriving, had spread outside the walls and nearly up the hillside. If attack came, all the women and children would have to be gathered within the protection of the walls. Either that, or they must be sent away inland until the attack ended. One way or the other, if he thought they stood in danger of being overrun, it would be his duty to see that happened.

He made these kinds of decisions now, not Da—even though in name, Da remained chief. And would, so long as Quarrie could assure it.

Gathering the women and children into the fold would mean they'd need sufficient food. Fortunately, they had a well inside the walls. But there needed to be enough weapons, also.

The Norse were not known for launching a siege. They were hit-and-run attackers, bringing blood, destruction, and often flame, seizing whatever they could in the confusion.

Could he defend against an attack? He stopped where he was, outside the great hall, to contemplate the question. It depended on how many longships came. It might be one—a scouting party or a lone venturer. It might be a trio or as many as ten.

Whether or not he thought he could defend their land would make the difference in bringing the women and bairns inside, or sending them away. He could not bring them in only to be overrun and see the lot of them slaughtered.

The women would include Norah. And her babe.

That thought hit him like a punch to the gut. It had not stopped hurting yet. At one time, he'd believed that Norah's children would be his own.

He knew better now.

"Quarrie?"

His mother stood leaning out the door of the hall, striving for his attention. She looked weary and drawn, not having obtained any more sleep last night than he. She it had been who'd helped hold Da down throughout all those long, dark hours.

Dark in far more than the lack of light.

"Son, have ye had breakfast?"

"Nay, no' yet."

"Then come away in."

She would seek to feed him, never mind her own exhaustion. Always thinking of others, was Ma. He followed her reluctantly into the hall, which lay dim and empty, full of shadows and the scents of countless fires and countless feasts. Quarrie's ancestors had been here so long, no one could remember when this chunk of rock had not been theirs.

How dare the accursed Norse try to threaten them from it?

"Sit," Ma said. "Eat."

The place she had set, not bothering to light a fire, looked pitifully small in the great room. Quarrie sat, and she settled opposite him. Though he felt hollow inside, the bannock cake she offered did not tempt him.

He rubbed his hands over his face.

"I wanted to talk wi' ye," Ma said.

"Aye." They needed to talk. Rationally, if it were possible to set aside their emotions. Likely not.

He lowered his hands and looked at her. A lovely woman once and still, despite all the trials she had borne. The loss of several babes long ago. The loss of Quarrie's younger brother, Kyle, in battle two years past. And now—Da.

He did not favor her, his ma. She had honey-gold hair and pale gray eyes. He took after Da, copper brown and hazel. Her pale skin—

Now bloomed purple on one cheek.

"How did ye come by that bruise?" Quarrie caught his breath. "He never struck ye? Da?"

Her eyes met his for an instant and promptly filled with tears. "He did no' mean to. His arms were flailing. He caught me—"

Quarrie's remaining interest in his breakfast fled. His da, for all his strength and ferocity in battle, was a gentle man with women and in fact had drummed that lesson into his sons.

We are here to protect our women, always, lads. Especially the women we love.

As he loved ma.

He had not meant to hurt her, nay. He had been off his head last night. That did not make it any better.

"Ma—" Quarrie began, but did not know what to say. He had been there. He should have protected her.

"'Tis all right." But her lips trembled. "He is sleeping now. I had to gi' him double the draught the healer left. I hated to do it, but—"

"Aye." He had begged her, last night, to summon the healer. She had refused to get the elderly man out of his bed till early morning.

"'Tis just that he is in so much pain," Ma half wept. "It turns his mind."

It had turned Da into a stranger, a man they barely knew.

"We ha' increased the strength o' the draughts to where he is either near senseless, or—like he was last night. The healer says if the draughts cease to work, we will ha' to restrain him. Quarrie, that will kill yer father."

It would. Yet they had in fact already restrained him last night with their own limbs, if not by binding.

"I think"—Ma raised her eyes to Quarrie's—"ye should take over for him. Tak' the place o' chief officially, is wha' I mean. Now, at the beginning o' the season, in case there is trouble."

Quarrie's stomach clenched so violently that he wanted to vomit.

"I ken fine," she went on in a voice that trembled, "ye are already performing all his duties."

"Why no' just carry on that way, then?" he asked hoarsely. Because his taking the title of chief from his da—that was like admitting Da would never get well. That they, as a family and as a clan, would not overcome this horror that beset them.

"Quarrie, I do no' think your father will grow well."

It was as if she stole his thoughts from him. He might not look like her, but he and his ma were a lot alike.

She was at her breaking point. Staring into her eyes, he could see that.

He was very nearly at his.

"I think," she said softly when he did not speak, "the people need this. They need to see ye at the reins."

"They do see me." Every day in a hundred ways.

"Aye, so. But they need to see someone standing at their head." Tears now trickled, unheeded, down her face. "Someone strong."

"Da is strong." The evidence of it lay in that bruise on her cheek.

"Aye, he is. He always has been. He gave me two strong sons. 'Tis time for one o' them to step into his place."

"Ma—" Quarrie pushed his breakfast away. The wave of nausea that threatened arose and swamped him. "Folk love Da.

They will understand."

"Quarrie, they ha' barely seen him since winter. They canna follow a man they canna see." When still Quarrie said nothing, she shook her head. "I suggest ye meet wi' members o' the council today. Put the matter to them. See wha' they say."

"I can do that."

"I will attend wi' ye, if ye like." She leaned forward and laid her fingers on his arm. "I will urge them strongly to make the right choice."

There were no right choices, in a world gone wrong.

CHAPTER THREE

Hulda Elvarsdottir narrowed her eyes against the glare of dawn and gazed hard at the strip of land. Naught but cold rock it was, with a gray keep crouched at the midpoint of the headland, dwellings spread out from it higgledy-piggledy like errant children at their *móðir*'s skirts. It did not look like much of a target, yet blood had been spilt there. Norse blood.

"Duck in behind the island," she told Garik, the helmsman. "Swiftly now."

She did not want to be seen. Not yet. The Scots had quick eyes, and like all along this rocky coast, they kept good watch.

Garik obeyed, but Ivor rolled his eyes at her, his lips set in an insolent line. Ivor, her second-in-command.

Curse him.

When she had talked her *faðir* into letting her make this venture, taking one of his longboats and returning to the Scottish coast—and a long, hard argument it had been—he'd agreed only if she'd take Ivor along with her.

Ivor had been second-in-command to her brother, Jute—and his close friend, though Hulda had never understood why. They'd all grown up together, but she had never taken to Ivor, finding him crafty and sly and all too often cruel. No matter; he and Jute had been blood brothers sworn.

So she undertook this voyage lumbered with him.

Thus far he had questioned everything she did. Disapproved of most of it, and of the whole venture in deed, if not in spirit. He wanted revenge, *ja*, for Jute's death. He merely did not think Hulda could achieve it.

Who else, though? She and Jute had been born less than a year apart and were close as twins. He'd taught her everything she knew about fighting. About sailing.

A great deal.

She had not been with him last year when he was killed. Here, upon this stretch of shore. She'd been off sailing with Faðir, raiding farther north.

Ivor had been here. Another reason Faðir wanted her to bring him.

"He knows the coast, Hulda. And he is a strong sword."

He was. A vicious one. She sometimes thought Ivor killed for the sake of it, even when he did not have to. Did he not know slaves were more valuable than dead men—and women?

"If you are going to attack," he said now, in full hearing of the whole crew—the men she commanded—"then attack. Morning is the best time, when the lazy bastards are still trying to lever their asses out of their beds."

"I know what I am doing," Hulda told him. She had a plan, one Ivor would not like. Nor would Faðir, truth be told. But this was her venture, her chance to avenge her brother.

Ivor needed to learn he must accept her decisions. Answer to her will.

Perhaps a punishment, if he continued to speak out so freely against her. He did not think her woman enough to do that. He would learn.

She had questioned many of those who had accompanied Jute on his last voyage, and had a good idea what had happened to him. She had also gathered knowledge of these islands, clustered like sleeping dragons off the shore. Many of them, like the one behind which they now hid, were small and uninhabited. Rocky and barren.

"There." She gestured to a narrow inlet that pierced the rocks ahead of them. "Can you take us in?"

Garik eyed the rocks that flanked the inlet. Nodded. He was young but an excellent helmsman. A good crew all round, but for Ivor.

"Are you mad?" Ivor asked now, baring his teeth at her. "You cannot take us in there. You'll scrape bottom."

"Take us in," Hulda ordered Garik again.

On a wild day with high seas and storms pounding the rocks, it would be impossible. And if weather came, as it did so often along this coast, ja, they would be trapped. Foolish, as Ivor said.

But no one would see them tucked in there against the isle, not from any direction. If it stormed, they would just have to sit tight. For days if need be.

Would that not drive Ivor to a berserker's rage?

Once Garik had them safely within the rocky arms of the inlet, she walked to the rail and stood looking out as the men dropped anchor and prepared to settle. Not much to see but those stony arms, more stones on the shore, and the rough green turf of the barren island. From here, she could not even see her goal. Her target.

As she might have predicted, Ivor was not done with her. He approached her with that swagger he so often employed. A tall woman, she nearly matched him in height, him being a not especially tall man. So their eyes were nearly on a level when he glared into her face.

Dark eyes, Ivor had, brown tinged with red, unusual for their race. It was rumored his mother had been a slave from the eastern lands, some place called Constantinople. He'd inherited her dark hair, though he had his father's brawn and cunning.

Hulda could not say for sure, since the woman had died long before ever Ivor and Jute became such fast friends.

As she had many a time, she wondered what Jute had seen to like in the fellow. His slyness, perhaps for, ja, Jute had possessed a measure of that also. His cunning and his dark sense of humor.

"Before you begin to rant at me," she said, "I will remind you of who is in charge of this war party."

"It is not a war party," he retorted. "It is a pleasure cruise, so far."

She drew a breath and wondered how best to deal with him.

Before she could speak, he said, "Your brother died out there."

"Which is precisely why we are here."

"Skulking."

"We are not skulking. We are the cat waiting for the mouse, which does not know it is there."

That made him blow a breath between his teeth. "Cats! I came for vengeance."

"And you shall have it."

"We are Norsemen. We do not play at games."

"You want to redden your sword?"

"Ja."

"And you shall. But it will be done my way."

"Women," he mumbled under his breath, but meant for her to hear.

Ja, to Hulda's knowledge he had extensive acquaintance with women. Young maids, older widows, even the jarl's daughter, so it was rumored, and all manner of slaves. Jute used to speak of it when he thought Hulda could not hear, and sometimes when she could.

She narrowed her eyes at him. Faðir joked sometimes that his daughter had the most intimidating stare of all his warriors.

"Pity the fellow she weds," he'd said, "if ever she deigns to accept any husband."

She had no time for following after men. They made her impatient with their bluster and their insistence on being right. Rarely, since she'd grown from a girl to a woman, had one turned her head.

There had been Karl. That thought arrested her where she stood. Karl had betrayed her. And then he had died. Swift justice, that, but it just went to show…

She did not need a man.

"I thought," Ivor said roundly, "we came here to attack."

"You thought that, did you?"

"Ja. It is why I came."

Hulda deliberately took a look over one shoulder and then the other. "Do you see a fleet of longboats?"

Ivor's expression settled into a glower.

Hulda went on, "That is a strong settlement out there. So strong that when my brother came last year with three boats, he met with defeat. You think we can batter them with one?"

"Then why are we here?"

The rest of the crew, with the boat at rest, had moved in close and listened. Hulda spoke to all of them.

"We are here to take revenge on the man who killed Jute. But we will be clever about it. I mean to negotiate."

"Eh?"

"Those who were there at Jute's death—you yourself, Ivor, say they think it was the leader of the settlement who struck Jute down. The chief. That man will not know how many ships we have hiding here.

"A good chief will surely sacrifice himself to save his people. It is what these Scots do."

Ivor studied her face. "You are mad."

"And once he agrees to deal with us, we shall betray him."

CHAPTER FOUR

ALL DAY LONG, Quarrie could not shed his feeling of disquiet. As if trouble hung off on the horizon, waiting for him.

Half a score times he climbed up on the walls to look out over the blameless sea. He questioned the guard until they began eyeing him doubtfully.

The days had been growing longer, and that was an advantage for them. Just as the Norse could get their boats to sea come spring, so also did the gloaming give defenders hope of spotting the longboats. Yet as evening drew down, Quarrie's uneasiness merely increased. He could not claim to have the Sight. And he was not sure what he'd seen—thought he saw—that morning, but...

Something was out there.

He remained worried enough to bring it up in the meeting of council, the one Ma had requested to discuss Da's condition. They met just at nightfall, there in the hall.

Not a council as such, naught so formal as that. These were but men who over the years had become Da's advisors, and his friends. A few aging warriors. The smith, Ronold. The persistent wee priest who insisted on saving them all.

They exchanged glances with one another before turning their eyes on Quarrie.

"Master Quarrie," said Fergus, who looked after the armory, "wha' is this all about? 'Tis no' the Norse already?"

It was, though Quarrie did not want to bring that up yet.

Before he could speak, the wee priest spoke up. "The blessed father who passed by yesterday—he is an itinerant fro' Ireland, ye understand—said the Norse have sacked the church at Oban. No' much to steal, but they left many dead."

"Abominable," old Morchan said. One of Da's longstanding cronies, he would remain pagan to his grave, though that did not keep him from great indignation over any slight to a Scottish church. Any excuse to fight.

For the most part, the fledgling Celtic churches here in Scotland were not rich. Not like the ones farther south. But they were easy targets, and some of the brothers were taken as slaves.

Most men in Scotland would be hard pressed to say which was worse, slavery or death. As for the women…

"If and when the Norse show their sails," Quarrie said, "we will be ready to fight. Wha' I brought ye here to discuss is the chief's condition."

A moment of complete silence ensued. Quarrie found himself faced by almost identically dismayed expressions.

"He is getting better, surely?" said Fergus then. "I ken fine that wound he took was a dire one. I was fighting near him when he got it, and saw him take that Norse bastard's head in spite o' it."

Another man, Connor, said, "The healer assured us all then, wi' time and rest the chief would be right as rain."

Aye, the healer had said that. But the blow, from not a sword but a Norse axe, swung hard, had cut nearly to the bone.

Quarrie looked the men in the eye. "Aye, so the healer did hope. So we all hoped. But ye ken poisoning set in. The wound did no' heal clean. In truth, it refuses to heal at all."

"Still?" The word came in a hush.

"Still."

"The chief is a gey strong man," declared one of the advisors. "A bull."

He had been.

"I will no' lie to ye," Quarrie said steadily. "'Tis why I ha' called ye here, to speak out the truth. My father's great strength wanes. He canna stand on the leg, and the pain"—he did not want to speak out the rest of it, though it must be said—"the pain is driving him mad."

Appalled faces turned to him.

Before any of them could speak, the door of the hall rumbled open and Ma slipped in. Her footsteps made no sound as she walked down the length of the chamber to the gathered men.

She did not strictly belong here in the midst of a meeting. Yet every man there knew Airlee MacMurtray adored her. They themselves honored her. They stood and waited for her to join them.

As if she'd been listening outside the door, she began, "I pray ye will listen to and heed my son. I believe 'tis time he should step into the place he has been holding these many months wi'out the title."

"But, mistress, Airlee is our chief. We each and every one o' us swore fealty to him."

Ma looked around at them with her calm gray eyes. Eyes that had become unaccountably fierce. "As has Quarrie sworn fealty to him."

"Aye, so. No one would question Master Quarrie's loyalty or his heart. But 'tis Airlee we follow."

"Ha' ye followed him to his bed?" Ma asked. "When is the last time any o' ye went there to see him? D'ye ken the state he is in?"

Not a man there, and they the leaders of the clan, said a word back to her. They must have heard the commotion coming, at night, from the chief's quarters. Had they denied what that meant?

"Ye, Morchan," Ma challenged the oldest of Da's friends. "When is the last time ye called upon yer chief?"

"To tell ye the truth, Mistress Einid, it has been a while. The last time I did go, he seemed discomfited to see me. As if—" The man ran out of words.

"He is embarrassed and shamed that he canna get out o' his

bed. That he can no longer stand for his clan as he has for so long. The pain is unbearable. Nay draught nor drink can stem it. 'Tis I and Quarrie who ha' been there day and night as he's struggled beneath the weight o' his injury."

The men stared at her in dismay. Still, no one else spoke.

"We begin a season," Ma went on, "that may hold much of fighting and strife. I am here to tell ye, since the chief will no', out o' shame and distress tell ye so, he will no' be able to lead ye through it. He has a fine son." She indicated Quarrie. "One I mysel' bore him. I call upon ye to let the torc pass to Quarrie."

The men began to murmur, a groundswell of muttering at first and then everyone speaking at once. Protest. Acknowledgment—aye, Quarrie was a fine lad, but Airlee remained their chief.

By the time the full of them had their say, Quarrie knew the truth. They were not likely to accept him as chief. Not while Da was still alive.

They would follow him, aye. They might take orders from him if they believed those orders fell within the lines of what Da would do.

But Airlee—muddled or not—would remain Chief Murtray till death.

He stood with an impassive face and heard it out. Ma stood silent also, her expression stricken and her eyes full of tears.

"Go to see him," she urged when they quieted down. "See him, all o' ye, and mak' yer own judgment. If ye wait for your chief to hand off leadership o' this clan to Quarrie, 'tis a thing he will never do."

Too stubborn by half, was Da. And no more ready to believe he would never go to battle again than were these men.

But he would not. And the incipient madness, the same Quarrie had witnessed last night, told the truth.

Da would not want these men to see that. By the same token, they could no longer hang back from accepting Quarrie as leader. Not if the worst happened.

"Mistress," said Fergus heavily, "if the chief will no' hand off leadership o' the clan to his son, how can we tak' it fro' him?"

The other men mumbled again, in agreement.

One of the tears welling in Ma's eyes spilled over and trickled down her cheek.

They looked away then. They no more wanted to see her weep than they wanted to see their chief on his back, weakened.

That was the true reason they had not gone to see Da for so long. They would rather lie to themselves.

Quarrie stepped forward. Ignoring the disappointment in his heart, that after nearly a year leading the clan in truth, these men still refused to acknowledge him, he said, "If an attack comes from the sea, we maun be ready. I urge ye spread the word. Talk to yer women. Have them pack up wha' they may need if we see sails out there upon the water. They may be better off awa' in the hills than here." He added deliberately, "Should we fall."

Unthinkable that women like Norah, for whom, despite himself, he still cared, might be stolen away. That children might be slaughtered. That the huts huddled around the keep might be burned to the ground.

"We will no' fall," Ronold declared roundly. "How many generations ha' we been fending off those bastards? Ha' we ever fallen?"

"Nay." Quarrie stared the man full in the eye. "And how many times over the years ha' our women and children taken shelter out upon the breast o' the land while we fought for them here? 'Tis best to be prepared, wha'ever ye think. For when attack comes, it comes swift and hard."

He looked from face to face before he added, "I do no' fear the Norse any more than my father. Gi' me a chance. I will lead ye against them. But I will first seek to spare every life under my care."

They nodded. This, they would accept.

They began to file out. Quarrie stood like stone beside his mother and waited. Not till they were alone in the big, echoing hall did Ma slump and say into her raised hands, "They did no' listen. They did no' believe me."

"They do no' want to believe." Neither did he. He did not want to accept that his big, bluff father, who could roar with laughter and work hard every morning at training before tending the cattle, had become a man who roared instead with pain and threw things at the wall in madness.

He and Ma had been there. They had seen.

He took his mother in his arms and let her weep, a storm of tears kept in far too long. It needed out, the way a storm needed to break.

"Hush now," he bade when the worst of it ebbed. "We will carry on as we ha' been."

His position in life did not matter. So long as he stood strong.

CHAPTER FIVE

THEY SPENT A cold night out on the water, it still being early enough in the season for a chill to come with the dark. In this case, it felt as if the icy air had followed their longboat down from the north and now gripped them in its claws.

Going viking, as Hulda well knew, was an elemental business, subject to every sort of change in the weather and the sea. Being trapped aboard a boat with a score of males was likewise elemental. They fell subject to their elemental urges—anger, pride, hunger, lust—and seemed to give very little thought to any of it.

And folk said women were subject to their moods…

Hulda had known these particular men all her life. For this venture, she and Faðir had between them selected each man. Yet she was already sick of their childish jokes, their careless bickering and complaints.

Men, ja, were like the weather. One could do naught but put up with it.

These men—all but the despicable Ivor—had been chosen for their reliability, their skill at sailing, and their strong backs when rowing became necessary. If they did not overly question her orders, it was a bonus. But they, like any good Norsemen, had come along on this venture for profit. Bored near to death after the long winter, they'd been apt to jump aboard any vessel heading out of the bay.

Still, she would have to offer them something.

The settlement where Jute had died did, indeed, look large and no doubt wealthy. Also well defended. She would have to be careful if she meant to satisfy her men. She would have to be smarter than anyone else involved.

She got very little sleep and was up before the sun, staring out at the ocean and the rocks of their little isle. The men, other than the two guards she'd set for the end of the night, still slept, wrapped in their cloaks, snoring and farting.

Garik, who was one of the crew members Hulda could best tolerate, soon got up and came to stand with her at the rail. He was young like most of the crew and had been a friend of Jute's. Well, everyone in their settlement at Avoldsborg had been a friend of Jute's, him being well liked.

Garik towered over her even though she had a decent height. He had very fair hair, clear blue eyes, and a number of tattoos that had been poorly applied.

He nodded at Hulda before leaning on the rail. "Going to be a clear day," he said.

"Ja. We will move out of the inlet in a while and let ourselves be seen."

"I wanted to say, do not listen to Ivor. You know what he is like."

"I do."

"He will try to undermine your authority for the sake of it. He did the same to Jute."

"Did he?" That made her eye her companion.

"Ja. I was on that voyage, when Jute died. Here in these waters."

The very reason Hulda had brought him, as well as some of the others.

"Jute and Ivor were great friends. Yet Ivor loved to needle him."

"Ivor loves to needle everyone."

Garik agreed, "It is how he is made. Do not let him discourage you. If you think you can win this through negotiation or sleight of hand—do so. We are but one ship.”

“And it is a strong settlement.”

Garik shrugged. “Ja. I was fighting on that shore not far from Jute when he went down. These are not defenseless holy men.”

That made her eye him again.

“And Ivor—” Garik began, and paused abruptly.

Another man had joined them at the rail. Was it Hulda’s imagination, or did the clear morning darken a whit?

Ivor asked, “Did I hear you speak my name, Garik?”

“Ja. I was but saying to Hulda, you must want vengeance more than any of us, Jute having been such a good friend to you.”

“I fair thirst for it.”

Hulda nodded. Behind them, the rest of the crew were coming awake, grunting and coughing.

“But,” Ivor went on, “it seems we hang here like that cat outside the mousehole.”

“Ja,” Hulda told him, “and today the cat will show her face.”

“QUARRIE—A WORD, IF ye ha’ a moment.”

Quarrie paused and faltered when the words met his ear, just as if he’d hit a stone wall.

Last night had been peaceful—doubling up on Da’s draught seemed to have worked—and he’d managed to catch some sleep. But it had made him late coming out to begin the day’s first rounds.

He’d had the most curious dream…

About a woman, it had been. He dreamed about women only seldom. When he did, it was usually the sort of dream that beset most men from time to time. Of spending himself in passion, usually—disquietingly—with someone he knew.

This had been different, very different.

She’d stood before him, close, her hands lightly gripping his forearms. And a sight to behold with a wild mane of brown hair swirling around her, and eyes of bright silver. Her gaze fastened to his.

She spoke to him, and her voice wove in and out of him like an ancient song remembered. Lightly accented yet familiar, her voice was, and rooted in his soul.

"Always you say, my love, that you will find me—no matter where. No matter when. This time mayhap it is I who shall find you."

"Quarrie?" The voice speaking his name here in the cool, quiet morning was also familiar. He spun to find Norah at his elbow.

Norah, holding her wee bairn in her arms.

Emotions speared through him at the sight of her. Only, surely, because he had not expected to find her here. He was over her, was he not? He no longer loved the woman. He could not say he'd ever loved her. He'd been *attached*.

She was a lovely thing. Small and delicate, with large gray eyes and dark-brown hair. A rosebud mouth. Sweet buds at her breasts also, and he had tasted them. Och, aye, he had.

He'd once believed, aye, he would wed with her. That she would birth his bairns. Now she stood looking up at him with another man's babe in her arms.

The child of his close friend.

He told himself all he felt now was an echoing sense of betrayal. Of anger.

Both of those emotions made him look at Norah coldly as he said, "Mistress."

She made a face. She could be mischievous, could Norah. Or coy. Now she appeared chiding, or perhaps rueful. "How long are ye going to stay angry wi' me?"

Forever, perhaps. Or just till he stopped caring. "I am no' angry, mistress," he lied, and accompanied it with a stiff bow.

"Then why d'ye no' call me by my name?"

He had no answer for that, but her name still would not leave his lips. "Wha' is it?"

"Corban says we are to prepare for a flight to the hills, we women and children." She jiggled the babe in her arms. "Have sails been sighted? Already?"

Quarrie looked at the child. A wee lad—of course she would give Corban a son—he had dark hair like hers and big, solemn eyes.

Corban. Supposed to be loyal to him.

"'Tis best to be prepared at this season. Should attackers appear, I would ha' an orderly flight rather than a panicked one."

"I suppose that makes sense."

"If I can do naught else for ye, mistress, I am needed on the walls."

He made to step past her when she reached out and touched his arm. "Quarrie, I want to explain—"

She had explained it all before. With tears and desperate wailing, she had. How she'd never meant to betray him. How she and Corban—who, like the rest of them, had known each other all their lives—had suddenly felt something springing up between them.

Quarrie just bet they had. And he knew precisely what.

"Quarrie," she said again, "people canna help who they love."

Nay, he supposed not. But they could help going behind the back of someone who trusted them. Who expected naught but honesty. Who did not see the knife coming before it sank in between his shoulders.

Well, that was the thing about a knife in the back, was it not?

He made himself look into her eyes, deep in. Lovely eyes they were, tipped up a little at the outer corners and fringed by dark lashes.

"Do no' be angry wi' me," she repeated. "Ye used to look at me so kindly."

Aye, and he'd learned that lesson, had he not? Not to go blithely giving his heart away.

She whispered, "I did care for ye—"

Aye, mayhap just not enough.

He detached his arm from her grasp. "Excuse me, mistress. I am that busy."

He had time to see tears fill her eyes before he walked away.

By heaven, did he not have enough troubles without adding her in?

$$\text{━━◆━━}$$

CHAPTER SIX

"**M**ASTER QUARRIE? MASTER Quarrie, come quick."

The call came from the top of the wall and carried a note of urgency that had Quarrie's pulse speeding. The guard was about to change, with the dawn. One of the men set to depart, it was, who cried out.

The fellow's name was Lohr, and though barely twenty, he had a serious nature and showed a lot of promise.

Even as Quarrie's feet thundered up the steps, he called again, "A sail!"

Och, by all that was holy, no.

"Where?" Quarrie gasped out even as he joined Lohr and the other members of the night guard, including Borald, who stood at the line of wall that faced west.

Another soft, clear morning it was, and rare enough to have two in a row along this stretch of coast. Rain came swiftly here, in frantic bursts as swiftly gone again, and the wind could threaten to pluck a man from the parapet.

This morn, though, looked like a dream, utterly still with the light reflecting out on the water. The islands clustered there gazed at their own images like a woman gazing into a glass.

Far too lovely a morning for incipient death.

"Where?" he repeated even as he saw. *He saw.*

It hung out beyond Oileán Iur the way a hawk hangs in the sky, motionless, just before swooping in upon its prey. An apt enough comparison—indeed, the stillness of the image had

Quarrie blinking his eyes and then blinking again.

Was it really there?

Other men came running up the stone stairs, crowding the wall.

Far enough off the boat was, to make Quarrie doubt himself. Near enough that—

"They want to be seen." He said it aloud. Whoever commanded that boat knew as much about these distances as he. Showed himself in the bright light of the morning. Wanted them to know he was there.

A threat? A dare?

"Just the one?" he asked Lohr. "Ye ha' seen only one sail?" A vital question. One boat, and he had a chance. A flight of them—

The very thought turned his stomach.

"Aye, only one," Lohr said grimly. "So far."

What did it mean?

Quarrie narrowed his eyes against that reflected light. The keep faced west and the sun rose behind them, stretching over the hills to the east. The sail—most of what he could see of the boat—showed black. Unmoving.

Borald came pushing in beside him. "He wants for us to see him, aye. That's deliberate, that is."

"Aye." Quarrie breathed it. But why? Such attackers came swift and hard. They did not float there like something out of a dream.

He thought again of the dream he'd had, of the woman with the brown hair. No ordinary dream, that. But he could not waste time contemplating such things now.

To Borald he said, "Mobilize the men. See everyone armed. Spread word among the women for them to be ready. Keep them fro' panicking, if ye can."

He spared a fleeting thought for Norah and her wee boy. His every instinct was to protect them, despite the pain.

Borald rolled his eyes. If a group of Norse boats hung over the horizon, there would be no holding back the panic.

He dashed off. Another body came pushing in beside Quarrie. Coban. His former good friend.

Coban was as fair as Norah was dark, with a rough-hewn sort of face and a wide mouth now set in a grimace. Arguably one of the last people Quarrie wanted to see.

"Are they movin' in?" Coban asked.

"Nay. No' yet. Just hanging there."

"Why?"

"The devil knows."

"They must know we can see them."

"Aye." A game it was, Quarrie decided. He would much rather deal with what was, terrible as that might be.

The men around them began to mutter.

"I do no' see any other sails."

"Is he movin' to attack??

"Nay."

It seemed unreal as the moments trickled by and trepidation grew. The sail on the horizon continued to hang while more and more men and, aye, a few women crowded the walls.

"He's moving!" cried someone who must have very sharp eyes indeed.

Was he? Quarrie's gaze narrowed instinctively and then—the sail was just gone.

Men exclaimed. They cried out. To be sure, the sail could not possibly have disappeared.

He had moved back behind the island.

A game of cat and mouse, it was. He had waited there till he was sure the light was strong enough that they would see him from shore.

A chill of apprehension chased its way slowly up Quarrie's spine, leaving his whole body cold. What was this? Whatever it was, it could not be good.

HULDA LIFTED HER chin and closed her ears to the protests all around her. From Ivor, she'd expected it. From the others, nay, though now they were all complaining.

They wanted to fight.

She—she wanted the man who'd killed her brother. She wanted him dead, ja. She would prefer to take him home to Avoldsborg in chains.

So she let her crew's hard words wash over her the way waves washed the rocks of the shore. Those waves might do some damage, ja, but it would take a while.

A beautiful morning it proved to be, and the land beyond looked just as fair. The harshness of winter fast withdrew and the green of spring spread apace. In the distance, away toward the heart of the land, blue hills floated in the clear light. What mysteries awaited there?

The stories, as she knew, abounded. Her people had been taking captives, slaves, from these lands for generations. From them had she learned the Gaelic tongue. Having learned the tongue, she had listened to the stories.

They wove some fantastical ones.

Her faðir possessed a Celtic harper, taken from farther north. A talented man he was, who, after a few beatings and some threats to break his fingers, had settled in to entertain them.

Garan, for that was the man's name, insisted his homeland had a spirit and a heart deep within those blue mountains, lying there as beneath a fair woman's breasts. A mysterious heart.

Cursed if Hulda did not half believe him.

Did not such things also exist at home? There were the trolls who lived deep in the mountains, who—more—were made from the mountains. The elves who inhabited the forests and dales. The gods who oversaw all and whom one might encounter while out rambling.

Why, then, should she disbelieve Garan's stories? Unreasonable, that would be.

She seldom felt happier than when listening to Garan's music.

If happy could be the proper word. His music called up something from within her and gave her…peace. Perhaps that was better than happiness. A kind of dreaming peace.

She needed that now.

The men were bored, she knew that. She had not chosen them—or Faðir had not—because they liked to sit on their asses and whittle. Another day spent hiding between the arms of the little island might well drive them over the edge.

Garik came up beside her, and she turned to gaze into his eyes. A very fine young man, was Garik, with that far-seeing blue gaze and a face to rival Baldur's. Indeed, had she not sworn off men, she might well be interested.

She had sworn off men.

His eyes now held a rueful light. "Captain, are you looking for mutiny?"

"Nei, not in the least."

He cocked his head, not having to ask the question.

"Ready the *færing*," she told him. "We are going ashore."

CHAPTER SEVEN

B Y LATE AFTERNOON when the call came, Quarrie knew what must be happening. Or he *thought* he knew.

Since dawn he had haunted the walls, up and down so many times he'd lost count. In between he had fielded questions. Everyone who could catch hold of him had asked, much as Norah had, whether they must prepare for attack.

Even his mother had drawn him aside. "Son, are there sails—"

"A glimpse only, Ma."

"If we come under attack, can ye hold them off?"

Quarrie had met her gaze with his own. "I will do all I can." Including spend his life if necessary.

She hurried on as if she did not hear him. "Because I think yer father should be taken awa' wi' the women, if they are sent to the hills. He canna fight. He can barely stand. But—"

"Ye will ne'er persuade him of it," Quarrie told her. Abandon the keep during a fight? Was there a force on earth that could convince the chief to leave?

"But he canna fight," she repeated wildly for her. A composed sort of woman, this, she had lifelong been a foil for her husband's intensity. Driven beyond that now.

"He would ha' to be carried," Quarrie said. "Can ye see him letting his men carry him awa' to the hills?"

"Nay." Her hands twisted together. "Nor do I wish to see him slaughtered in his bed."

"Ma, I promise ye I will do all I can to defend this place with my own heart's blood, if that is what it takes."

"I know ye will. And ye are a fine warrior. The best we ha' seen, so yer father always says, for generations."

Da was not so bad himself, before his injury, so Quarrie reflected. Witness the fact that he had taken the fierce Norseman's head last season.

"Then trust me," he bade Ma. "We do no' even know as yet that this is an attack."

But when the call came from the walls, aye, his entire being ran to the defense, even as his feet carried him up to lean out and stare just like the guards.

Borald was there, leaning out so far he looked to tumble over, and turned a burning gaze on Quarrie.

"There," he said. "Look!"

The sail was back, a dark shape now against the early afternoon light.

"It came out fro' behind the island," said one of the other men. "We were all watching."

It hung there as it had before. And then it began an approach.

Narrowed eyes followed it with fear and dread. A single sail. Not so intimidating except for the fact that, as it drew closer, the silhouette became unmistakable. The big, square sail. The long, sinuous shape of the craft raised at bow and stern.

"Wha' in God's name are they doing?" someone wondered aloud. "Showin' themselves in broad daylight."

"Is there but the one?" another man asked.

Only one they could see. Anything could lurk behind the island.

"Wha' should we do, Master Quarrie? Send the women and bairns awa'?"

"No' yet."

A single ship. It might be overflowing with Norse warriors the way a grain store overflowed with vermin. But he should be able to hold them off. He should be able to protect this place he loved.

He barely breathed as they watched the longboat come in. It sailed gracefully over the still water, catching its own reflection. Like something out of a dream.

Or a vision.

When they could see it clearly, it paused. Quarrie noticed then that though the sail was up, there were men at the oars. He could see other men on deck. One at the tiller, a couple hurrying about. One standing beside the prow, gazing landward.

Staring at them.

The commander of the vessel, no doubt. He wore a helmet that caught the sun and a fine cloak, and was no doubt heavily armed. He gave no audible commands, made no gestures. Stood like stone when the vessel halted and the men threw anchor.

"What is this?" Borald asked.

Quarrie could not imagine. Not an attack. Not anything he comprehended.

The men on the longboat hauled something around. A curragh it was that they had towed out. Faint cries echoed over the water. Two men descended into the curragh before the commander, motionless till then, followed.

"They are coming in," someone said in total disbelief.

"Get men on the shore," Quarrie called, but men were already there. Members of the guard and some clansfolk all staring.

Quarrie said, "Get yer weapons. I am going down."

THE SETTLEMENT GREW larger as the færing approached, rowed by strong arms. Hulda had chosen two of her best men, level heads who would not go off before she commanded, but good fighters in a pinch.

They might all three be about to die.

She watched the scrambling on the shore—brought about by their presence—and marveled at the fear produced by one longboat. Such was the reputation earned by her countrymen.

Order and chaos she saw before her. Armed men chased away what must be the ordinary occupants of the place. Her fingers played about the hilt of the sword she wore.

One man emerged onto the rocky shore, standing firm at the place toward which the færing headed. She eyed him closely. Her opponent?

Was this the man who had killed Jute?

His stance argued authority, legs wide and feet planted on the stones. *His* stones, that attitude seemed to say. *You shall not pass.*

"Hulda," Garik said from behind his oar, "are you sure this is a good idea?"

"Ja," she lied. The closer she got, the less certain she felt.

Details came into view. The stronghold, up on the rise and out of reach from the sea, was a fine one built all of stone, the thatch on the roof weighted down with more rocks. Many were the other dwellings scattered around it. A stout guard stood backing the man who waited for them, and she could see they were heavily armed.

She could not see their faces clearly as yet, but would bet they held distrust.

The man waiting for her had brown hair lit to red where the sun struck it. He wore no helm but had a sword at his side, his hand on the hilt. He was tall, gracefully built.

A typical Gael, she told herself. One she would have no difficulty killing if it came to that.

Just a Gael. One on a rocky stretch of Scottish shore. Who had likely killed her brother.

"Halt," she told the men, and they shipped the oars. The small boat drifted. Everything on the shore froze.

"Who is leader of this place?" Hulda called over the waves, bellowing so the words would carry. She called in the Gaelic tongue, not considering them intelligent enough to know hers. "I would speak with him."

The man with the brown hair took a step forward, which put his toes in the foam. "I am he. What do ye want?"

Familiar was the cadence of his speech. Hulda's own nurse, Aoedh, had been a captive who spoke so. Like music, sometimes.

She tossed back her head. "I have five more ships waiting behind yon isle. If you wish to spare your settlement, you will speak with me."

A man dashed up to the brown-haired commander. They conferred briefly before he stepped away again.

"We ha' naught to say to ye. Be on yer way."

"You would prefer to watch your homes burn? Your people die?"

"Only try for it," he said.

He possessed confidence, she had to give him that. Ja, he it must be who had taken Jute's life.

"You would let me kill scores, when I want but one?"

"What one?"

Hulda floated there and did not say.

He called, "I value all my people."

"And yourself? What value do you set upon your own life, Gael? Are you worth more than your folk?"

That caused him to rear back a little. Aoedh had told her many stories. Her people prized the valiant. The tales teemed with self-sacrifice, or one for all.

Was this man not likewise valiant?

She bellowed again, "Let us talk about it."

"Madness," said Garik, behind her.

Ja, maybe she was about to die. But she did not think so. These Gaels loved their honor too well.

Before the man on the shore could reply, she called, "May I have your pledge of safe conduct for me and my men, until our talk is done?"

He hesitated. Her boat had floated in closer and she could now see his face more clearly. A woman needed to see a man's eyes before she could judge him.

He seemed to make up his mind all at once, as if the answer came from beyond him.

"Aye. Come awa' in."

CHAPTER EIGHT

THE NORSEMAN SPLASHED through the water without regard for the breaking waves. Of average height he was, and of slender build, with long strides that ate up the distance between him and Quarrie.

Quarrie experienced a moment of unreality, of time slipping in its steady pace so it felt he glimpsed another age, or perhaps events that had not yet happened or could not happen at all. An illusion possibly caused by the afternoon sun in his eyes that struck glare off the Norseman's helmet and set the sea to sparkling. But it shook him.

It shook him.

Two other men came behind the first, one of them trailing the line of the small boat. They did not advance far but stood in the foaming breakers.

A hush fell behind Quarrie. Not one of his people but trained their eyes here, yet there was not a sound besides the pulse of the sea, like the pulse of the world.

"Are you commander here?" the Norseman asked in Gaelic with his gaze also hard on Quarrie.

He nodded.

"Good. I come to you with the offer of a bargain." The man said it boldly, just as if he did not stand the focus of as many weapons as gazes. A strong, ringing sort of voice he had that called out, but the sound of it started an odd feeling in Quarrie's chest.

He backed up a step. He did not want to, yet instinct made him do so. "Wha' sort o' bargain could ye offer me?"

"I will spare your settlement. Your people."

"Och, will ye then?" Quarrie's eyebrows shot up. This man spoke his language well, and that was but one of the chain of surprises.

He must be in his bed and dreaming all this. That was it—he'd never yet come awake this morning.

"Ja. I want but one man. You hand him over to me and I will go away with him, spare the rest."

Quarrie flushed with heat, brought by disbelief or mayhap pure aggravation. He shook his head. "What man?"

"I do not yet know. He might be you."

The Norseman took three more steps forward out of the sea and onto the shingle. Onto the soil of Scotland. Quarrie looked into his face and saw—

He was not a *he*. He was a woman.

The realization shocked him so, it made him blink. Made him wonder if he was mistaken. For the person facing him was tall enough to be a man. Dressed like every Norseman Quarrie had ever seen in leggings and boots—now wet—a long tunic covered by metal and leather mail. A sword and several knives, including one strapped to a leg.

His gaze returned to the intruder's face, trapped beneath the helmet so he could see very little hair. The few wisps he could see were pale as flax. But many Norsemen had hair that color.

The features—the features were all wrong for a male. Strong, aye, with a straight nose and a firm chin. But the mouth—that mouth was feminine, and no beard had ever marred that skin.

Her eyes—they looked pale in the strong light. Not blue so much as gray.

"Ye're a woman," he said, nearly under his breath.

She heard. So did the men behind her, who stirred. Big brutes, they; he could not doubt their gender.

"Hulda Elvarsdottir is my name," she announced. "We are

from Avoldsborg in Norge. As I tell you, I have five more ships in my fleet, but we have not come to raid, at least not here. Not this trip."

"Then why do ye come?"

"For vengeance. I have told you I want but one man." She splashed out of the water till she stood beside him. She was not as tall as he. He was built long, so once her feet came level with his, he found himself looking down at her. Yet he could not deem her aught but…

Formidable.

He'd never seen a woman to match her. Nor imagined one.

"Which of us d'ye seek?"

"May we sit and speak of it? I have your safe conduct."

Quarrie had not given it, not precisely, yet she had given him no reason to strike her down. He did not know how to handle this. He'd never had a woman walk out of the sea in full armor to challenge him. Like an old tale it was, one Danoch the harper might tell.

His thoughts scrambled. He did not know how to choose. He dared not choose wrong.

"If I say no, ye mean to return to yer ships and attack this settlement, is that so?"

"I will burn it to the ground."

"And ye trust in any safe conduct I offer, that I will no' merely kill ye?"

She lifted sandy brows. "If I do not return, my men have orders to attack."

Her men. They followed her, this woman.

That gave Quarrie a kind of thrill. Surely caused by apprehension.

"Aye, so, I suppose ye had better come and talk."

HE LED HER to the hall because he did not know where else to take her. People stared. They stood grouped all along the way, some gaping, and inside, Quarrie wanted to do the same.

Just as part of him wanted this woman, this savage stranger, to be impressed by the stronghold his ancestors had built, that he worked so hard to defend. But when they paused outside the gate, Hulda Elvarsdottir's expression revealed nothing.

She had courage, he had to acknowledge that, walking straight in here alone, for she had barked at her two men in her own tongue and they had stayed with the boat. He might say she had balls of iron, if she'd had…

At the gate she paused and looked back, perhaps measuring how far into enemy territory she had come. A tiny frown hovered between her brows.

After looking down at the small boat and her two waiting men, she glanced at Quarrie. "You have not told me your name."

"So I ha' no'. Forgive me. Quarrie MacMurtray, I am." He bowed slightly.

"You are jarl of this place?"

"Nay."

"Not jarl. Chief."

"That is my father. Come in."

Borald stood at the door, fully armed, his eyes nearly bugging out of his head.

"Let us in, man," Quarrie told him. "And watch the shore. The lady has come to talk."

"Lady?" Borald's eyes flew to their visitor and narrowed. His face lit with astonishment. Aye, her disguise was very good.

If it was a disguise.

The hall stood dim and empty. Someone had lit a fire that morning, Ma most likely, but it had nearly gone out now. The servants would light it again before supper.

Quarrie's steps sounded loud, his companion's a bit lighter. Her weapons jingled. He saw her look around, but she did not comment.

When they reached the hearth, Quarrie turned to her. "Now, what is all this about? Ye maun admit 'tis an unusual—"

She pulled off her helmet. Quarrie lost all his breath.

Her hair, pale, ashen blonde, fell all around her face. It had been braided tightly to fit beneath the helm. It had to be, for there was a lot of it. The plaits came down like golden rain.

It changed her astonishingly, turned her in a wink to pure woman. Quarrie felt precisely like he'd been thumped hard in the chest.

He knew her, surely? As she turned to him with the helmet in her hands, there was something so familiar about her…

But nay. He had never seen this woman before.

"Pray, sit," he invited her, treating her, aye, like a guest because he did not know how else to treat her. "Will ye tak' ale?" Did a man offer a female warrior ale? "I will call the server."

He did so, signaling to Seonad, who stood concealed in the door that led to the rear alcove. Behind her, he could see a guard lurking.

They thought he was likely to have his throat cut.

Mayhap he was.

But when he turned back, Hulda Elvarsdottir was taking a turn on her heel, staring about the room as if fascinated. Surely they had such large halls where she dwelt.

"Please, mistress," he said, "let us sit. Say wha' ye will to me."

CHAPTER NINE

THE HALL WAS large and dim, and it felt oddly familiar, as if Hulda had been here before.

Only she had not.

To be sure, she had set foot upon Scottish soil elsewhere. Had fought and held the longboat off other shores. She had even been in the halls of other chiefs, helping Faðir to sack them.

Not like this one.

A sharp little shiver traced its way down her body. She told herself it came only of being so daring, taking this mad step alone with no men at her back.

Mad, ja.

But it was not just that. In some curious way, she knew this place. The very air smelled familiar. And even while walking up from the shore, the path lined by foreign faces, the ground beneath her feet had felt...well, as if she'd trodden it before.

And this man, this Quarrie MacMurtray...

She turned her head to look at him as he returned from instructing the servant. He, too, felt—

Ach, but she was overwrought. This step she took—this bid to have her way without bloodshed—played with her senses.

What sort of Norsewoman was she, to want victory without bloodshed?

He was tall, with a lithe yet powerful build. Wide in the shoulders and fluid in his movements. She would bet he might be quick in battle. A worthy opponent.

He had a mane of red-brown hair that had gleamed like fire in the sun outside and was now muted to something far more ordinary. A face strong in the brow and cheekbones, sharp at the jaw. He was curiously pleasing to look upon.

His eyes, out in the light, had looked green, and that was a magical thing. The elves, so the sagas told, often had eyes of green, as did those who carried elven blood.

This man, this Gael, could not possibly have elven blood.

She had not expected to be attracted to the man who had killed her brother, and she did not like it. But ja, as she figured, it must have been this man or his father that he said was chief, who had slain Jute. For Jute's men had told her it had been the leader here who had done the deed.

A man with a fiery-brown tail of hair, they'd said.

She sat next to the hearth and set her helmet beside her. Quarrie MacMurtray sat opposite her, both of them still heavily armed.

If it came to blows, if he betrayed his implied vow of safe conduct, could she best him? Mayhap, but then she would have to fight her way out of here.

If his honor broke, she was lost. Curious to rely upon the honor of an enemy.

"Mistress, why do ye no' tell me—"

The servant hurried in with the ale. Hulda felt glad. She needed the moment to gather her wits. His voice was like…

Music. Light and strong, and he sang the words she'd only learned to speak with difficulty. A beautiful language, his was.

"Thank ye, Seonad. Ye may go."

The woman scuttled off as if pursued by a monster. Hulda raised her cup and smelled the ale. Poisoned?

"Why do ye no' state wha' ye want o' me?"

"Ja." That she needed to do. Before coming ashore, she'd had the words all lined up in her mind. A challenge, she would make of it. A bid to persuade him. The sacrifice of one against the lives of many.

But this place played with her mind, scattered her thoughts. As did this man.

"Near the end of the last raiding season," she began, "we came here. My faðir's crews did. There was an attack. A battle down there on the shore."

"I remember." A curious look came into his eyes. His steady gaze did not waver.

"You were there? You fought in that battle?" She had been right. He was the man. That must be why she had these strong feelings toward him. Her inner self knew he had killed Jute.

"I was there."

"I was not. I was fighting with my faðir elsewhere."

"The women o' yer clan fight?"

She hesitated to answer that. She owed him no explanations. Yet she held his gaze and said, "I do. I fight my own battles. Always."

Thoughts flickered like light in his eyes. Again, she failed to identify them.

"I was not there," she emphasized. "My brother led that attack. He was killed there on your shore."

The very place where she had landed, mayhap. She might have walked across the spot where his blood flowed over the stones.

"I was very fond of my brother." That did not begin to speak to it. She had laughed with him, teased him, admired him. He had protected her when she was very small. He had taught her all she knew of sailing, of fighting, and of the sheer hard work involved in both. "I come now to avenge him."

Quarrie MacMurtray's brows flew up. Now she saw astonishment in his eyes. "I see."

"I come with a fleet." The lie flowed from her smoothly. "Mostly my brother's friends. We can take this settlement apart stone by stone, or I can allow you to buy my leniency."

"A price? Ye want a price?"

"I do."

Now she could see his thoughts racing. He had very expressive eyes, did this man. "We are no' that rich a settlement. We ha' many people for whom we maun provide."

"Rich enough. We have sacked, burned, and slaughtered for less. Yet I am offering you a way to avoid the slaughter. We need not redden our swords at all."

His thoughts reeled, she could see that. This man would not be good at keeping secrets.

"I ha' never heard o' your people acting so."

She shrugged. "We sail for gain. What fool would lose her men to battle if she could get what she wants without? Give me what I seek and we will sail away, trouble you no more this season."

His hands clenched into fists. "What is your price?"

He expected Hulda to name a measure of gold. She knew very well that gold from Ireland got traded among these isles. Or silver jewelry. He might pay her in weapons, though his smiths could not be so good as her own, who possessed fire magic. In gems. She could beggar his settlement with her demand.

Instead she leaned toward him and said, "But one thing will buy the safety of your settlement. I want the man who took my brother's life."

COLD DRENCHED QUARRIE from his head downward, a clammy sort of chill such as might accompany a sickness, when the woman spoke. For an instant the air around him wavered, becoming too bright even though the chamber remained dim. Through the glare of it, he saw the woman's face, only her face, and heard a murmur at the back of his mind.

This could not be happening. None of it.

That seemed so irrefutable he expected to awaken in his own bed. To sit up and think, *Och, that was a mad dream.*

Dreaming would explain so much. The woman in a Norse warrior's clothing. Her arrival this way. The sense he had that he knew her.

Had always known her.

Impossible, for surely she was like to no one he had ever met. Those uncanny, pale-gray eyes that watched him so carefully, that weighed his every reaction.

She wanted the man who had felled her brother. Without question, that had been his father.

Och, by all that was holy! What were his options? He could refuse and give her safe conduct out of here. Go to battle over it. A total of six ships, she said she had. 'Twould be a battle for the ages, one he did not know he could win.

If he tried, it would be costly. Widespread death and destruction. Even if he did fight them off, what would be left?

He could hand over their price. *Nay.*

He could persuade her it had not been Da, but another man who had felled her brother. *Him.*

"How can we be certain who killed yer brother? I remember the battle o' which ye speak." He drank deep of his ale, refilled the cup, and drained it again. She had not touched hers. Did she fear it poisoned? "It was mad confusion there on the shore."

"My brother was the leader of the men. First onto the shore, he would have been. Fiercest in the fight. His friends who were with him said he fought the leader, here." Her pale eyes met his again. "Do you say you do not remember?"

He could not say that. He remembered the fight, aye, and the Norseman's axe blade sinking into Da's leg. The stroke Da had made that took the man's head.

She narrowed her eyes at him and asked very carefully, "Did you see who felled him?"

"I did."

A breath escaped her, one that betrayed her emotions, though she kept an iron control. "Then you can hand over the man to me. We will go. Leave you in peace."

"Ye will leave us for the season."

"For the season." She waved a hand. "You have my word on that." Her tone implied that her word was cast in iron. "After that, I cannot say. My faðir has many warriors, many boats. They go where they choose."

They were a plague upon the world, but he did not say that. A season was a season and could give them time to prepare. It might give Da time to recover. If he did not recover, he might at least die in his own bed surrounded by those who loved him. Not hauled away among strangers, subject to every sort of punishment they could devise.

Quarrie had heard stories. They all had.

Hulda Elvarsdottir shifted for the first time. "Do you know the man who killed my brother? You say you were there."

"I was."

"You saw."

"I did."

"Then name him."

"'Twas mysel'."

CHAPTER TEN

"YOU ARE THE man who killed my brother?" From the moment she'd laid eyes on him, ja, Hulda had suspected it. The foremost among his men. A fine warrior, possibly fighting in his father the chief's stead. Who else could have bested Jute?

Besides, the way she felt about him—that was her inner knowing telling her so.

But now that he admitted it, she did not want it to be him. Regret took hold of her by the throat, and for the first time she wavered in her resolve.

For if he handed himself over to her in order to save his people, what she had planned included debasement. Ridicule. Humiliation. Pain and, at long last, death.

His gaze held hers, unflinching. "Aye."

She jerked up her chin. "Describe his death to me."

That surprised him.

"I would be sure I have the man who should pay the price for Jute's death."

"I took his head. The battle fell apart then. When his men withdrew, they took his body but his head remained here."

A particular source of grief to her. She had been away, ja, a member of Faðir's crew, and not come home until Jule's body had been laid out in state. Covered in wounds. As always, he had fought hard.

"Tell me what became of his head."

He did not want to. She could see that. "A trophy, mistress. It remained above our gate for some time."

Another long breath escaped her. "And then?" She wanted to hear it all, her brother's fate.

"Burned."

"At your orders?"

"Aye. 'Twas the decent thing to do."

"Decent?"

"Mistress, I can give no part o' your brother back to ye. I regret so, but that is the way o' it. If ye come here to our lands seeking battle, ye maun reap the results."

"This is a thing all warriors know." All honest warriors.

"It is."

"I have an offer for ye, Master—" She paused in an effort to remember his name.

"Quarrie MacMurtray," he reminded her.

"Son of the chief here."

"That is right."

"And where is he, your chief?" His father.

"Indisposed."

Hulda narrowed her eyes at him. She did not know what that word meant; it reached beyond her understanding. For the moment, she let it go. "He did not fight in the battle that took my brother's life?"

"He did."

"You fought alongside him?"

"Aye."

Hulda studied him, letting her gaze move from the mane of fire-kissed brown hair to the tense face, to his bared arms and knees. He bore scars in plenty. A warrior, aye, and it was not unreasonable to believe he was the man.

But something inside her, that bone-deep instinct, still was not certain. Or did not want to believe it.

As a woman, she was in the habit of listening to her instincts. They set her apart, often called disrespect down upon her, yet she'd learned to heed them.

Somewhat here was not quite right.

"Quarrie MacMurtray," she said solemnly, her tongue tripping over the unfamiliarity of the name, "I have come here to right a wrong that was done. My faðir, a powerful warlord, has sent me with many longboats to accomplish this. So I make you this offer. Hand yourself over to me and we will, as I have stated, spare your settlement. You will have my word as a Norsewoman on it."

His face tensed to white and a hard green light glittered in his eyes. "Why should I hand mysel' over to ye when we might well fight ye off, as we did last year? Come at me wi' yer warriors, and it just may be ye who lies down on those stones wi'out yer head."

Hulda made herself shrug. "You may fight us off, you may not."

"We did, as I say, last time."

"Last time we came with but three boats. This time I have six."

"Where are they, then?"

"They lie off behind yon island." If he knew these waters, as he must, he would know there was an inlet there, and that she could well speak the truth. If he did not believe her—why, still he must doubt. "If you choose to fight and we attack," she told him forcefully, "it will cost you. In blood. In fire and destruction. If you give yourself over to me, the punishment will land only where it belongs—upon the man who took my brother's life."

He was not a stupid man, this Scotsman. He would have some inkling as to what must befall him if he turned himself over into her hands. The voyage to Avoldsborg in chains. The march through that settlement. The tribunal, the sentencing. The torture.

By the time he died, he would be praying for it.

Had he the courage to hand himself over for that?

She leaned toward him slightly. "Surely you wish to spare your settlement our fury?"

"Fury, is it?" He stared into her eyes, deep. She could still see the thoughts moving there, but no fear.

No fear. A warrior, this man, to the heart.

How could she, daughter of countless warriors and no frail flower herself, fail to respond to that? To admire it?

"Ja," she said, ignoring what surged within her, or trying to. "All up and down these coasts you have felt our fury."

"As your brother felt ours, mistress."

It felt like a slap in the face, or as if he spat in her eye.

"Your brother came here seeking a fight. 'Tis what he got. He paid the price."

Dismay seized Hulda by the throat. She could not fail in this. She had argued long and hard with her faðir for this opportunity and the lend of the one boat. The crew. She could not return home empty-handed.

By the same token, having seen this settlement up close and having met its defender, she was certain she could not best them with but one boat.

In hatching this plan, she had counted on the honor inherent in these men who inhabited the islands, many of whom had in the past stood and sacrificed themselves. She had not imagined a standoff.

She pushed to her feet, abandoning her mug of ale. "I will give you until tomorrow morning to make your decision. Talk with your advisors, your chief." If he was here. "Contemplate what is best for your people. I will return for your answer."

He said nothing, though those bright eyes narrowed.

She jerked up her chin. "My safe conduct will hold till then?"

"It will."

She turned and stalked her way out of the hall, her spine tingling. This would be the moment he would sink a dirk into her back, if his honor broke. In truth, this would tell her what ilk of man he was, this Quarrie MacMurtray.

Her hand hovered over the hilt of her sword. She was very quick, and if it came to single combat, here and now, she would have to do Jute proud. She would not get away after she killed

Quarrie MacMurtray, but it would be a debt paid.

He did not attack her from behind. They went out into the beautiful morning and she stood for a moment seeing it for the first time from a defender's perspective. The strong gate. The slope leading down to the sea. She could see her two men waiting there, and the færing. The longboat beyond, floating on the mirror of the sea like a dream.

She must walk down that slope to rejoin her men looking unafraid, even though there would be five score blades waiting to take her life along the way.

Beside her, Quarrie MacMurtray raised a hand. A gesture, was it, providing her protection? Whatever the case, he did not accompany her back to the shore, only so far as his gate, and by the time she reached her men, her legs wobbled.

Sure she was, that she had lost.

"Well?" Kettel's eyes stabbed at her. "Have you finished your negotiations?" Clearly he disapproved, but she must forgive him that. His wait on the shore, prey to all those swords, must have felt a long one.

"For now, Kettel. Only for now."

"Let us leave here," Garik said. "My flesh is creeping."

"Ja," Hulda agreed. In her heart, she knew she would be back again.

CHAPTER ELEVEN

I N THE GREAT hall with his father's advisors once more gathered around him, Quarrie related all that had been said in the meeting with the Norsewoman, omitting nothing. They listened with incredulous, disbelieving faces and barely waited for him to finish before bursting out with objections and opinions.

"Six longboats, ye say? But we dunna see them."

"Hidden behind Oileán Iur, so she says they are. Waiting."

Several of the older men shuddered. They had seen enough of Norse invaders to dread the very idea of such an attack.

"They will cut us to pieces," said Borald.

"Nay so!" cried Morchan. "They will no' find it so easy as that."

"I did no' say 'twould be easy."

"We maun send the women and children off at once. Why should this Norsewoman keep her word and wait for morning to attack?"

"And—a woman!" cried another man. "Why would they send a woman? And what kind o' leader should she be for a fleet o' six boats?"

"A competent one, fro' what I could see," Quarrie managed to fit in before they were off again.

He let them rage for a time, getting the most of it out. Ma had come in and stood quietly at the door that led to Da's quarters.

"We maun ready our defenses," said Morchan at the last.

"Call up all the men. Distribute weapons. The armory is well stocked. If we reinforce the gate—"

"Yet most the dwellings lie outside the walls. They will come wi' fire, as they always do."

"Aye, we maun resign oursel's to losing much o' the settlement—"

"Unless we gi' them wha' they want."

Quarrie said it quietly, but it silenced everyone there. Ma took a step forward into the room.

"This woman," Quarrie went on far more calmly than he felt, "has asked for only one man."

"Ye canna believe her, lad!" Morchan cried earnestly. "'Tis a ploy. A way to get us to lower our defenses."

"How? How would it lower our defenses to hand over one man?"

"Ye are talking about a sacrifice."

"Aye."

"And wha' makes ye think if ye hand over one man, they will no' tak' him and then burn us to the ground anyway?"

Quarrie did not have an answer to that, not one he could present to these men. He simply believed Hulda Elvarsdottir.

He did not know why.

"'Twould be an agreement founded in honor."

"A Norseman has nay honor!" Morchan howled. "Yer wits must be addled if ye think different."

"'Tis a gamble," Quarrie agreed. "A risk I am willing to take."

"Nay." Ma spoke for the first time.

"Lad"—Morchan stepped up to Quarrie—"think on it. 'Tis a sentence o' death, whether they come back and attack us or no'."

It *was* a sentence of death. A quite painful and horrific death, without a doubt. One more terrible than Quarrie could likely imagine. Looking at it squarely, he asked himself if he had the balls. He loved his home, but—

Had he the balls?

"Besides…" It was Borald who once more stepped up to face

Quarrie. "They want the man who slew their leader down on the shore, last year."

"Nay," said Ma again.

This time Quarrie glanced at her. "No' to worry, Ma. I will no' turn Da over to them. I told them 'twas I who killed yon leader."

"But 'twas no' ye," Morchan said doggedly.

"The Norsewoman does not ken that. She was no' there. Besides"—a spasm passed through Quarrie—"I think they want a scapegoat. Someone upon whom they may loose their displeasure and hate. It need no' be Da."

"'Twas your father took that young man's head."

"And received in return the blow that besets him yet. Is it no' my duty as his son to accept this in his place?"

"I am no' sure it is." Borald looked angry now. "'Tis your duty to defend this clan."

"As I will be doing."

"Mayhap, mayhap no', depending on the honor o' some woman who thinks she is a warrior! This clan needs a chief, Quarrie." Borald shot an apologetic look at Ma. "Ours is dyin'."

That statement hung in the air of the hall the way a curse might. Aye, they had all thought it. Worried over it. Whispered it, mayhap. Even discussed it in ones and twos. But…

"All the more reason," Quarrie said determinedly, "for me to tak' responsibility. I canna hand over to torturers a man already at his last."

"Torturers," Ma repeated.

"Mistress Einid," Morchan said, "'twill no' be an easy death in Norse hands. We ha' heard the accounts o' wha' they've done to the monks. To their prisoners and to their slaves. I say"—he turned to eye Quarrie—"we should fight. Who says we may no' win?"

There were mutters of agreement.

One of Da's old friends said, "Aye, when she returns in the morning, let us meet her wi' cold iron."

"Six longboats," Quarrie said.

Again, Ma stepped forward. She was not a tall woman—not like Hulda Elvarsdottir—and looked tiny there surrounded by hulking men. She raised her gaze to Quarrie's face and spoke clearly. "I say we put the matter to yer father. Is he no' still chief? Should he no' have a say?"

"Nay, Ma. He is no' fit."

"He is no' well, perhaps, and he is suffering. Ye, son, have been taking many o' his duties. But for ye to make a decision o' this importance wi'out so much as consulting him—well, he would never forgive ye."

Quarrie writhed beneath these words. With Da so ill, he had sought to trouble him as seldom as possible with clan matters. He did not want to take this to him now, mainly because he knew what Da's decision would be.

Everyone in the chamber watched him, avid to hear what he would say.

"Nay," he told Ma, struggling with it.

"Son"—she stepped up and touched his arm—"should ye turn yoursel' over to this woman in his place, if they haul ye awa' to death or worse, wha' am I to tell him? Wha' when he asks for his lad?"

His lad. That nearly brought Quarrie to ruination.

"Tell him I serve this clan. And him."

Slowly, Morchan shook his head. "Mistress Einid is right. We canna go behind the chief's back in this. He is, for good and all, still chief."

"Let us tak' this to yer father," Ma said. "Master Morchan, yoursel', and me. Quarrie, 'tis his right to ha' a say."

Quarrie's every protective instinct rose in protest. But he could feel the will of each man there, his father's advisors, align with that of the aging Morchan.

They wished to protect him, these men who had known him from a child. Who had helped to raise and train him.

"Aye, so," he said, wondering how he might persuade his

father, a man who, despite the changes that had come over him this past year, possessed a valiant heart.

A sigh went around the chamber. Ma looked relieved—and agonized.

"Meanwhile," Borald said, "we will use the time to prepare. Alert all the men, ready the families to leave. Organize the armory."

Prepare to fight. Borald's words told Quarrie he too felt certain what Da's decision would be when the matter was put to him.

If ever Quarrie had argued anything with his father, it must be now, when he argued his right to spend his own life for this place he loved.

CHAPTER TWELVE

THE SWIRL OF water around the oars sounded loud in the quiet as the færing made its journey over the sea, quiet as a pond, and back to the waiting longboat. No one spoke on the way, though Hulda's companions shot her close looks.

Was it regret that kept them silent? The fact that they thought her three parts mad?

As mayhap she was.

She had not been quite right in her head since Jute fell. It was as if, upon his death, a force had been set loose inside her, one that insisted she seek justice. Now that she had seen the place where he had died, her tall, bold brother—when she'd beheld the very gate where his severed head had been displayed until the crows finished with it—she lusted even more strongly after that justice.

It would not be easy to attain. The settlement was a strong one. She should have begged more ships from Faðir, at least two, and more likely the six she'd told Quarrie MacMurtray she had.

Quarrie MacMurtray. What to make of him?

An attractive man, and no mistake. She had not expected, nei, to feel drawn to him, one of these folk responsible for the death of someone dear to her heart. The very man responsible.

Having battled all her life for a place of honor, of legitimacy among men, she did not waste much time desiring them. Ja, there had been Haakon. And only look how that had ended. She had sworn never, never again.

Just as she would ask no man to fight her battles for her, she would trust no man ever again with her heart.

Yet there was something about Quarrie MacMurtray. What was it?

As they rowed steadily and strongly to the longboat, she pondered it. Was it his appearance?

No question but that his appearance was pleasing, in an odd and foreign kind of way. All that copper-brown hair, and those eyes, glinting with green. But more, much more than anything about his appearance, it was the *feel* of him. A certain steadiness. A strength. A familiarity…

But *nei*. It could not be so. A man from outside her world. Beyond her blood and her understanding. It could not be.

He it was who had taken her brother's life. The brother who had known her best. Who had indulged her, who had trained her when no one else would.

For this man, she could afford no feelings besides hate.

Then why did he pull at her so? Was it, after all, because she wanted revenge upon him? Had her mind twisted it into something more?

So it must be, for she could not want the man who had quite likely killed her brother.

The færing bumped gently up against the side of the longboat and ready arms helped her aboard, even as the smaller craft was drawn behind. Anxious faces met her gaze, and she wished—ach, by Odin's eye she wished—she might have just a moment to settle her mind before having to make explanations to them all.

"Wait," she told Ivor, who had been hanging over the side as they came up, his expression hard as flint. He did not agree with this scheme of hers. He had made that much clear. "Let us return to the island before we speak."

He ignored that. "Where is the captive?" he called almost before her feet hit the planking of the deck. His voice held a sharp edge of sarcasm. "Has your great plan gone awry?"

"Not yet." She hated having to explain herself to any man,

and Ivor more than most. "It is called negotiation, Ivor, because it is not accomplished all at once."

He nearly spat with derision. "And so we are left languishing here? Waiting again?"

"How long?" asked another of the men, and Hulda realized how edgy they all were.

"I have given him—the leader there—until morning to decide whether he hands over the man who killed Jute to me."

"Such leniency," Ivor exclaimed. "This is what happens when a woman is put in charge. Our blades become rusty."

"Your blades," she retorted, "are still plenty keen. We will have our prize."

"And if he does not hand the man over, this leader?"

"Then we will attack and your blade will no longer thirst for blood."

They exchanged looks, this crew of hers.

Trym spoke. "I say we go ashore and explore this isle. I am tired of sitting and playing at draughts."

"There is naught on that island," Ivor objected, "but thistles and chiggers."

"I would like a fire tonight," Trym said, "if we are staying."

"Go ahead and build your fire," Hulda said. "Build several of them." The smoke would be visible from the settlement across the water and would lend verisimilitude to her claim of a large force.

That was, if Quarrie MacMurtray was watching. And she believed he would be.

DA WAS UP and pacing his chamber—if painfully—when Quarrie, in company with Ma and Morchan, went in. An astonishing sight, since it had been days since the chief had found the strength to leave his bed. He had even managed to get himself partially dressed, which made Quarrie wonder if he meant to venture out.

He and Quarrie looked enough alike to leave no question they were father and son. They had the same tall, lithe build, Airlee having gained a little more bulk over the years than Quarrie had yet attained. The same heavy, thick mane, though Airlee's showed more gold than copper, Quarrie having got some of his red from Ma, and since his injury Da had grown a crop of gray. They had the same far-seeing, hazel eyes, Quarrie's tending more to green. The same effortless strength.

That was, Da *had* possessed that strength.

He whirled now to look at them, moving on his good leg. Quarrie, who had seen the condition of the other, could not imagine how Da managed to stand. Fever burned high on his cheekbones.

"Wha' is going on? Somewhat is. I can feel it."

No doubt he could. He was a fine chief with good instincts. And the madness that sometimes claimed him when his fever burned high in the night did not appear to beset him now. His eyes looked clear and sane.

When none of them answered him, he demanded, "Are we under attack?"

"Nay, Chief Airlee," Morchan said. "Though sails ha' been sighted off shore."

"Sails?" For most Da's life, the Norse had been a threat, a promise of loss and destruction. "How many?" When again no one answered him, he switched his gaze to Quarrie's face. "Quarrie?"

"We believe there are six longboats."

"Six." Except for the spots of fever, Da's face paled.

"I ha' had words wi' the Norse leader, who wishes to negotiate."

"Wha'?" Da waved a hand, a sweeping gesture. "There is nay negotiating wi' those savages. All they want is plunder."

"This is different."

"Pray sit down, my love." Ma urged Da to a rug by the fire. It must pain her as much as Quarrie, seeing him on his feet.

Da went down with a grunt, every movement agony.

Ma spoke into his face. "Ye should no' be up."

"No one came when I called. No' even the servant."

"I am sorry, my love. We were all in the hall. Here, will ye tak' the draught the healer left for ye?"

"I am no' a child to be dosed. The draught clouds my mind. If attack is imminent—"

He could not fight, much as he might wish to. All three of them there could see that.

"When were these sails sighted? Why did ye no' come to me at once? Morchan? Am I no' still chief o' this clan?"

"Aye, Airlee," Morchan said.

"We are here now," Ma continued, "fresh fro' Quarrie's meeting wi' the Norse leader."

Da grunted, leveled his hard gaze on Quarrie's face. "Tell me."

Quarrie did, pulling no punches with it. In his opinion there was nothing to be won in doing so. As chief, aye, Da must have his say.

Whether that say would hold sway was another matter entirely.

Da listened with a hectic frown coming and going on his brow. "But," he said immediately when Quarrie finished, "'twas I who killed the man. The Norse leader."

"Aye, Da."

"Everyone who was there fighting on the shore knows 'twas I. How can ye suppose to tak' the blame?"

Quarrie said nothing.

Airlee MacMurtray went on, "If anyone should be turned o'er to these savages, it is me."

"Nay, Da."

"This woman…" Da's eyes quickened. "Ye say she is a warrior?"

"Aye."

"A curious thing. There ha' been strong women in our own past, if the old tales are to be believed." His eyes took on a faraway look. "Those who wanted to mak' their own way in the world. But a Norse marauder—"

"However unusual it may be," Morchan said, "she is here and making her demands. Chief Airlee, ye will agree wi' me that Master Quarrie canna be allowed to hand himself over—"

"That I do agree."

"He is far too valuable to us. Especially—"

"Especially wi' me dyin'." Da's gaze met that of his friend and ally, unswerving. "Nay, Einid," he said to his wife, "do no' weep. D'ye think I do no' ken my fate?"

"Ye will grow well," Ma insisted. "'Twill but take time."

"There has been time," he told her savagely. "A fall, a winter, a spring. I do no' grow well."

It was indisputable. Against his orders, the tears in Ma's eyes overflowed.

"Long ago," Da said in a much calmer voice, "I swore mysel' to this clan. As a lad, I did. To live for this place and the people who dwell here, a family. I swore to die for this place, if I must."

His fevered gaze touched each of the three faces in turn, those closest in the world to him.

"It seems that time has come."

CHAPTER THIRTEEN

HULDA SLEPT BUT fitfully that night, and in snatches. Wrapped in her cloak on the deck, she rose from time to time in order to pace before lying back down again.

A clear night; the sky arched overhead with a hundred-score stars, bent like a rainbow. She almost expected Faðir Odin to come striding down that arc to go walking upon the earth, here among men. To mayhap come and sit on the deck beside her and give her advice like a trusted friend.

Tell her how to handle these emotions that beset her.

When she left home, she'd had but one goal, to make those who had killed her brother pay. She had begged Faðir for the chance. It sometimes seemed she had begged most her life for her place in the world. There was a force inside her, a desire that said she would allow no one else to fight her battles. To die for her.

A great and terrible force.

She sometimes thought Jute was the only one who understood, her strong and wise brother. He had looked at her and seen more than a girl needing protecting. He it was who had supported and empowered her.

Then he had gone off from her, and not returned.

Unbearable. The very thing she had fought all her life to prevent.

It would not be enough to punish the settlement where he had died. She wanted the man, the very man by whose hand he had died. Had she met him today?

She did not feel certain. Her instincts were good, sometimes uncannily so. And her instincts about Quarrie MacMurtray said—

Ach, but they said far too much.

He might be hiding something.

She got up once more and went to the rail. Most of the crew had gone ashore to sleep and settled on the stretch of land above the rocky shore. She could just glimpse their swaddled forms in the light from the fires they had lit, as the stars began to fade.

Only Garik and Lars had stayed aboard with her. Lars always slept like a rock, in all locations and weathers, but Garik came now and stood beside her, looking out.

"You are worried," he said, not a question.

She slanted a look at him. Among the youngest of the men he was, but a talented helmsman, and she felt comfortable with him, glad he'd accepted a place among her crew.

"Ja," she said. "I am worried."

"What is it that worries you?"

A score of things, but she could not tell him that. A crew must have confidence in its captain.

"Ivor worries me."

That made Garik grin. "Ivor worries everybody. He is, you understand, like two men in one."

"What do you mean by that?"

"Ah, well, there is the reasonable, affable Ivor who will sit with you in the ale hall and tell dirty stories. Then there is the other one, who on a raid will split children on his blade with glee. I saw him do it to an infant once, still in its mother's arms. Down farther south, that was."

"No wonder they hate us, these people."

"It is not important that they hate us so much as fear us. It accomplishes half our task, so my faðir says."

"Rarely do I encounter the Ivor who tells stories in the ale hall. I see only the disagreeable Ivor, all too quick to criticize me."

"Ja, but it is you, Hulda, who command this voyage. That, you must remember."

He was right.

"What answer do you think you will get from the Gaels?"

"I think," Hulda said very slowly, with her eyes on the water, "this leader of theirs, this Quarrie MacMurtray, will turn himself over to me."

A LONG NIGHT passed with agonizing slowness, much of it spent by Quarrie in his da's chamber, where the man in question strove mightily to disguise his pain. Determined Da was to hand himself over, come morning. And for that, he would have to be on his feet.

Quarrie felt for Ma, who suffered as much as if she shared Da's pain. He would not take the draught from her, and she got less sleep than Quarrie, and that was not much.

Morning came still and clear. Quarrie went out to walk the walls and speak to the guard, which he had doubled the night before.

"Any signs o' movement?" he asked the men there.

"The smoke fro' their fires. Look."

Aye, if Quarrie narrowed his eyes he could see the thin threads of gray, streaming upward. It must be true, then, the tale of the six ships.

He knew the island well. In times gone by, he and his friends had taken a tiny boat and gone there to fish. To take some time away and pretend at being grown.

He knew the inlet. Was there room for six longboats?

They were clever craft, he knew. Narrow enough to fit between the stony arms of such an inlet, and they did not need much draft. Could sail up rivers, it was said. Floating weapons.

He cursed them one and all.

Borald came up and joined them on the wall, taking the stairs by leaps and bounds. He cast a questioning look at Quarrie but asked nothing here before the guardsman.

Not but everyone doubtless knew everything he and the Norsewoman had discussed by now.

"Signs o' movement?" Borald asked.

"No' yet."

"The women and children will be ready to leave this morn, at your order."

"Aye."

"I ha' chosen a number o' men to accompany them awa' to the hills."

It would not be easy out in the open, especially for women with small children and the men who accompanied them—a hard task, and yet they might be the only men of MacMurtray blood left alive when this was done.

"Send them," Quarrie decided. "As soon as we see those sails on the move." Better to be safe than sorry.

Borald nodded.

Quarrie let his gaze stray from the sea and wander over the settlement, blessed by the soft morning light. Would this be the last time he saw all these buildings standing? The place he loved, before fire took it.

He had few illusions. If he handed himself over, it would be to torture. Merciless abasement before a no doubt more merciful death.

Better him than Da.

Da would be up on his feet and moving this morning. If he could manage it. Quarrie needed to go and check on him.

"Stay here," he told Borald. "Keep watch."

"I will no' stir, no' before we see sails."

Quarrie heard Da yelling even before he entered the chamber. He hurried in to find Da struggling to get out of his bed. Ma strove either to assist or restrain him, along with the ghillie who served as Da's manservant.

Da's agony, though, thwarted his efforts.

Kalen, the ghillie, cast Quarrie a relieved look when he came in. "Best call the healer, Master Quarrie. He is in a lot o' pain."

Did Quarrie make up his mind as to what he must do at that moment? Or had it already been decided?

"Ye go for the healer," he bade Ma, and took her place, attempting to ease his father back down.

Kalen's appalled eyes turned to Quarrie. "He says, does the chief, he means to turn himsel' over to the Norse."

"Get awa' fro' me!" Da threw them off with unexpected strength. "'Tis exactly wha' I shall do."

"Nay, Da—"

"Am I no' still chief here?" Da's eyes burned fierce, and fever seared his cheeks. A determined man, and a very sick one.

"Da, let me meet wi' this woman first, and see wha' may be bargained."

"I will be at that meeting."

"Nay."

"The next man what says *nay* to me will feel my fist in his face."

Kalen backed off a step, clearly believing it. As did Quarrie.

"Hulda Elvarsdottir," he said, "is expecting to deal wi' me." He had a sudden image of her—that strong, oval face with its sculpted, somehow brutal yet still beautiful bones. The gray eyes, pale as water.

The way she looked at him.

"Son." Da reached out and seized a handful of Quarrie's tunic. Since he could not succeed in getting out of the bed, he drew Quarrie to him. "If ye think I will let ye turn yoursel' over to those savages and pay the price for a deed I committed—"

Gently, Quarrie freed himself from his father's grasping fingers. "We do as we must for the sake o' this clan. It does no' matter who pays the price."

"Lad…" Agony twisted Da's features, and he spoke in a low growl. "I am already three parts spent. Nay good to this clan. Whereas ye…"

Whereas *he* would allow Da to die, if die he must, in his own bed with the woman he loved beside him, if Quarrie had aught to do with it.

CHAPTER FOURTEEN

THE NEW DAY dawned clear, as Hulda saw when she dragged herself up from the deck where she'd had little sleep, but clouds gathered far out on the western horizon. The voyage south had been fair, as had these past couple of days waiting here to deal with the Gaels. But she knew very well how rain liked to play among these islands and could feel the moisture riding upon the breast of the water, beginning to breathe across its surface.

The men returned early from the island while she still contemplated breakfast, with Ivor in their lead. Ivor wore a scowl, and the first words from him were, "I am going with you to this meeting. I think it best."

"Nei," she told him. "You will stay here and command the party if I do not return."

That made him shift his weight and eye her impatiently. "You think they will hold you?"

"That depends, does it not? On whether the man believes I have five more ships in hiding." Quarrie MacMurtray seemed an intelligent man, but he was also a desperate one. And he, just like she, had no doubt chased his thoughts all night.

She did not enjoy chasing her thoughts. Like the men amid whom she'd grown up, she usually tended to make her decisions swiftly and then keep to them, considering the matter done.

Naught was as usual here. Her feelings were all stirred and would not stop with clamoring at her. Her feelings toward Quarrie MacMurtray—

Why should she have any feelings for him?

Yet she did. She did. Even though he may well be the man who had killed Jute. Even though she might have to watch him die after immense suffering. To perform the deed herself.

As the one nearest to Jute in blood, that would be her right.

Ivor scowled still more deeply. "I will not go back to your father and tell him you were killed upon this shore. You had best let me go with you so I can prevent it."

Ja, Faðir was a powerful man in Avoldsborg. Not the jarl but close friends with the jarl and considered one of his cronies. And a man of great wealth, which he had amassed by a combination of ruthlessness and good sense. Faðir would not be happy if she failed to come home. He might well take it out on Ivor.

"I will go with the two men I took yesterday," she told him, "and rely on the Gael chief's honor."

"His *honor!*" Ivor sounded incredulous. The other members of the crew had gathered to witness this battle of wills, looking curious rather than alarmed. Despite their youth, they had seen much, these men, and were surprised by little.

"These vermin have no honor," Ivor declared, which was not truly fair. Though he had slaughtered them and taken many captive, he did not know them.

Quarrie MacMurtray has honor. She did not say that aloud. Could not tell how she knew, save by the way his eyes had met hers and, ach, the feel of him.

She could not wait to lay eyes on him again.

That thought shocked her. It shook her.

She told herself things might well have changed overnight. He could have people talking in his ear, as did she. His honor might well have bent.

"I will come back," she told Ivor, told all the men. "I hope with the man who killed Jute."

Trym grinned at her. "We will sharpen our knives."

The rain had crept in from the horizon before they left, and the scent of it accompanied them as they set out, taking only the færing this time. The men, used to being out in all weather, rowed hard. The settlement grew steadily larger as they rounded the island and approached the shore. A haze of smoke spread out above it, making it look misty and indistinct, like something out of a dream.

Surely Hulda had seen this place before. Before yesterday, that was, when she'd approached in the longboat. Ja, surely that was what she remembered. Why did she have a sudden vision—or memory—of approaching in a different boat with a man at her side, a man and a great, gray hound, and fear in her heart of a terrible battle taking place?

No battle occurred here now, not yet. But as they drew near, she saw that people waited on the shore.

Quarrie MacMurtray did.

He stood square, front and center. Legs planted on the shingle, hair gleaming red in the morning light. She could not mistake him.

For an instant, she felt time slip. The remorseless grip she kept upon the order of things failed her and flowed through her helpless fingers like water.

This had all happened before. *He* had happened before, in her life.

It felt like her heart would tear asunder. What was she doing here? She should turn around. Flee. She, who so seldom ran from anything.

But the men rowed on and she did not give them the order to stop. The færing grounded on the shingle. Kettel leaped out to pull it up.

Hulda stepped out with dignity, and as she did the rain found them.

As at some signal spoken by the gods, it swept up from behind and engulfed them. It crashed over them in a curtain, spreading up the shore, and filling Hulda's ears with sound. Drops upon the water, upon the stones.

She looked into Quarrie MacMurtray's eyes.

"Well? Have you made up your mind, Master MacMurtray?"

"Aye, mistress. I will go wi' ye. For I am the man who killed yer brother."

It felt as if the stones quickened beneath Quarrie's feet as he spoke those words. As if he had spoken them before. But surely then he had said, *Mistress, I did not kill your brother.*

Another time. Another place. But it all blurred around Quarrie, even as the scene blurred from the falling rain, lending a terrible unreality to this thing he did.

It would become real soon enough.

He turned to Borald, who stood beside him. Agony shone from his friend's eyes, and his hand hovered above the hilt of his sword. *Ye lead them,* he told his man silently. *Make a defense if need be.*

But he hoped what he did, this terrible step, assured no need for that. Bought their safety with his life.

"Take him," Hulda Elvarsdottir said, and her boatmen seized Quarrie, manhandling him unnecessarily.

Half a score of men, including Borald, stepped forward on the shingle. Quarrie threw back his head.

"Stand back!"

This was naught, he told himself, as Hulda, now with her sword drawn as if in defense of him, drove him onto their small boat. The two men sat to the oars and drew them out into the sea. And Quarrie prayed, as they moved off from the shore, prayed he would be able to withstand the pain that would come, endure it like a man.

The faces and the sights of the place he loved—loved right down to the marrow of his bones—fell away from him. The two Norsemen rowed, and Hulda Elvarsdottir sat behind him with her blade pricking the small of his back.

He had no illusions but that she would stab him. She would, in the blink of an eye, despite whatever it was that existed between them.

At the last, through the rain that beat down and the smoke from the settlement's fires, he saw his ma come running down to the shore. He knew, even though he could not see, that she wept.

No one aboard the boat spoke. It would have been hard to speak anyway, for the clatter of the rain. The craft was well built, light and agile. The men rowed well. Mistress Elvarsdottir stayed alert. As they rounded the small isle, Quarrie distinctly felt her tense.

Now, Quarrie thought, now he would see the fleet of Norse ships standing proud round the back of the wee isle, likely in the small inlet that lay there, where he and some of the lads used to go and swim. Now he would likely die there.

If he was lucky.

He tried and mostly failed to block memories of the stories he had heard, all the ways the Norse could make a man suffer. Suffer for their enjoyment.

Aye, death would come welcome.

It used to be, long ago, that when a warrior died he had hope his spirit would fly away to the land of *Tír na nÓg*, to remain ever young and ever happy. Quarrie did not want that. Rather he would hope his spirit, loosed, would fly the short distance over the water to that stretch of stony shore he loved, to abide there for an age, and another age.

There could be no better reward. He had only to endure what must come first.

He turned his eyes to the island and blinked. Shock and outrage had him starting to his feet in the small boat, making it rock violently. For no fleet of longboats sheltered in the lea of the island. Only the one—the single dragon boat that had approached the settlement.

He had been fooled. The woman had nay honor, and had deceived him.

Bright and sharp, he felt the point of her blade in his back. "Sit," she hissed, "for the sake of the gods."

CHAPTER FIFTEEN

"THIS IS NOT the man." Ivor barked the words as soon as they got Quarrie MacMurtray onto the longboat. A very angry Quarrie MacMurtray he must be, and perhaps abashed also. Hulda, sitting behind him on the færing, had not been able to see his face when they rounded the isle and he caught sight of but one ship standing there in the inlet. But she had seen his whole body stiffen, tensed for fight.

She had lied to him and he knew it. What would he make of the ruse? He would be enraged, ja, bitterly so. She knew she would, in his place. He had turned himself over to her for no good reason, since she did not doubt he and his settlement could have fought off the number of warriors she had at her command.

She half expected him to strike out as he was hauled aboard, to fight the men who handled him, but Kettel had bound his hands and taken his sword, and though he no doubt had other weapons stashed about him, he could not reach for them.

Now he stood on the deck of her boat and, staring at him through the rain, Ivor said, "This is not the man."

"What?" Hulda returned stupidly. Anger of her own, and heat, and a certain chagrin crawled up through her—for she had known it, in her heart she had. She turned her gaze on Mac-Murtray. So he had lied to her also.

His gaze met hers with a glint of green. *I trusted ye,* it said. Though the gods knew why he should.

She had wanted to trust him also—Freya knew why. So now

they were even, ja?

She turned a face to Ivor that she hoped did not betray her chagrin. He was the last man to whom she would display weakness or folly.

"He told us he was the man and turned himself over to us."

Ivor stepped up to her, his aggravation palpable. "Did I not say you should have taken me with you? I was there on that shore when Jute died. I saw the man who battled him and took his head. It was not *him*." Ivor swung round to sweep MacMurtray with another glare. "Had the look of him, ja, but it was an older man. One with authority. Mayhap the chief of the place."

Hulda too looked at MacMurtray. She and Ivor spoke in their own tongue, which she doubted he could understand. But he was not a stupid man and must garner much from Ivor's gestures and tone.

And ja, he must have expected this, if he thought anyone who accompanied her on this voyage had also been on that previous one.

His chin jerked up. He stood defiant. He must have some inkling of what they would do to him. He had sacrificed himself— for whom?

The person who had truly slain Jute.

"This is what happens," Ivor carried on in front of her men, her crew, "when a woman is put in charge. You do not think with your head."

"That is not true," Hulda said with calm she did not feel, as dismay weighed upon her. She always used her head. Except...there had been something else in her exchanges with MacMurtray. Some undertow of emotion.

Had she let it distract her?

She eyed MacMurtray once more. He stood proud and composed. And what was she to do with him?

"Kill him," Ivor pronounced precisely as if he heard the question in her head. He made a strong motion with his hand that MacMurtray could not fail to understand.

"Nei." Hulda spoke instinctively, a visceral reaction.

Ivor swept her with a scornful look. "What else is to be done? He is not the man. If you wish to follow through with your plan, you will have to go back and secure the man who took Jute's life."

"Ja. I will exchange this one for him."

"What? Like a ribband you do not like?" Ivor sneered, all the scorn that must have been simmering in him since the beginning of this voyage coming to a head. "He will have to die. He has seen we do not have six longboats, eh? Foolish woman."

She could not let MacMurtray go back. Not if she were to maintain her ruse, and her leverage.

She could not watch him die.

That last thought shocked her more than anything that had come before. What was wrong with her? Had she not seen countless men die? Women. Children.

Not him.

She swallowed hard, trying to gulp back the emotions on the rise before they choked her.

She could not save him.

One of the crew, Bjorn, who had been so bored since they arrived, said, "Can we not make some sport of him before he dies? See how much pain a Gael can endure."

Ja, such was their way when they found little else to do. Not this time, though, if she could prevent it.

Could she prevent it?

She turned a glare on Bjorn. "And how would that honor Jute?"

"He would have enjoyed it," Bjorn said sullenly.

"Listen to me, all of you," Hulda shouted in Norse. "I am still in charge of this voyage, as my faðir placed me. No man makes the decisions here, but me."

"No man makes the decisions," Ivor muttered, "and that is the problem."

She turned on him. "Do you want to return to Avoldsborg having defied me?"

"Nei, mistress. Kill him swiftly, then, and toss his carcass over the side. I no longer care."

"Fool," Hulda accused in turn, her mind emerging from its fog and beginning to work again. "He is worth more to us as a hostage. We can ask a price for him or exchange him for the man we want."

She turned to MacMurtray, who remained as motionless as if carved from stone. The rain had now soaked him—as all of them—to the skin. He did not flinch from it, or from her gaze.

In his tongue she said, "Ivor here was fighting on the shore when my brother Jute was killed. He says you are not the man who slew him."

Some of her men could follow the conversation, ja. Most of them had slaves.

"Ah," MacMurtray said. He directed a look of what might be regret at Ivor before switching his gaze back to Hulda's face.

"You lied to me," she said, less forcefully.

"As ye did to me. Unless"—he took a deliberate look around—"the rest o' your boats are invisible."

"They may lurk behind another island. You do not know."

"I do not. Though where would be the sense in that?" His eyes met hers, glinting green between dripping brown lashes.

And just like that, she wanted to kiss him. Wanted it with an unprecedented longing that tore through her like pain. Ach, by the gods! By Freya's heart, she almost knew how it would be. His lips warm through the cold rain. The feel of them, heady and familiar.

She must be going mad.

Shaken, she asked, "Whom are you protecting?"

He seemed to contemplate that, standing tall while the rain ran down his face like tears. He might lie to her again. He might tell the truth. It scarcely mattered, when it came to what she felt for him.

What did she feel for him? Desire. A need to protect. A devotion that—

Nei. That could not be.

He said, "It might be any number of men fighting on the

shore that day who killed your brother. I will tak' the punishment for any o' them."

"Nei." She strove mightily to master her protest. "My man says it was an older warrior." She narrowed her eyes. "Your faðir?"

The briefest narrowing of *his* eyes betrayed his reaction. Ah, so it was.

"Does it matter?" he asked. "Ye wish for vengeance." If he could have spread his hands, he would. "Here ye have it."

"I want the man who did the deed."

"Ye canna have him."

"Then we will destroy your settlement."

He continued to gaze at her steadily. "Wi' one boatload o' warriors?"

She tossed her head, contemplated attempting to continue the delusion, and gave it up. "I can send back home and bring the number I promised." Another lie. Faðir had indulged her in this. He would not be pleased with how it had gone.

And she asked herself, not for the first time, did Faðir not also want vengeance for the death of his son? Jute, of whom he had been so proud. Over whose headless corpse he had wept. Faðir, whom she'd never before seen cry.

He had seemed to recover from the loss far more swiftly than she. Jute could not be replaced. Her own heart would not so swiftly leave go of him.

And yet...she did not want this man to die.

She said, "Someone in yon settlement will want ye back. They will bargain to get ye."

"If that was so, would they have let me come awa' wi' ye? Nay, mistress. Ye will ha' to vent yer spleen on me, or no one."

Determined he was, to sacrifice himself. Even among a race of men noted for their reckless courage, Hulda could only respect that.

She turned to Lars and Garik, whom she trusted. "Guard the prisoner. Trym and Bjorn, the three of us are going back—to bargain."

CHAPTER SIXTEEN

HULDA ELVARSDOTTIR'S TWO boatmen did not look happy with her when Quarrie watched them go over the side of the small boat. They did not want to row to the settlement through the rain.

In fact, none of the Norsemen looked particularly happy with her, and the one who had argued it so vehemently—a big, rawboned man whose wet hair looked dark brown—wore an ugly grimace of dissatisfaction.

Was he the one who had witnessed the death of her brother? Likely so. He had the look of a warrior, with scars on his hands.

They searched Quarrie for weapons, taking his sword, the knife from the small of his back, and the *sgian-dubh* from his boot before lashing him to the mast. He sat there, legs thrown out before him in the pelting rain, and regretted the loss of his sword. Da had given him that when he turned sixteen, replacing the poorer weapon with which he'd trained up till then.

He wanted that sword back almost as much as he wanted his life. Not as much as he wanted to preserve Da's life, though.

He figured things were about to end for him. Here on the deck of this boat, or mayhap on the island. Better on Scottish soil than foreign oak planks. His spirit would have less trouble journeying home.

Curious, though, for he'd thought to have more time. The wheel of his life had barely turned. And yet if this was the purpose he was destined to serve, he would *dree his weird*, and serve it.

The Norsemen stood around him and conversed in their own tongue. They seemed to be complaining about the course things had taken, or perhaps about Hulda Elvarsdottir's actions. Mayhap they argued about what to do with him.

Aye, he had heard the stories. They could cut out his beating heart. Haul his lungs from his body. As a final insult, castrate him.

They argued over it a while, the brown-haired man working himself up to quite a fervor, during which time the rain pounded down. Their tongue sounded guttural and strange. Odd, he could not even discern what would be coming to him.

At length, the brown-haired warrior—had Hulda called him Ivor?—hunkered down in front of Quarrie and spoke in Gaelic so heavily accented, Quarrie could barely understand.

"You will tell us all you know, eh, stupid Scot? Who killed my friend."

His friend, had Hulda's brother been?

Not giving Quarrie much time to answer, the Norseman struck him in the face. It was a hard blow that bounced his head off the mast and made him see shooting lights.

So it begins, he thought before the man struck him again. Again. Face. Head. Body. Quarrie fought the desire to vomit and sought to keep his senses. Set himself to endure. This was just the start.

The battering—for it could not truly be called a questioning—went on for some time. Ivor—if it was indeed his name—did ask a few questions. *Who killed Jute? How many are your warriors?* But his clear intention was to work out his aggravation.

The rain washed the blood from Quarrie's face and down his tunic. The other Norsemen did not take part in the battery but stood and watched.

Quarrie did not speak. He did his best not to grunt when the blows landed. He spat and swallowed blood, raised his gaze to the skyline and tried to imagine himself home.

When Ivor grew tired and pulled a knife, one of the other men stepped forward. They began to argue in their own tongue, an argument not difficult to follow. Ivor wanted to cut him. The other man, younger, objected and at length went so far as to spread his arms in front of Quarrie in a gesture of protection.

Ivor turned away in disgust.

The deck rose and fell. Quarrie fought down his sickness and thought about the fact that he was not going to die—yet. How long would Hulda be gone?

Would whomever she spoke with at home bargain for his release? This had not gone at all the way he had intended.

What if Da, in turn, gave himself over? Those at home still did not know the Norse claim of six ships was a ruse. Da would want him released.

Nay, this had not gone the way he'd meant, at all.

After a time, the rain slackened. Even here in Scotland, among the isles, it could not continue so forever. Quarrie shivered as a wind blew across the deck and found him. The skin around his eyes swelled. He ached.

The Norse settled down to argue some more, to play at draughts, and eat. Though they directed glances at Quarrie, they did not approach him again, not until the young man who had forbidden Ivor from cutting him came and hunkered down with a cup in his hands.

He let his gaze slide over Quarrie doubtfully before he jerked his thumb at himself and said, "Garik."

Quarrie nodded.

Garik held out the cup. "Drink?" He clearly possessed very little Gaelic. What he did have was rough.

The liquid in the cup could well be poisoned. Yet…this fellow had defended him.

"Aye."

The man held the cup to Quarrie's battered mouth. It contained sour ale. It stung, but Quarrie gulped it down anyway.

The kindness performed, the young man rose and left. Quarrie closed his eyes and prayed.

Funny, how quick the prayers came in such circumstances.

Before a battle or, indeed, during one when a man stood knee-high in the water fighting off intruders—or when, as now, his life teetered on a knife's edge—he tended to try to bargain. *Only let my strength hold out. Let me be quick enough. Let me live.*

Only now, he did not know for what to bargain. His end here would not be good. But the last thing he wanted was to see his father hauled up over that rail and put in his place.

And still Hulda did not come. She did not come.

HULDA STOOD KNEE-DEEP in the surf, arguing with a member of Quarrie MacMurtray's guard. A line of them had gathered, but one of them spoke, a tall, rangy young man with light-colored hair and a veiled expression. He did not want to let them land the færing.

Not even to negotiate.

Stubborn these people were, and apparently thick as an oak plank. That was, Quarrie MacMurtray did not appear to be stupid, despite the fact that she'd succeeded in deceiving him over the number of her ships. Stubborn? Mayhap.

Right now, aggravation had her longing to kill them all. The day wore on. She was getting nowhere. And her crew—that was, *Ivor*—could be doing anything to MacMurtray in her absence. Any cruel and vicious thing, to afford some amusement. MacMurtray could be dead by now.

She called upon her patience and, fighting to keep her hand from her weapon, tried again.

"I wish to see your chief."

The tall guard muttered something she did not hear, speaking to the man next to him before spitting at her, "And I ha' told ye, ye canna. Ye ha' had all ye will get fro' us." Something dark brewed in his eyes. "Save the edges o' our swords."

Odin curse the man! "List to me. We hold one of your men."

"I ken fine ye do! I watched ye tak' him away from here against our liking, if ye maun know."

"I wish to negotiate now for his release."

"Ye be mad." The man repeated it to his companions. "She is mad."

By Freya's heart! "I have told you"—tried to tell him—"he is not the man we seek. We would trade him for the man we do seek."

Could he not understand?

"If you will not deal with me," she went on, hard as iron, "we will call out our fleet of boats to attack."

He blinked at her.

"Do you not want your man back?" *Fool,* Hulda added in her head, though she did not allow the word past her lips.

"Aye, we want him back. He is a good friend o' mine and one o' the foremost men this clan can boast. But ye made yer bargain, ye bitch, and 'tis all ye shall have of us."

Hulda turned and pointed dramatically out toward the island. "He shall be slain. And then we shall fall upon you and yours like wolves. Is that what you want?"

The guard's face grew stark. "Quarrie MacMurtray knew when ye hauled him awa' out o' here that he would die. It seems his courage is brighter than yer honor. Did ye no' promise to leave our settlement be, if he gave himsel' over to ye?"

"Ja." Hulda was forced to admit it. "Only because we thought he was the man." With dignity, she added, "I do not wish vengeance for vengeance's sake, upon the head of one who did not commit the deed."

For the first time, the fellow hesitated. Imagining the fate that might befall Quarrie, perhaps. Stark grief stood in his eyes.

For a moment—just a moment—Hulda hoped. They would negotiate on. She would find a way to release Quarrie Mac-Murtray.

Then the tall guard said, "We promised him no' a one o' ye would set foot on this shore again." He stepped forward and drew his sword. The other Scots who formed the line stepped with him. Hulda had no choice but to step back in the water.

"Begone," the guard said. "And God ha' mercy on that brave hero ye hold."

Hulda stole a glance at her two men who held the færing behind her. If they tried to fight it out here, they would all die. Three of them against all the swords of the settlement.

She would end her life on the selfsame strip of Scottish shore as Jute.

Was his spirit here? Did any part of him linger? His head, so Quarrie claimed, had gone into the fire.

A fit end.

Surely his spirit had flown away with the Valkyries. There was little to fear in death, save a loss of honor, and failure to fulfill one's promises.

She had promised her faðir vengeance. She had promised it to herself. Now, unaccountably, Quarrie MacMurtray stood in the way.

She spoke to her men in her own tongue. "We will go." And louder to the stubborn guard, "You have brought your fate upon yourselves."

Nei, she could not defeat them with the crew she'd brought. But the season was early, and she could always return.

CHAPTER SEVENTEEN

THE RAIN HAD ceased, and behind heavy gray clouds the light moved steadily to the west. Quarrie, shivering intermittently, slumped against the mast, half mad with his thoughts and with questions that had no answers.

He would die, that much was certain. If Da gave himself over to Hulda in a misguided attempt to ransom him, likely they would both die. The only uncertainty was what would come ahead of death.

He hoped he had the strength and courage to face it bravely. If she brought Da, and these savages made Da watch him die—well, he must then die bravely for his father's sake. At the end of it all, Da should be proud of him.

If they made him watch Da die—

Nay, not that. Please.

The deck of the ship was narrow and he was positioned prominently so he had to endure the stares, the curses—identifiable even in a foreign tongue—and kicks from all who passed. He had no way to evade any of it, and as the time passed, he could feel his endurance wane.

What if his men killed Hulda there on the shore? What would happen then?

He did not doubt that the fellow with the brown hair and the vicious eyes would take control of the boat. Quarrie's death would be hard and long and terrible.

He closed his eyes for a moment, and a deep shudder took

him. Would he pass beyond prayers then? Did a man who hung on the very breath of pain forget how to pray?

The crew aboard the longboat grew impatient. They went repeatedly to the rail and looked out. At last there came a shout.

Did Hulda return?

Quarrie's heart struggled in his chest and began to beat hard. No chance for escape. They had left his hands bound behind him and also lashed him round with stout line.

He heard excited calls from the crew and the hull of the smaller boat scraped alongside. He strained to see over his shoulder. If they hauled Da aboard…

They did not. Hulda Elvarsdottir came clambering up first, and then one of her men. The other likely secured the boat.

A fast and furious bout of question-and-answer followed. The voices of the crew integrated with Hulda's lighter tones. Anger. Still another argument broke out.

They argued much, these Norse. Quarrie barely noticed, so strong was his relief that Da had not come.

Da had not come.

Thanks be to whatever powers ruled the heavens and the earth. The whole point of this was for Da to perish, if perish he must, in his own bed with Ma at his side.

Then why should Quarrie, for just a moment, feel like a small, abandoned lad?

Because he was going to die here. Most terribly. And even though it was a choice—a sacrifice—he'd made, he had thought in the back of his mind that his father might want to save him.

Foolishness, that. There was no sense in both of them dying.

Feet padded across the deck and Hulda moved into Quarrie's field of vision. As might be expected, her men followed, still arguing in their own tongue. A fiery argument it was.

The brown-haired man railed at Hulda, no doubt for coming back empty-handed. She answered in a tone that shouted, *I am in command here.* Others of the men joined in, or tried to. The two of them were locked in on one another.

Until, that was, Hulda glanced at Quarrie.

They were beginning to lose the light by then and clouds lowered, but she could not fail to see the damage he carried.

A swift demand. *What happened here?*

Volatile answers from her men.

What did you do to him?

The brown-haired man answered.

Hulda came to Quarrie swiftly and hunkered down. Her gaze, pale even in the dying light, inspected him swiftly. She spoke in Norse and then said, "I told them not to harm you."

He believed her. The harm would come later. Soon.

The brown-haired man stepped up behind her. He spoke in very rough Gaelic, no doubt for Quarrie's benefit, "He got but a taste of what he has coming."

Hulda sprang to her feet and faced him. "I gave you an order, Ivor."

He shrugged. "He will have to die, either way. And we are bored. Kill him, mistress, so we can go home."

Hulda said nothing.

"This has been a bad venture from the first. I should have known. Be assured, I only came with you because your faðir asked. Him, I respect."

Implying that he had no respect for Hulda.

"I thought you wanted vengeance for Jute, your good friend."

"That too. Now I am bored. Let us kill him and pull anchor. We can drop the corpse on the shore of the settlement as we pass." He bared his teeth. "Without its head."

One of the men, listening to this, spoke in Norse. Another chimed in.

"Ja," Ivor agreed, and added in Gaelic, "After we find out how much pain he can endure."

"In the morning," Hulda thundered. "I need time to think if this is the best plan."

"It is the only plan. He deserves to die."

"Does he?" Hulda drew herself up to face Ivor. "He has

shown courage."

"Not yet, he has not. Mayhap he will, though I doubt it. See?" He looked around at the crew. "This is why it is a bad idea having a woman in command. They are not hard enough, eh?" He made a lewd gesture, pumping a hand at his own loins.

Hulda said something to him in Norse. The crew stood down.

For now.

Come morning, it would be a very different story. Quarrie had only the night ahead to live.

HE DID NOT sleep. The voices of the crew kept him alert in case Ivor argued his point and they came for him sooner. Came to take him. But he did let his mind wander away from the deck of the boat, back to the place he loved.

Mayhap if he thought hard enough on Scotland, that was where his spirit would linger once he died. For he wanted no other heaven.

He called up memories of days he had known, all he would have now. Shivering against the mast, he relived them. Bright mornings setting out for the hills on a hunt with the scents of salt air mingling with wild thyme all around him. Bonfire nights when the flames leaped from hilltop to hilltop and the connection he felt with his ancestors flared strong. Times under the stars when a visiting harper came to tell stories of all the places he had been, and played music with the power to transport Quarrie like magic.

He wanted all that. He wanted it all his life. But a warrior could not choose how he died. And a warrior did not always fight with a sword in his hand. Sometimes his only weapon remained courage.

He needed to remember that when they came for him. When

they cut him or flayed him or set whatever challenge they desired. He would die like a warrior.

And when the agony ended, he would fly home.

Dimly, he heard the guard change—the men who had been standing went to their rest. Others, only dimly seen, took their places.

A shadow moved beside Quarrie, close. His whole body jerked to life, his heart beginning to pound sickeningly.

"Be silent," a voice hissed at him. "Hold still."

A knife. It glinted in the dim light, and he thought, *Och, so it ends here after all. Quick or slow?*

The rope binding him to the mast was cut with haste. A sharp blade it was, as he found when it moved to his bound hands, nicking his skin but only out of haste, with no intention to harm.

He gasped involuntarily. He'd been bound a long while, and it hurt to move.

The shadowy figure moved closer to him and asked, "Can you swim?"

He knew her then. Recognized the inflection of the whisper. *Hulda.* She did not mean to haul him up and kill him, but—

"Go," she whispered. "Go now while Garik and I are on watch. You will have to slip over the side." She asked again, "Can you swim?"

"Aye." Could he? The shore was a long way off and his arms were numb. "I can. But mistress"—he reached out and touched her arm—"why—"

"They will kill you." She seemed to feel it explanation enough. Perhaps it was.

She dragged him up. She was strong, and he could feel her determination.

"My sword—" he began. It meant much to him, and he wanted it back.

She shook her head violently. "Nei. Go. Now." Yet her hands continued to clutch at him, and when he would have stepped away to the rail, prepared to leave with nothing but his life, she leaned up—and kissed him.

Quick and hard and fierce was that kiss, so fleeting that, as she towed him to the rail, he almost thought his blasted mind had imagined it.

For why would she kiss him? Why let him go, for all that?

Soundlessly, he slid into the water and began to swim.

CHAPTER EIGHTEEN

A FORTUNATE THING indeed for Quarrie that the rain had ended and the sea had calmed. Else he never would have been able to swim so far in deep swells.

As it was, the ocean stretched out flat before him all the way to the shore, which made no more than a distant line in the dark. He did his best to move silently, for sound would carry on such a still night. Hulda's man, Garik, must be in on the escape, but if the wrong member of the crew—say, Ivor—stirred and rose, they could well come after him in their small boat. Club him down right here in the water.

Hulda. Why had she done what she had? For the life of him, Quarrie could not say. He was battered, the recipient of kicks and blows, and his body hurt when he pressed it into motion. But the desire to live made a wondrous elixir, and he kept on, floating from time to time to rest and gain strength. A cold wind snickered across the water and he shivered uncontrollably. But at least, come morn, those bastards back in the longboat would not be cutting out his heart.

At the very end, when the shore drew so near he could make out separate details of the settlement, his strength flagged at last and he did not think he would make land. A stout guard had been set, as might be expected of a settlement that believed a fleet of six enemy boats hung offshore. Someone spotted him and, not knowing who he was, called up half the guard to watch him nearly drown.

It was Borald who waded out to him and, seeing the truth, called other men to help. They dragged him in, too weak to stand, and watched as he coughed up seawater onto the shingle.

"Master Quarrie! By God, we thought ye lost."

"As did I," he managed to croak, and sat back on his heels to breathe.

A circle of men—*his* men, thank God—surrounded him. Others looked out to sea.

"Did ye escape?" Borald asked. "Shall we expect them to be comin' after ye?"

They might well try. Quarrie was not sure what would happen now. To him, or to Hulda.

Hulda. Her lips on his, fierce as a brand, claiming him. Seeking, searching, giving. He'd never known aught to match it.

"Help me up," he bade his men.

They did, with eager hands.

"By heaven, they did work ye over," Borald said, appalled.

"And no mistake," someone else muttered.

"How did ye get awa'?"

"Did they beat ye and cast ye into the sea?"

"They meant to kill me come morn and toss my corpse in the foam. The woman who commands them released me instead."

That brought a hush of silence. Clearly, the men did not know what to make of it, no more than did Quarrie.

Giving up, Borald said, "Let us get him warm and dry. Seumas, ye run for the healer. Come."

They half—in truth, more than half—carried him up from the shore and into their own hall, where they kept a good fire for the guards to take turns warming themselves.

As they set him down on the bench, he said to Borald, "She has my sword." There seemed something significant about that, as if some instinct told him he could trust her with it, or as if all this had happened before, long ago.

Borald swore viciously. "I ken fine wha' that sword means to ye."

"Aye." So it did.

They stripped off his wet, bloodied clothing without ceremony and wrapped him in someone's plaid. Drachan, the healer, arrived and clucked over him in distress. He treated the wounds to Quarrie's face and head, and the bruises spreading across his body.

"Ye mean to tell me, Master Quarrie, ye swam all the way fro' Oileán Iur in this condition?" he marveled.

"Aye."

"There is a story in it, I do no' doubt."

"They meant to kill me come morning. But listen"—Quarrie seized Borald's arm as sense trickled back into him—"there is no fleet o' six ships. Just the one we saw."

The faces around him stilled, eyes staring incredulously.

"Wha'?" someone gasped.

"'Twas all a ruse." On Hulda's part, he did not doubt. "A means to bargain for the vengeance they sought."

Angry mutters greeted this information.

"But," Borald objected, "having got their hands on a means o' vengeance—ye—why did this woman then let ye go?"

"I canna tell," Quarrie said. Or perhaps he could, if he dared to. There was something between him and Hulda Elvarsdottir. Or was such a thought just madness?

Whatever the case, he did not doubt his story would be all over the settlement before dawn.

"Run," Borald bade someone standing by, "tell Mistress and Chief Murtray their son is returned. Wake them if ye ha' to. They will want to know."

He turned even as a man dashed off, and fixed Quarrie with a stern eye. "Ye be sure there is nay fleet o' longboats?"

"Nay, but the one."

"Then rest, sleep, and leave it in my hands."

To Quarrie's surprise, he did.

HE WOKE FEELING worse, if possible. Every part of him hurt, and when he sat up, his ribs screamed at him. Several blows and kicks had done real damage there.

A few off-duty guards remained on hand playing at draughts and watching over him. They came swiftly when he roused.

They did not ask how he felt. It must be obvious. Both his eyes had swelled and one side of his jaw ached. Indeed, every bone in his body joined in the miserable chorus.

I might have been dead. That thought speared through his mind. For aye, clear morning light flooded in the open doorway, and he could hear bustle from outside.

Would he have survived till morning, on the longboat? He might well have been floating on the tide by now, headless, had she not saved him.

He had to digest that thought; he could not get around it.

"D'ye want anything to eat?" asked one of the men.

He shook his head. But when the man shoved a mug into his hand, he drank, remembering the ale the Norse helmsman had given him.

"Yer ma was here to see ye," another man, Gavin, said, "but ye were flat-out asleep. She asked ye should go to her and the chief when ye awakened." He eyed Quarrie doubtfully. "Are ye able?"

"Aye." *I might have been dead.* But he could do any damned thing, since he was not. "Gi' me another cup o' ale and I'll go."

It was not a quick or easy journey up to his parents' quarters in the keep. The clansfolk who were out and about kept stopping him, exclaiming over his state, and demanding confirmation: "There is nay fleet?"

He assured them again and again. The main gate stood open, and his ma came hurrying out to meet him.

"Quarrie!" She embraced him hard, which hurt, but he did

not mind. "Och, only look at ye!"

"Ma, it might ha' been worse."

"Come. Come. Yer father wants to see ye."

Da was up on his feet hobbling with the help of a stick, his face livid with pain. He too came and embraced Quarrie, saying roughly into his ear, "We thought ye dead."

He had been, good as.

"Sit," Da told him, taking it as an excuse to lower himself beside the fire. "Tell us all."

An interesting experience, following the emotions in Da's eyes as he listened to the account. There was anger, aye, that Quarrie had gone against his wishes and given himself over in his place. Anger also that the Norse had played such a ruse and fooled them with the threat of a fleet. And vast relief that his son, however wayward, had returned to him.

It was Ma who, when Quarrie flagged, said plaintively, "But I do' no' understand why this woman let ye go, after coming all this way to seek vengeance for her brother."

"I was no' the right man," Quarrie said soberly, "as her crewman did tell her."

"Aye, but fro' all we ken of these people, they might as well ha' slit yer throat anyway. Wha' do they care for a single Scottish life?"

"Aye," Da put in, "and she had reason to be angered. She did come and try to bargain wi' us for your return—something I did not find out till afterward. Your man, Borald, kept that standoff on the shore fro' me."

Good man, Quarrie thought.

"I would ha' given mysel' over, sure, to ransom ye," Da added softly, as if to himself, "had I known."

"I am that glad ye did no'. I ha' nay an answer, Da, to why Hulda Elvarsdottir behaved as she did." Only that something existed between him and the Norsewoman. Something more than mere attraction, though aye, that played a part in it.

He had not, after all, told his parents all. He'd left out the kiss that he could still feel like a brand on his torn lips. That kiss had awakened something inside him. He just could not identify what.

"Foolish wench," Da said. "She must know ye will tell all of us she has but one boat, that we can surely fight off."

She might well be a foolish wench, but, by heaven, had there ever been such a woman?

CHAPTER NINETEEN

AFTER HULDA WATCHED Quarrie MacMurtray slip over the side of her boat into the water and bob away, his head looking very like that of a seal moving through the quiet ocean, she wrapped herself in her blanket and rolled up, preparing to sleep. Ja, she was meant to be on watch with Garik, who stood astern, steadfastly gazing in the opposite direction.

There would be retribution to pay, especially on Garik's part. She had spoken to him about it, and, steadfast heart he was, he had been willing to weather any blame that might fall on him.

Hulda would have to make sure it was not much blame. Letting MacMurtray go had been her choice and her decision.

She did not sleep, but lay thinking. *Thinking.* A thousand notions crowded her mind. Questions. Sensations.

Ja, she wanted vengeance for Jute's death. She still hurt over that, and someone had to pay. Not Quarrie MacMurtray.

Why? Blood was blood, and Scottish blood easy to spill. She had worked hard talking her faðir into allowing this journey. She had just scuttled it. They could have taken home the Gael's head.

Nei.

Not him.

But why not?

She lay with her eyes stretched wide open while the crew members snored around her, and contemplated it. Came up with only a few answers and more questions.

Why had she kissed him?

Ja, that was the question of questions, was it not? A hostage. A Scot. And her mortal enemy. She had gifted him his life and taken a kiss in payment.

The urge had come from deep within. A source as vital to her as the need to breathe, to stay alive, to direct her own life. There had been an overmastering need to touch him. To taste him. To tell him—

What? That in some curious, heretofore undiscovered way, she knew him? Desired him?

Nei, neither of those things. *Remembered* him.

She could not possibly remember the man. She had never before set foot on this stretch of shore. Had not been there when Jute died. But ach, by Freya's heart, she remembered…

Nei, it was nonsense. Fancy. Anyway, it was not he who drew upon the strings of her memory so much as some elusive details in him. The way he turned his head, mayhap. A glint of light in his eyes. The timbre of his voice.

Gone now. Gone. She wondered if—hoped—he had made it back to his settlement. A long swim, even if through calm sea, and he had been battered. What if he had drowned?

Nei, and nei, she could not lie here and worry for him. The next time someone got up to piss—

An outcry came. Alarm and fury. At once, the whole of the crew was on their feet as if under attack.

"He is gone! The prisoner is gone!"

In the way of such things, everyone spoke at once. Hulda, also on her feet, let them exclaim until, predictably, Ivor stepped forward and turned on Garik. "You it was on watch. What happened?"

Garik gaped at the sliced ropes left on the deck where the prisoner had been. They had talked about this beforehand, she and Garik, in fierce whispers. He would play stupid. So would she.

"He is gone?" Garik asked, doing a good job at the stupid.

"As you see!" Ivor roared. "Where were you that you did not give the alarm?"

"I was at my post, aft."

"And did you not see him?"

"Nei. I was watching the water. Looking out for signs of attack."

All eyes turned to Hulda. "You also kept watch," Ivor said accusingly. "You did not see?"

She yawned. "It was quiet. He was securely tied and injured. I took my rest."

Mumbles greeted this, and a few grumbles of outrage. Ivor's eyes nearly bulged from his head. "Careless! It is not to be believed!" He stooped to examine the ropes. "These have been cut. Someone"—he leveled an even harder gaze on Hulda—"has freed the prisoner."

"The work of Loki, perhaps?" Garik suggested innocently.

Ivor glanced around. "Do you see Loki here on the deck of this longboat?"

"He tends to come and go," Garik said.

Hulda drew a breath. "The prisoner must have had a knife— one of those wee black ones—hidden about him. Who searched him when he was brought aboard? You missed a weapon. He has cut his own bonds and slipped over the side."

One of the men moved to the rail and looked out as if thinking he could spot the miscreant. Hulda hoped he could not. These men were capable of going after Quarrie with the færing and clubbing him down.

"A long swim," the man said. "And he was battered. Tir willing, he did not make it so far."

Tir willing, he did.

A terrible thought came to Hulda: she might never know. Not know if the man lived or had died. A long, hard shiver convulsed her. It should not matter.

It did.

He or someone of his blood killed your brother. That is all you need to remember. Let the rest of it go.

"You were on guard," Ivor flung at Garik, "and should be

punished. Step up!"

Hulda moved before Garik could. "It was my responsibility, that watch. If you will take up with anyone, it will be me."

"Gladly." Ivor moved closer and spoke into her face. "You do realize he will tell all his warriors we have but one boat, ja?"

"If he makes it to shore," said the grim watcher at the rail.

"*If*," Ivor spat. "Our chance here is spoilt. What is to be done now, other than slink home like kicked dogs?"

"What, indeed," Hulda replied.

"This voyage," Ivor raged on, "has been a disaster from the first."

"Blame yourself," Hulda fired back. "You said he was not the man."

"So he was not. I also said to kill him anyway. You listen to half my advice and not the other. Tir spare us from the madness of sailing with a woman in command."

Hulda's eyes narrowed. "You question my ability to lead?"

"I do. And for the welfare of us all, I feel I should assume command from this moment forward."

A rare anger licked up through Hulda, blooming from the base of her spine to her head. She did not fire up often. She had learned that a woman competing in a man's world—where tempers were often quick and volatile, fueled by male pride— could not afford to. She reached more often for reason. Persuasion. Now Ivor's words tapped the most fundamental part of her.

She drew her sword. It left its scabbard with a sharp snick. "You challenge me?"

Ivor's eyes narrowed. Even in the dim light, for morning had barely come, she could see the thoughts moving in them. If he challenged her, he challenged her faðir who had placed her here, and Faðir was a wealthy, powerful man. Close with the jarl. Dangerous to cross.

But Ivor was angry and impatient, eager to vent his spleen and take out his frustration upon someone.

Her.

"If you can best me," she hissed at him, "then you can take command."

Jute had taught her to fight, and Ivor knew it. He had jeered at the start of her training. Not of late.

"I say the crew should decide."

"That is not how it is done."

"It is."

"Not aboard my boat. I am in command. Unless you can depose me."

No one surrounding them made a sound. The soft lap of the tide against the side of the longboat grew loud. As did the beat of Hulda's heart.

Ivor snorted. "Let us leave this place. Sail home with your failure. You can see what your faðir thinks of the wasted time and cost of this voyage."

He did not want to face her. Whether because he thought he could not best her, or because he thought he could and feared the consequences of humbling Elvar's only surviving child.

She sheathed her sword, thinking he was right. She could do nothing now but return home, and Faðir would not be pleased. In the north, summer months with their navigable weather were precious and not to be wasted. In the time this had taken, they might have sacked a church.

Still and all, she would have to argue hard when she got home. For more longboats and more men, and a return voyage.

Because she just had to return to this stretch of shore.

<hr>

CHAPTER TWENTY

QUARRIE STOOD AT the highest point of the walls that encircled the keep, his eyes narrowed in a fixed stare upon the sea.

It had cost him something to climb all the way up here in his battered state. To be sure, the healer and his ma both had given him strict instructions to stay abed. But when Borald had popped into his chamber to say the longboat was on the move, he just had to see.

As it was, he nearly missed it. By the time he reached the best lookout point, the vessel had rounded the island behind which it had been hiding and sailed northward.

Away.

The sail once more made naught but a black shape on the horizon, one that for the distance seemed to move but slowly. Difficult to tell, at once, in what direction. But aye, north and away.

The breath left his body in a great rush, painful for his bruised ribs. Indeed, the rafts of black and blue had bloomed magnificently across his chest and sides where he had been kicked. Surprising he had no broken bones, and Drachan had raised his eyebrows at what he termed such strength.

"I dunna ken, quite," the man had said in amazement, "how ye swam so far."

Neither did Quarrie, thinking back on it. The memory had attained an air of unreality, the floating, the buoyancy of the water beneath him, as if it had willingly brought him home. The scent of it all around him and the clap of it in his ears. Scotland had drawn him in. The water had carried him home.

What, though, of Hulda Elvarsdottir?

His eyes narrowed farther, as if he could spy her aboard that speck of darkness riding the sea.

Why had she let him go? He still had no answer to that. Why not just slit his throat, as her men had no doubt wanted?

Why had she kissed him?

Such a kiss, fast and fierce, that had reached inside him, clutched at the very roots of his soul. He would never forget.

Just as he would never see her again. At least, he had better hope he did not, for next time he would surely have a sword in his hand, and she a sword or axe in hers, and they would be expected to kill one another.

Despair touched his heart, a kind of searing disappointment such as he had never known. Aye, he'd felt dark emotions before, after a battle when he'd surveyed their dead. When Kyle had died. When he'd realized Da was not going to get well.

Naught to match this. And he did not understand why.

She was but a woman, was she not? The enemy. Seeking vengeance for her slain brother.

Only…only there was more to it.

"Good riddance," said Borald, beside him.

"Aye."

"Too bad 'tis only the start of the season. They will be back, or others like them."

She would not be back. "Keep good watch," Quarrie bade his captain.

"Aye, and ye need to tak' your rest. I only thought ye would be glad to see them going."

Quarrie returned to his quarters, moving slowly. His fellow clansfolk stopped him all along the way exclaiming over his condition or marveling at his escape from the viking longboat.

"Monsters they are," cried one woman. "Naught but savage monsters."

He gained his quarters at last, and the bed beckoned. He lay down with a groan. Difficult to sleep during the day. He was used to being on the move throughout daylight. Now his body screamed in protest at the very thought.

He drifted off only to imagine he was back aboard the long-boat and lashed to the mast, the deck shifting beneath him with the craft's agile dance at anchor. The fists and feet came at him again, striking and dealing pain along with disparagement.

He awoke with a start.

What had she told her crew, Hulda, when they woke and discovered him gone? The fellow on guard must have been in it with her. But the others would be enraged, would they not? Cheated of their entertainment. Even if she was in command.

It bothered him that she might take on trouble for his sake. But she was not his to worry over.

He slept again and dreamed what did not feel like a dream. He stood outdoors in the sunshine at the side of a roundhouse such as his ancestors might have built long ago. How he knew it for such, he could not say, for he'd never seen such a structure whole, only the ruins with the stones scattered.

One existed here at Murtray, in fact, predating the present keep.

In the dream, sunlight had warmed the stones. He stood near a washing place as familiar to him as his own name.

What *was* his name?

Not alone, he stood facing a young woman. An ordinary enough young woman she might be—a wee bit above average height, slim as a willow wand, with a mane of yellow hair and a pair of wide, true-blue eyes now filled with worry. Naught ordinary about her, though, for the sight of her, the very feel of her, raked up his emotions into a storm of protectiveness, of devotion, of love.

He loved this woman, if love could describe the power of what he felt. She loved him.

In the dream that was more than a dream, he reached out and

captured her hands, raised them one after the other to his lips and dropped kisses into the palms. Leaned forward to kiss either corner of her mouth. Her cheeks. He dropped a kiss at the center of her brow, inhaling as he did so, her scent. Drawing in the feel of her.

A benediction. A blessing to keep her safe. *Even though she sailed away from him.*

He awoke with his heart pounding, surprised to be in his own bed and not standing outside the little roundhouse. So real had it been. So real had *she* been.

He lay there struggling to breathe and wondering, had he ever loved anyone the way he loved that maiden standing in the sun? It made what he'd felt for Norah a shadow, or a delusion. And this made Norah's rejecting him…och, nothing.

Indeed, any lingering hurt for that evaporated like dew before the sun. That had not been love.

Shaken, he lay and took stock of himself. Where had he journeyed in that dream? And who was she? It could not feel more real. The skin of her palms against his lips. The twitch at the corner of her mouth, the softness of her cheeks.

There had been grief in it, though, all tangled up with the love. And there had been fear in it, right alongside the devotion.

He struggled to his feet. His room had gone dark while he slept. Night had come. He could not remember the last time he'd slept the day away. His body protested his movements, trying to drive him back into the bed.

He pushed his fingers through his hair, desperate to think. Naught had changed. He was still the son of Chief Airlee Murtray and would himself be chief one day—if he survived. He had been very fortunate to escape death at the hands of the Norsemen. But his life would continue in the way it mostly had. Waking and training. Keeping watch. Filling in for Da as best he could.

Nothing had changed, though everything had.

Where was she now, Hulda Elvarsdottir? He tried to picture the narrow boat out upon the dark sea. She would not be afraid to sail. She was not afraid of much. A woman like no other.

Except…

Had there not been a thread of what he'd sensed in Hulda Elvarsdottir in the woman he'd kissed outside the roundhouse? Possibly many threads bound up together, the same that had drawn him to Hulda without cause or reason. The same as had anchored him to the woman he'd blessed with his kisses.

He crossed to the narrow window of his chamber. Outside lay darkness, a flare of light from a watchfire. His window faced the sea and he could feel rather than see it moving restlessly, an eternal movement. As eternal and as unstoppable as time.

Keep her safe, he beseeched the sea, and perhaps time itself. He did not know which of the two women he meant.

✦

CHAPTER TWENTY-ONE

THE VOYAGE HOME to Avoldsborg was grim and silent. The crew had hoped for spoils—they always hoped for spoils—and returned home empty-handed. They felt they had wasted their time.

Ivor remained angry at Hulda, whether out of damaged pride because he had failed to take up her challenge, or just because their mission had been fruitless, she could not tell.

But he acted sullen and surly. He tried to take out his temper on Garik, faulting him for the Scotsman's escape, until Hulda had to intervene.

None of this was Garik's fault, though he alone of the crew knew the truth about MacMurtray's escape. Ivor was capable of getting the helmsman alone and forcing that truth out of him. Hulda must make sure that did not happen, if only in return for Garik's loyalty.

MacMurtray. She could not get the Scotsman out of her mind. What was it about him? He was good enough to look upon, ja, straight and tall with that lithe, well-muscled body. But so was many a Norseman, and they did not turn her head.

It was not that.

Though his eyes… There was something about his eyes. They spoke to her. As if, almost, he could tell her things without words, which was as well, since words were not entirely easy between them.

Not that it mattered. They had no future, she and Quarrie MacMurtray.

If she ever returned—and it would take a good deal of talking to win Faðir round—it would be to burn MacMurtray's settlement to the ground.

There could be no other way.

She mused upon that during the journey home, since she seemed able to do little else. Most of the voyage was calm, but north of Shetland, when they turned toward Norge, they were caught in the teeth of a storm that pounced upon them like a cat on a vole.

Indeed, it played with the longboat in the same way a cat might, letting them think several times they had escaped the worst of it, only to bat them back again. Heavy seas raked the deck. They almost lost a man—Sven—saved from going over only by getting his leg tangled in a line.

When it was over, Sven's leg was snapped like an alder twig, and the rest of them wetted to the bone. The boat limped into the bay under oars with none of the high spirits that should accompany a return.

"A bad voyage from beginning to end," Ivor pronounced as he went ashore, speaking to his fellows but making sure Hulda could hear. "I am sorry I ever joined it."

Hulda lingered to speak with the harbormaster after the crew was gone and make sure repairs would be underway. She was not eager anyway to see her faðir.

When she reached the stony path that led up from the shore, she found that Garik had waited for her.

She eyed the young man with some surprise. Clothing plastered to him, fair hair sodden, he maintained his customary calm expression.

Her stomach tightened. He was a loyal man, ja. Yet he alone knew the truth of what she had done.

And he, like the rest of them, had earned only minimum pay for this voyage.

"Let me buy you a drink," he said easily as they began walking together.

She gave a tight smile. It occurred to her that Garik alone treated her as if she were neither female or male—just someone with whom he chose to sail.

"You wish to buy a drink for me?" At the end of a voyage, it was usually the other way round.

"You look like you need one." He shrugged.

"It might not be a bad idea. I will now have to go to my faðir and report we have had a wasted voyage."

"Ja." Garik said nothing for a moment. Their boots crunched in time on the stone. The storm had clearly moved through here also, and the sky looked dark as the beginning of night.

"Will you go back?" Garik slanted a look at her.

Hulda shook her head slowly. "If I go back, it would require a fleet of boats. An actual fleet, not a ruse. That is a strong settlement."

"But I think you will want to go back."

Hulda stopped walking and gazed at him. She did not wish to insult him by asking if he meant to betray her. But she wondered.

"I had an idea," he said. "It may be a mad idea, but—"

"Sometimes those are the best kind."

"Then come have a drink. We will discuss it."

The ale hall was busy and loud. Other members of the crew had reached it ahead of them. There were cries of greeting, men wanting to know how the voyage had gone. They quieted just a bit when Hulda came in. She understood how they felt about a woman going viking. It was not unheard of. Tales of fierce shield maidens abounded in the sagas, and were the Valkyries not female?

Rare, indeed, for a woman to command a boat, and most of the men laid it at the feet of favor on the part of her faðir. As if she had not earned her place sailing with Jute and, ja, with Faðir himself. They would likely never believe she had earned it.

Ivor, thanks be to Odin, was not there. Garik indicated a bench in the corner and went to fetch their drinks.

Hulda sat and tried not to shiver. Their bench was too far

from the fire—but private. She listened to some members of her crew telling tales of their voyage. It would be all over Avoldsborg by nightfall.

A humiliation, for certain. Faðir would not be happy. *She* was not happy.

Garik came back and put a mug of ale in her hand. He looked thoughtful.

"They talk," he said with a jerk of his head at the members of the crew.

Ja, and what if they knew the truth, that Hulda had let their captive go?

"I am curious about something," Garik said.

Here it comes, Hulda thought. *He will press me over his silence.* "What is it?"

"I think I understand why you let the Scotsman go. His end would have been long and bitter, and he was not the man who killed Jute." When Hulda said nothing, he went on. "Someone like Ivor might say he should have died even though he was the wrong man. Someone needed to pay, and he was a Scotsman. It is enough."

"Ja."

"A head brought home in vengeance is a head brought home in vengeance."

A silence fell, broken when Garik said, "Me, I despise Ivor."

That made Hulda slant a look at him. "Do you?"

"Ja. He is a bully and a braggart with very little honor. I would not wish to sail with him again."

"Oh?"

"I would, though"—he leveled a look at her—"wish to sail again with you."

Hulda sighed. "You will have a long wait. I doubt I will be able to talk my faðir into another such venture very soon."

"That is just it." Garik took a deep drink from his ale cup. "I have an idea. It may be, as I say, a mad idea, but I cannot seem to stop thinking on it."

Just as she could not seem to stop thinking on Quarrie Mac-Murtray. "As I say, mad ideas are some of the best. Tell me."

"I am a good navigator, nei?"

That she answered readily. "You are one of the best I have ever known."

"Yet because I am young, I am seldom offered the place I deserve. Only you offered me such a place. There are many like me, younger men who get pushed aside for those with more experience. The old men say we have not yet proved ourselves and they will not hire us."

"A pity. So?"

"So what if you did not have to ask your faðir for a boat? What if the rest of us did not have to beg for places on a crew?"

"Garik, I am not following."

"My friends and I have some wealth laid aside. Some earned from past voyages but most gifted to us by parents and grandparents. You may have the same."

She did. Not enough, yet, to build a boat of her own. "Go on."

"There are enough of us to man a crew. If we put our wealth together with yours, mistress, we might have a boat of our own, with you in command. Beholden to none but each other."

It was the dream of everyone who went viking—to sail for himself and not an overlord or patron. She eyed her companion. "How young are these friends of yours?"

He shrugged. "Young. I am the oldest."

By Odin's eye! A bunch of green boys for a crew? "But they have sailed?"

"Ach, ja, they have with fathers or foster fathers or brothers. We have talked about it, see. We all want a chance. We need a leader."

"Some of your friends may not want a leader who is a woman."

He shrugged. "You give us a chance, we give you a chance. Do you not see? That is the beauty of it."

It *was* the beauty of it.

She huffed a breath. "Everyone in Avoldsborg would think us raving."

"The reason I proposed it as a mad idea. What do you say, Hulda?"

She did not know what to say. She drank first before venturing, "It is an expensive proposition. Would we have enough to build a boat, even if we pool what we have?"

"Mayhap."

"And if we did pool what we have, and we fail as we did on this voyage, we will lose everything."

"We would still have the boat. And we are young. We could build up again."

"Garik, I do not know. It takes months to build a boat. By the time we do that, the raiding season will be at an end."

"Ja, but we know of a boat. Frode's."

Frode was an old man, a warrior well past viking and, ja, mayhap half mad, whose boat had been wrecked in a storm last year.

"That is far too damaged."

"*Was* too damaged. Frode has been making repairs with the help of some of my friends, who have skilled hands."

"You think Frode would sell?"

"Ja, he will never sail again even though he wants to. Dag, who is his great nephew, can talk him round. Think about it." Garik gave Hulda a wise look. "We could raid the smaller targets, and after we build some wealth—well, then we can go back to Murtray, ja? Where," he added deliberately, "I think you kissed that captive goodbye."

Hulda's heart leaped. He had seen that, had he? She'd thought the deck too dark.

"Something, ja, to think on," she told him with calm she most certainly did not feel.

✦━━━⟨≋≋≋⟩━━━✦

CHAPTER TWENTY-TWO

"W HERE IS THE head of the man who killed my son?"
Faðir bellowed as soon as Hulda entered the chamber
where he worked. A bright place, it was, that displayed both his
wealth and his power. A good fire burned, and as Hulda had not
dried out much during her time with Garik, she went directly to
warm herself.

"I do not have it," she said.

"I know that already." He pushed back from the table where
he sat. "Eager tongues could not wait to bring me the news on
equally eager feet. *Dottir*, you promised me."

He got up. Elvars Andersson was a tall man, well built, with
his daughter's pale-gray eyes. Eyes that, so he prided himself,
could see far. He did not like failure or disappointment.

She faced him boldly. "I did so promise."

"You have failed me."

That made her flinch.

"I gave you a charge, my dottir, to avenge my son! Others
scorned me, laughed at me for doing so. Put a woman in charge
of the voyage? Pah! But your heart was as agonized as mine. I
thought I could trust you with it."

"You *can* trust me. Always."

"Then where is his head?"

"We captured a man we believed was Jute's killer."

"And then you let him get away. Ja." Faðir tossed up his
hands. "I have heard this too."

"Ivor was here." She should have known that as Jute's trusted friend—the very man Faðir had chosen to send along with her—Ivor would run at once to him. She had made a strategic mistake by delaying with Garik and not going to Faðir at once.

"It does not matter that the prisoner got away. Ivor himself told me he was not the man."

"So, it did not occur to you to use him to bargain?"

"That did occur to me, ja. I tried to bargain. The Scots would not talk to me."

"So you let him escape." Faðir cocked a sharp eye at her. "On purpose?"

Hulda sighed. "The crew would have killed him. The wrong man. There would have been no satisfaction in it."

"Ivor says the crew did not mean to kill him—merely make him suffer."

"They had already done that."

"You are soft," Faðir declared.

"Is that also what Ivor says?"

"It is."

"And you will take his word without even speaking to me?"

"I am speaking to you now."

"But your mind was made up already when I walked in here." Anger made Hulda add, "I no longer trust Ivor."

"I do."

"He undermined my authority throughout the voyage. He did not accept my orders."

"Perhaps with good reason."

"There is no reason for a leader to be disobeyed." She did not mean to shout it, but it came out that way.

Faðir did not appreciate her raising her voice at him. Hulda knew that very well. Her frustration cried out on its own.

More calmly, she said, "The leader deserves respect."

"Even as I deserve respect from you? Not to have you come in here bellowing at me—"

"I am not bellowing."

"—and interrupting me." Faðir shook his head gravely. "It seems I have made a dire mistake. Ivor warned me before you left. I listened to my heart."

So that was it. Ivor thought he would advance to leader when Faðir planned his next voyage. So he had set out to destroy her.

"Now my ship is damaged by storm and I have gained naught in vengeance for my son's death."

Hulda dropped her head. "This is true."

"You have failed to avenge your brother."

These words hit Hulda like physical blows. She said nothing.

"Did you know," Faðir asked after a few moments, "it was Jute who came to me and argued for you to take up battle training? *Let me train her, Faðir,* he said. *She wants it so badly. And why should a fierce spirit be limited by gender?*"

Had she a fierce spirit? Hulda wondered. She remembered, as a girl, longing to take up a sword, ja, but not so much because she felt fierce. It had been because she desired, with a deep and fundamental longing, that no one, no man, should sacrifice his safety, his life for her. She would defend herself.

Some part of Jute had beheld that longing, even though she doubted he recognized the reason behind it. Ja, in their world, women gave life and men took it. Things, though, were rarely so simple.

"Jute stood up for you," Faðir said heavily, "and so I gave you a chance. This is how you repay him?"

Hulda nearly doubled over with pain. She missed her brother, and at the beginning of the voyage just past would have said there was nothing she would not do for his sake.

Then she had gazed into the Scotsman's eyes.

"Faðir," she said desperately, "I miss Jute more than I can say, and I want revenge for his death. But I want it against the man who did kill him."

"They are Scotsmen! Does it matter who wielded the sword that took Jute's head? Foolish girl, you kill them all!"

When Hulda said nothing, Faðir went on, "I should have

commanded the voyage myself. I am not too old to avenge my son."

"I will go back," Hulda said then. "Attack the settlement. A strong settlement it is, well defended. With six boats—"

"Six boats?" The scorn in Faðir's voice near flayed her. "You think I should place you in command of even one boat again? Get from my sight."

"Faðir—"

"Go to your *móðir*, where you belong."

Hulda went out into the air, heart pounding and cheeks burning with shame, Avoldsborg spread out before her eyes. Bustling, prosperous. Founded in blood.

She could not have slit Quarrie MacMurtray's throat, not even to spare her faðir's condemnation.

Ah, but she had fallen in Faðir's eyes. He would not soon listen to her again.

She walked through the gathering twilight around the back of the hall to the family quarters and let herself in. Her móðir worked there beside the hearth, clad in her familiar haus dress, a linen cloth covering her hair. A tall woman, she had gifted Hulda her height and her strong build, though Hulda had her faðir's pale eyes.

"Dottir?" she said, and glanced at her woman, Rota. Rota had been with Móðir since her marriage, the two women thick as thieves. "Hulda, we heard that your boat had come in, delayed by storm."

To be sure, they would have heard. There were few secrets in Avoldsborg.

"I have failed to avenge Jute," Hulda announced starkly.

"Put aside your weapons," Móðir said gently. "Come and sit down. Rota, get her something to drink."

Hulda obeyed.

Móðir, as Hulda well knew, had been as destroyed by Jute's death as she. Her big, strong son, she had always called him. She had not asked Hulda to seek vengeance. More inclined to appeal to Freya for strength and sustenance, she had nevertheless refrained from interfering with Hulda's intentions.

Now, despite her soft voice, a hint of iron entered her blue eyes as she pushed Hulda onto a bench and took her hands.

"Listen to me, dottir. Vengeance will not bring your brother back. Nothing will."

"I know that."

"I am glad to see you returned. I do not need another of my children dying upon a foreign shore."

Nei, Móðir had never objected outright to Hulda's pursuit of training at arms. But Hulda had once overheard her saying to Rota, *A dottir should be a comfort to a móðir, close at hand.*

"Faðir is angry with me," she said. "He will not sponsor another voyage."

"Your faðir's heart is broken, just like mine. Just like yours. Jute was a son in a thousand. Your father expected grand things of him."

Hulda's lips trembled when she said, "Men go viking. They so risk not coming back."

"This is so. Rota, where is that drink?"

A cup was thrust into Hulda's hands. Móðir sat down beside her.

"Dottir, I believe it is time to give up all this nonsense."

"Nonsense?" Hulda raised her gaze to her mother's face, which looked worried. Weary. Wounded.

"Lay aside the weapons. The violence. The pursuit of blood. Be what you are."

"What am I, Móðir?"

"A woman. A quite beautiful one."

"Can a woman not be strong? Can she not fight for herself and those she loves?"

"We fight." Móðir gestured to Rota and herself. "In our own way, we do. Women possess the strength of the stones beneath the hearth fire. The stones that hold up the walls of our dwellings. It is no less for being quiet."

"And are you content to let the men you love die for you? I am not." Hulda would have leaped to her feet, but Móðir's grip on her hand kept her where she was.

"It is time," Móðir said again, "to lay aside your flaming sword. Marry. Have children of your own. One of them may fill the hole Jute has left in your heart."

Hulda said nothing. She blinked back the tears that filled her eyes.

"I thought," Móðir went on doggedly, "when Haakon courted you, that you would wed him and settle. Let her get it out of her system, I told your faðir. All will come right."

"Haakon showed he did not want me," Hulda croaked out.

Móðir shrugged. "There are other young men. Some who do not go to sea."

Hulda gazed at her mother uncomprehendingly.

"While you were away," Móðir said gently, "Gothrum came to talk with me. He asked if your faðir and I would approve his suit."

"Gothrum." Hulda barely remembered him. She and the others near her age had all grown up together. She should know them all. "The silversmith?"

"Ja. A talented man." Móðir's lip curled. "He has his eye on you."

"But—" Gothrum was tall, ja. Weedy. A bit stooped from the close work he did bending silver and gold wire into intricate brooches and chains.

"He asked me, honest and forthright, if I thought you would be interested. I said—"

"I am not."

"—that I thought—"

"I am not." Hulda had lent her heart to Haakon. She would not make that mistake again.

A vision of Quarrie MacMurtray arose before her eyes. Lips split and bloody. Eyes bruised, face battered. She had kissed those lips.

Nei, she wanted naught more to do with men.

"—he should place his suit before you when you returned."

A nice enough young man, Gothrum. But he had nothing she desired.

Looking her móðir in the eyes, she said insistently, if more calmly, "I am not interested."

With some of Hulda's own stubbornness, Móðir replied, "We shall see."

❖

CHAPTER TWENTY-THREE

Q UARRIE HEALED SLOWLY, his efforts aided little by his refusal to keep off his feet. Drachan implored him; his mother scolded him. None of it mattered a whit. Not even the complaints of his own body could hold him.

He became obsessed with keeping watch and might be found upon the walls at any given time, day or night. He forgot to eat and very nearly forgot to sleep. He hounded the men until they began to look at him tight-lipped with strain in their eyes.

He knew that if—when?—Hulda Elvarsdottir and her men returned, it would not be with a single boat but enough to storm the settlement.

He must be ready. No excuses for it.

When he resumed training with the rest of the men, everyone protested. Borald did, and the men themselves, perhaps because they could see what it cost him.

He did not care for the cost.

They heard tales of Norse attacks farther south, at Gallanach and Balliemore. A church was destroyed there and the resident monks slain. A settlement burned. While spring proceeded inevitably into summer, Quarrie's eyes searched ceaselessly for sails.

One day following training, when Quarrie still dripped with sweat, Borald took him aside. A warm, fair day it was, though Quarrie barely heeded the bonny weather.

"Let me ask ye somewhat," Borald began when the last of the

men had slogged off.

Quarrie withdrew his gaze from the sea. "Aye?"

"Are ye tryin' to kill yoursel'?"

"Nay. Why should ye—"

"Because ye're doin' a fine job o' it."

Quarrie focused on his fellow warrior. Friend. For aye, Borald was that. "What are ye on about?"

"Just that it hurts watching ye train. When is the last time ye slept? Och, I am no' talking about a nod here or there, but a full night's sleep."

"I—" Quarrie could get no farther.

"I will tell ye, then. Since before the Norse came. Quarrie, man, I understand yer caution. Yer vigilance. It does ye credit, but ye maun trust the rest o' us to tak' some of the weight."

"They will be back." Quarrie stared into Borald's blue eyes. "I know it."

"Aye, I do no' doubt that. Them or others like them. We will be ready when they do."

"They are destroyers." He thought of Hulda pressing her lips to his, her strong fingers clutching the front of his tunic. "Bad enough when they are seeking plunder. When they come in vengeance—"

"Aye, so. D'ye no' think we are ready?"

"I am no' sure we can ever be ready."

"Quarrie"—Borald drew a breath—"all our lives we ha' been aware o' what lies out there in that sea. We are no' about to forget now."

Forget. Forget the feel of her lips against his, soft in contrast to the strength of her? What would it be like to lie with such a woman? He could almost feel it.

Borald was eyeing him strangely. "D'ye ha' the fever, man?"

"Nay."

"No shame in admitting, if 'tis so."

"I do no ha' the fever." At least, not the kind Borald meant.

"Good, for ye do no' want to end up like the chief."

Nay, he did not. Da still fought hard. Up on his feet one day, grim and determined, awash in sweat the next night.

"Take the rest o' the day," Borald suggested. It was already late afternoon. "Ha' a few drinks, get some sleep. Eat somewhat, for God's sake. I do no' want to see ye up on the walls before morning."

Quarrie grunted. If he rested, the thoughts would pounce upon him. He would think of her.

But aye, Borald had a point. He hurt, he did constantly. He did not want to end up like his da.

He collected a jug of heather ale on his way home, not favoring the company to be had in the hall, and once in his quiet quarters drank more than he should, considering he did not remember what he'd had to eat that day.

He could not—absolutely could not—be sickening for want of a Norsewoman. One clad in men's clothing and armor, who fought with a sword. Madness.

Yet her pale-gray gaze haunted him. The flicker of light there when she looked at him. The deeper meaning behind it all.

He lay on his bed with his arm bent over his eyes. He slept.

He dreamed of her. He felt sure it *was* her, though once again, she was not Hulda Elvarsdottir. That is, she was and yet she wasn't. More, she was not the woman of whom he'd dreamed before, who'd stood with him in the sun by the washing place.

This young woman was strong like Hulda, aye, and had a bold eye. A flame about her. Hair of rich honey-blonde and eyes deep blue, like the far sea between Alba and Erin.

Now, why should he make that comparison?

Bradana. The name sounded in his mind as the woman in the dream turned to face him, desire flaring in her eyes. *His strong, Alban lass.*

An ocean divided them. Distance. Time. Nothing love could not span.

He reached out for her. *Adair,* she whispered into his mind, and came to his arms.

The scent and the feel of her at once inflamed and also satisfied him. The expression in her eyes stole his breath. He lifted each of her hands in turn and dropped kisses into the palms. Leaned to kiss each corner of her mouth, her cheeks. Her brow.

He awoke and lay trembling. No light in his chamber, no light anywhere save in his mind, which was full of her.

What did it mean? Two women. He had dreamed of two women who were somehow one, and a love that—

But he had no words for it.

Lying there staring into the darkness, seeing only her face in his mind, the love felt like pain. The pain felt like life, the one thing for which he might reach in all these days and nights he'd been given.

He needed to see Hulda Elvarsdottir again.

An impossibility. He did not know where in the wide world her boat had sailed. If he saw her again, it would mean she returned of her own accord. And if she returned, it would be with score upon score of Norse warriors to destroy him.

He would have to fight against her then. It was his duty and his birthright.

She had gifted him with his life there aboard her longboat. Mayhap that meant she would not return. For why come back merely to destroy what you valued enough to spare? There were targets aplenty along this rocky coast for her and her kind, if she would spare him.

That did not mean other marauders would not come from other places to the north and east. Vikings not Hulda Elvarsdottir. He must still be vigilant and watch for dark sails on the horizon.

Which meant he must get himself in hand, and start with taking better care of himself. He could not fall apart for want of a Norsewoman he'd met only twice.

Kissed only once.

Nor could he let himself malinger for the sake of two women he'd glimpsed only in dreams—two women who pulled at his spirit, who were somehow also Hulda.

He must put it all behind him, thank his stars he still drew breath, and go out to fulfill the duties that belonged to him. Live for this place as he had always done. Forget Hulda Elvarsdottir if he could.

Having lectured himself sternly, he rose and lit a rushlight by feel, against the darkness. He washed in his basin, thrusting away from him the memories of the bright dream and the woman beside the roundhouse. He put on clean clothes, groaning a little over his bruised ribs, and braided his hair, which had grown wild.

Then he went out into the dark and walked the settlement, quiet in the dead of the night.

By the time dawn broke in the east, he was on the walls again, looking out to sea for a glimpse of danger.

Not Hulda's sails, he assured himself. She would not return. But any others that could come swooping in like a dark bird above a battlefield, wings spread, looking for death.

All else was fancy and must be thrust away from him. He had been born to defend this place, naught more.

Best make his mind up to it.

⬗⬖

CHAPTER TWENTY-FOUR

"IT LOOKS VERY rough," Hulda said, narrowing her eyes against the strong morning sunlight. "I did not expect it to be quite so…battered."

Indeed, the longboat listed a bit to one side, giving the dragon at the prow a lopsided look. Compared to Faðir's ships—well, there *was* no comparison.

She no longer concerned herself with aught her faðir owned. She had moved out of his home four days ago, taking temporary housing where some of the warriors lived, but she did not like it there. They were noisy and crude and not overly clean. But it represented independence.

Following that move, she had gone to Garik and told him ja, she was interested in his offer to go in on a boat of their own. He and his brother, Helje, had brought her to this inlet some distance up shore from Avoldsborg, where the old man, Frode, kept the vessel he wished to sell.

Her first glimpse of it, though, dashed her hopes and made her question herself. A fool, Faðir had called her. Ivor, too. Were they right?

She glanced at Garik. In the morning light, he looked terribly young, too young to sail, though she knew very well he was a fine mariner. His brother, a couple years his elder, did not say much, though he was in on the proposed venture.

Garik met Hulda's gaze with steady enthusiasm. "She needs an overhaul, ja. It is nothing Frode cannot manage."

Hulda remembered Frode as a strange old man, elder to even her faðir. He talked to himself and he spat a lot. She had hoped, if she took Garik up on his offer, he would mostly deal with the old man on her behalf. Mayhap he still would.

"I somehow thought work on the vessel would be farther along," she said, doubtful. "How long will it take to finish?"

"Frode has been working on it. Not much longer. If we want it, we will have to put money in so he can finish."

"Ah."

Helje spoke for the first time, his voice deep. "One must start somewhere, Mistress Hulda."

"I understand that." She had not expected to start at so low a place as this. If she invested all she had in the longboat—well, it did not appear a hopeful venture.

If she failed—again—she would have nothing. Nothing. And she refused to go crawling back to Faðir.

There had been a terrible argument the day she left, Faðir threatening and Móðir weeping, taking Hulda aside and begging her not to go.

"I have already lost my son. Do not make me lose my dottir also."

"You are not losing me," Hulda had assured her. But ja, she could see that she was.

Hulda had held a big vision then of succeeding in this venture, launching a few bold voyages. Making Faðir eat his words about her. Looking at the slightly sad longboat in the narrow inlet, stranded there as if it had come home to die, that vision evaporated.

Was this truly the best she could do?

Frode's dwelling stood alone above the rocks that fronted the inlet. He had a son whom everyone considered slow, and no wife. The shed out of which he worked had been built just behind there, and he emerged from it now.

Grizzled he was, with a rat's nest of gray hair spilling down his back and salt-rimed clothing. Hulda had asked Garik how he knew the old man.

"Everyone knows him," he'd replied. "And a boy must learn the craft of boatbuilding somewhere."

Garik being a clever lad, she had taken his word for it. There was, so she reminded herself, a price for everything. Associating with the old man might be the price, in part, of her independence.

It might well be the price of seeing Quarrie MacMurtray again.

Still, she eyed Frode with misgiving as he loped over the rocks to them, a big, rangy, loose-limbed body now bent with age and likely the results of hard work. Boatbuilding, with all its attendant labors, was not an easy vocation.

He spat as he joined them. Hulda did her best to ignore it.

"Lads."

She was indeed dressed like a lad, some of Jute's stolen clothing cut down to fit and with her hair tightly braided, so she took no offense. Looking into the old man's face, which was deeply lined and frankly not too clean, she saw he had two different-colored eyes. Strange from birth, then.

"So you want to buy the *Freya*?"

Hulda sighed. Was not every second boat called *Freya*?

Garik gave her a look before treating Frode to a wide grin. "Ja, we do. And you promised you would make us a fair price."

"Did I?"

"Ja, sure, the bunch of us young men just starting out, like I told you."

"She needs a considerable amount of work." Frode squinted at the vessel. And spat into the water.

No lie, Hulda thought.

"Needs a new rudder. New mast, as you can see. Repairs to the deck. There was a fire—"

"A fire!" Hulda exclaimed.

Frode glared at her. "Just a small one."

Hulda began to say that she did not think it a good prospect for them. A picture of Quarrie MacMurtray flashed into her mind, face battered, eyes steady. Just the way he'd looked before she kissed him.

Days and days had passed, yet she swore she could still taste him on her lips.

"How long? To get it ready," she asked.

Frode hemmed and hawed. He mumbled to himself. He spat some more. "The big repairs—not long. The minor ones—"

"We could help with those," Garik said quickly. "Helje and I. And"—he gestured at Hulda—"you know I want to learn."

"She was a swift boat, once," Frode said. "Agile. Almost no draft. She would serve you well."

"Can you have her ready in a fortnight?"

Frode turned and stared at Hulda. Behind his bi-colored eyes, she glimpsed a certain lack of focus. In his thoughts, only? Or was that madness?

She said, "The season moves swiftly. We have only so much time."

"Ja," he agreed. "Summer is fleeting."

She stood there waiting while he pondered it, with the smell of the sea in her nostrils and urgency prodding her inside.

If he says he can ready the boat in a fortnight, she decided, *I am in. If he says it will take longer, I will withdraw.* Though the gods alone knew what she would do with herself then.

"Ja," he said. "A fortnight."

It felt as if Hulda's world shifted. As if, indeed, she found herself balanced upon some great wheel—that of Freya's chariot, perhaps—and she had to dance in order to keep her feet.

"If you help," the old man added.

The door of the shed banged on its leather hinges. Frode's son came out and headed for them.

As tall as his father he was, and twice as broad. A veritable ox of a man. He had light-brown hair and, as Hulda saw when he came close enough, two light-brown eyes.

"Bjarni," Frode said, "these fellows are going to buy *Freya.* They will help us get her ready quickly, ja?"

"Ja, Faðir," Bjarni said. He turned incredulous eyes on them one by one, lingering on Hulda's face the longest.

"I am not saying it will be easy, mind," Frode went on, and spat. "But Bjarni here is good for lifting."

Hulda just bet her was. The name suited him, his being big as a bear.

"And I have the skill we need in my head, my hands. The three of you will do the grunt work, eh?" Frode continued.

"There may be others," Garik said, "to have a share in the venture."

"We still have to agree upon a price," Hulda interjected. "If we are to supply labor, it should be less."

"But there is the matter of time." Frode eyed her. "I shall need to work day and night to finish in a fortnight."

"Faðir—" Bjarni began.

"Hush, lad. We are doing business." The old man squinted at the boat again and seemed to come to a conclusion. "She is doing no good moored there and would be better off about her adventures." He named a price that made Hulda suck in her breath. One even she could afford.

"Agreed," she, Garik, and Helje said all at once. At such a price, they could keep the venture among the three of them and no doubt share the spoils.

"Faðir," Bjarni said again, more forcefully, his gaze fixed on Hulda, "she is very pretty, is she not?"

Old Frode stared at Hulda and seemed suddenly to tumble to the truth of her gender. The ensuing look on his face made Garik begin to laugh. Helje joined in and then they were all laughing.

A good beginning, Hulda acknowledged. Mayhap it would be a successful venture after all.

CHAPTER TWENTY-FIVE

BJARNI BECAME HULDA'S shadow, at her elbow so often while she worked upon the *Freya*, she sometimes bumped into him. He had developed a fancy for her, that much was plain to see, and no matter how she tried to dissuade him, he would not be put off.

The other men thought it was funny. Hulda did not, since she never went out of her way to play with anyone's feelings.

It did, however, have its advantages. Bjarni was always at hand to do the heavy lifting, and she came to like him—the way she might a slightly perplexing younger brother, perhaps. She had absolutely no romantic feelings for anyone, save—

Nei, do not think of him.

She spent her days working hard on the *Freya*, learning more about boats than she'd ever intended, and both her days and nights *not* thinking of Quarrie MacMurtray. The second proved much harder than the first.

What was it about the man? He was just a man.

Nei.

When she grew tired and doubtful and annoyed with her companions, when she became uncertain about the crew she and Garik selected—young men, all—she told herself *Freya* was her means of getting back to Scotland. Eventually. And she labored on.

Her hands grew rough, her hair tangled, her body sore. For diversion from the hard work, she took some members of the newly selected crew aside for sword work. To measure their skills, she told Garik, but it was more than that. As a woman, particularly, she had to keep her own abilities at fever pitch. It was one of the things Jute had taught her.

"*Systir*, everyone who comes up against you will expect you to fail, ja? You will have to be twice as quick as the men, and three times as clever."

Her brother had been a wise man. Every time she picked up a sword or axe, she missed him.

The new crew, gathered mostly from Garik and Helje's friends and acquaintances, had never sailed with her and were not familiar with the notion of sailing under a female's command. So mayhap the truth was, at sword practice she also sought to show them of what she was made.

To a man, they were impressed. She heard them muttering about it to themselves and each other later.

I was not certain about sailing with a woman, but it is a rare opportunity to join a new crew.

The older captains take on only their cronies.

She can fight.

A rare compliment that, to be either topped or spoiled entirely by the one that came after.

She scarce seems like a woman.

Did Hulda not wish to be a woman? She had put all such things away from her, had she not? Driven by the relentless, inborn desire to look after herself, defend herself so that no one might ever be lost for her sake.

But ja, she *was* a woman, and upon rare occasions, and though she'd never admit it, enjoyed looking at a man.

She had enjoyed the kiss she had taken from Quarrie Mac-Murtray.

Since they'd worked on the *Freya*, hidden away in Frode's narrow inlet, no one in the greater settlement knew what they were about. Not until the afternoon they sailed her around to take a berth in the main harbor.

A gray day it was, with rain clouds stealing in from the west and not a breath of air stirring. They came in under the power of the oars and strong young backs, and in that regard Hulda was impressed by her crew.

On every voyage she'd taken in the past, there had been complaints from men taking up the oars, especially older men. This crew, enthused and energetic, did not seem to mind.

The harbormaster watched them come in, joined by the aging warriors who hung about the place and anyone else on hand. A strange boat coming in always drew attention. Some there recognized this vessel; some did not.

The harbormaster, a man named Hans who was close to Jarl Gudmund, stood with his arms akimbo and a scowl on his face.

"We will not get a good berth," Hulda said, standing next to Garik at the rudder.

"Who cares?" He tossed his head. "So long as they know we have arrived."

They did that. As soon as harbormaster recognized them, he directed them to a far slip and continued to glower.

When they came ashore in a group, he cried, "What is all this? No one informed me a new vessel would be taking up space."

"She is the *Freya*," Garik's brother informed him.

"I can see that. Battered she was, and barely seaworthy."

"She is seaworthy now," Hulda told him. "Under my command." She met his stare with a cool eye.

Someone in the gathered crowd scoffed. The harbormaster did not. Too close to the jarl and thence to Faðir he was, though Hulda did not doubt the story would soon reach Faðir's ears.

Indeed, a hint of respect lit in the harbormaster's eyes as he looked around at the crew. This was how things were done in their world. Men—and apparently women—seized opportunities.

"A young crew," he commented, shooting another hard look at Hulda.

"And a capable one," she returned, causing chests to swell.

"Does your faðir know of this, Hulda Elvarsdottir?"

She lifted her chin. "What has it to do with my faðir?"

She found out that evening when she was summoned to Faðir's house by one of his servants, who ran her to ground in the ale hall.

"Mistress Hulda," said the steward, who had known her from childhood, "your faðir requests your presence."

"I am too busy right now. Tell him I will come when I can."

"Mistress, he bade me tell you it is important."

She doubted that. No question but Faðir merely wanted to harangue her. He himself—though once a fierce fighter and avaricious viking—had not sailed since before Jute's death, preferring to remain at home and direct others.

"I will come in the morning," she said carelessly, "if I have time."

They meant to sail as soon as they could gather and load supplies.

The man looked pained, but he went away and bothered her no more. Not till the morning, when Hulda awoke in her despicable lodgings with a lamentably sore head, did she remember Faðir's request.

Or had it been an order?

She lay and wondered whether to grace him with her presence. The fact that he was family might well make her owe him that. Besides, she would like to see Móðir before she sailed.

The *Freya* might be lost. Not every boat that went viking returned.

She contemplated wearing a dress for the visit, and decided to go as the woman she now was—the commander of her own boat. She carried some pride when she entered her faðir's house to find him sitting at his breakfast, beside the hearth.

"So," he grunted at her, "you come in your own time."

"Ja. I am here. Where is Móðir?"

"Not yet risen. I do not think she slept all the night." To be fair, he looked as if he had not, either, face drawn and eyes holding an expression Hulda could not quite define. "She fears losing another child."

Hulda shrugged. "It is you who sent me to sea."

"I did not send you, dottir. I gave you permission to go. From a little child you have wanted a sword in your hand. I thought to let you work that out of your spirit and settle."

That made Hulda raise her eyebrows. Was it so? "You let me launch the last voyage—"

"Ja. I thought you needed that to stem your grief over Jute. I understand that grief. By Odin's eye, I share it." He fought down his emotions. "But you returned without the vengeance you sought. It is enough."

"It is not enough for me."

Anger joined the other emotions in his eyes. A reasonable man, usually, he hated to be crossed. "You have bought this boat of which I hear? Where did you get the means?"

"I have been viking from the age of sixteen. I put my wealth aside."

That made him grunt. Approval? Derision? She no longer needed his approval.

"An investment in a boat and crew is not a bad thing. Do not sail with them, though. Stay here and direct the venture."

"I sail." Away to the south. Toward Murtray.

"I forbid this."

"I am no longer a child. You cannot forbid me."

He got to his feet suddenly, visibly trembling. "It will cause your móðir pain and worry. Care you naught for her?"

"I care. To be sure I do."

"Then stay and glean riches off what your crew brings home. If they succeed. I hear they are very young."

"Very eager."

"And a hacked-together boat."

"The *Freya* is sound."

"Why must you do this, dottir?" It came as a cry.

Hulda was not sure she had an answer to that. "I am as I was made," she said.

"So you will blame me, will you? For overindulging you, perhaps. You will blame your brother for giving you training?"

"I blame no one." She lifted her hands. "Should there be blame for the woman I am?"

"Your brother always meant well by you. He loved you very much."

A mist of tears came to Hulda's eyes. "And I him."

Faðir turned his face away from her. "See your móðir before you go."

"I will." Because she was woman enough.

Her móðir received her more calmly than Faðir had, but the grief in her eyes reached deeper and touched Hulda's heart. When she wept at their parting, Hulda almost—*almost*—agreed not to go.

"You can move back home," Móðir beseeched her. "Here with me."

"And live under Faðir's thumb?"

"He wants you home."

"Móðir, I wish I could. I cannot."

Something drove her, a force she'd only begun to comprehend.

One that would not relent.

$$\text{---} \diamond \text{---}$$

CHAPTER TWENTY-SIX

QUARRIE CLAWED THE tumbled hair out of his face and tried to blink the grit from his eyes. The night just past had been a long one, the battle fierce. A battle fought not with sword and shield, but with will and determination.

Da's rages—and his fever—grew steadily more intense. Quarrie did not know how much more mere flesh could stand.

He left the chamber where his father had at last fallen into a restless sleep and stepped out into the larger room of his parents' quarters. Ma stood at the window staring out, her shoulders drooping.

His comrade-in-arms during the battle just past, she had been. And it had cost her.

He crossed to the window and stood beside her, gazing out. Dawn bled across the sky from the east, lighting the sea from ink black to misty gray. Any sails there? Quarrie had to admit that for once he scarcely cared.

"He is dying," Ma said, the words stark even though she whispered them.

Da had been dying a long while. Neither of them had wanted to admit it. A strong man, Airlee MacMurtray. Yet now that strength began to wane.

"One o' these nights," she went on, "we will lose him."

"Aye." Quarrie had feared it would be last night. Before the healer had come.

"It is the pain that drives him mad."

The healer had once more suggested they amputate the leg, which he insisted rotted from within.

"It will never heal," he'd told them in an urgent whisper, "if it has not by now. Best to take it off and try to stem the poison."

Quarrie had shuddered. Such an act would end Da's every hope of ever fighting again.

As would death.

It made him think of Hulda Elvarsdottir. Da might have slain her beloved brother, but by God, he had paid the price.

Everything made Quarrie think of Hulda Elvarsdottir.

He shrugged her out of his mind and put his arm around Ma. "Here now. Cry it out if ye need to. There is no one to see."

Da refused to let them reveal to their clansfolk just how bad his condition had become. So when Ma went forth and answered their questions about their chief, she had always to put on a brave face. Quarrie did believe her woman knew the truth, and that Ma must have wept in her arms many times.

Her next words to Quarrie supported that belief. "I do no' think I ha' any tears left." She rubbed at one of her cheeks absently. Da's flailing hand had once more caught her there. Such was his strength in his pain-racked rages, he had fair knocked her sideways.

Quarrie drew her in against him and held her tight. A few moments respite only. He knew very well that as soon as he left to go about the morning's business, she would be back beside the bed watching the man she loved sleep.

From the refuge of Quarrie's arms, she whispered, "Son, are we ready? If he had perished last night, or should we lose him during this night to come—are ye ready to be chief?"

A question Quarrie had tried to face these many days now. One he should not have had to contemplate for a score of years yet. Da was so strong, so vital.

Was he ready?

"Do no' worry yoursel' for that, at least," he murmured to her. "I shall tak' up my duty when the moment comes."

"I maun worry for it. All his life, he has lived first for this clan. When first we began courting—he said to me, Einid, we canna deal together unless ye understand, the clan will always come first. Our love second. I accepted that and ha' lived by it. Even now…"

Aye, even now Da put the clan first, his concern for the defense of it making him hide his pain. Mayhap that was what made the fever rages so terrible. They had to break through a lifelong restraint.

"I will be ready," Quarrie vowed.

She drew away far enough to gaze into his eyes. "We shall have to speak wi' him, ye and I. Later today when he wakes. Ye maun assure him ye ha' things in hand and will be the chief he needs ye to be, so that he can let go and—and cease suffering."

The tears in her eyes spilled over. What would happen to this woman after the man she adored was gone? She had lived so many years putting him and his duties first. Caring for him, these past months.

So perilous was love.

"Aye," Quarrie said softly. "I will come back." They would try to talk to Da before the fever ramped up for the night and brought the madness again. "Ye get some rest while ye can. Lie down beside him while he is quiet."

He should have followed his own advice, taken a few moments of sleep, however fleeting. Instead, after leaving his mother he choked down a breakfast he did not want and went out.

The sun was well up by then on what looked to be a clear, calm day. Quarrie's gaze moved at once to the sea. Before he could send it ranging far, a cry came from the walls.

"A ship. A ship!"

His heart leaped in his chest, and all the night's weariness flew. Nay, not an attack. Not now. He fairly flew up the treacherous stone stairs and joined Borald on the wall facing west.

"Where? How many?"

"But the one." Borald's face had settled into grim lines.

"There. Just come round Oileán Iur."

Quarrie's heart thudded still more violently. Could it be? But nay…

A black sail, aye, poised there in the strong morning light. Only it was not truly black—likely striped like the last one, which had been red and white.

He blinked to clear his tired eyes and blinked again. Not Hulda's ship, nay. This one had a different silhouette. Slightly smaller, and it sat differently in the water.

Not her, then.

How dare he think she would come back to him? They were enemies.

Were they not?

"Just the one," he breathed at Borald. Men were running along the wall, spreading the word. "Looks to be, unless others are hiding among the isles."

This one showed itself to them quite deliberately. Taunting them, perhaps, with its presence. Small and agile, it moved out from the isle, the same where Hulda's boat had taken shelter when he was captive on it, and headed southward under strong oars.

It would pass them by.

Men shouted now, all around them, giving the alarm. Quarrie stood transfixed.

It could not be her. It could not. At this time of year, with the full of summer upon them, scores of Norse boats might pass by. So long as they did not stop…

This one looked as if it would not. Indeed, it made a fine, braw show as it slid past the rocks that guarded the settlement, showing itself. The sails were plain brown. The dragon head at the prow showed stubby teeth in a grimace. The shields ranged along the side facing the shore showed a wealth of bright colors, as if newly made.

So close did the boat pass that Quarrie could see the people aboard. Most of them rowing. Someone at the tiller. Another figure striding the deck.

Nay. It could not be. He could not know her at such a distance.

Only he did. His spirit leaped to the knowledge, and his heart.

She stood gazing directly at him as the vessel slipped by, her eyes finding him on the wall. Fancy, surely. It could not be so.

The morning light made flax of her fair hair. He could *feel* her.

"Showing himsel' to us," Borald murmured. "D'ye think there are more?"

"Mayhap. Yet they are passing us by," Quarrie managed to reply.

"Aye, so, there may be others in hiding. This one may be taking our measure."

"Mayhap."

Had she returned with the promised—threatened—fleet?

"Prepare the guard. Keep watch."

Neither order was truly necessary. The men prepared on their own as word spread. But though they kept watch long after, no other boats appeared and the one slid away to the south, leaving not so much as a trail behind.

She had wanted him to see her. Quarrie could not dismiss that thought from his mind. All this while, had she held him in her mind even as he held her? Had he imagined it all? No proof that had been Hulda he spied on that deck.

Only he knew.

Later, when he returned to his parents' chamber, he found word of the sighting had penetrated even here. Da, now awake, knew of it, and they were the first words out of his mouth.

"A longboat? But one?"

"But one, Da," Quarrie reassured him.

"Showing itsel' to us, aye? But why?"

That was the question that remained in Quarrie's mind. He could think of only one reason. "Taking our measure, no doubt. Must ha' decided we look too strong to tak' on."

"There is danger everywhere. I maun get to the walls." Even

though night had not yet come, a fitful flush already stained Da's face—the fever flaring. He groaned. "If only I was no' in so much pain. Son, help me up."

When Quarrie did not move to obey, his father directed a stern look at him. "Lend me the strength o' yer shoulder."

"Da, I will not."

"Eh?"

Ma slipped past Quarrie and sat on the edge of the bed. She laid a restraining hand on her husband's chest.

"My darling, my dear one, ye ken how I love ye."

That stilled him and caused him to fix his gaze to her face.

"All these years, I ha' loved ye. Without fail."

"Without fail," Da repeated.

"I ha' watched ye guard this clan like a fierce father and watched ye fight for it time after time. Ye told me often 'tis why ye were born. And ye spared yoursel' naught in it. But I tell ye now, Airlee, it is time to stop fighting. Yer pain..." She moved her hand from his chest to his cheek. "Yer pain is more than any man should bear."

Da said nothing, but abruptly and quite disquietingly, his eyes filled with tears.

Quarrie did not know that he had ever seen his father weep. Och, tears of anger at times, or frustration. Tears shed when Kyle died or over the death of a loyal comrade, fallen. Naught like to this.

Ma went on. "Ye ha' a fine son to tak' yer place. Strong he is, and as steadfast as they come. Ye may trust in him and—and tak' yer rest."

Quarrie drew a breath. Might he become the chief his father was? Could anyone? But Ma could no longer watch this man suffer. Nor could he.

Da said, his gaze still fixed to Ma's, "The healer wishes to tak' my leg. Even then he says it may not cure me. The poison is all through my body. I am sorry, Einid. I was no' strong enough. I failed ye."

"Ye did no' fail." She leaned forward and kissed him full on the lips. "So braw a heart as yours could no' fail."

"What happened to your face? Your bonny face." He reached up and touched her cheek tenderly. "Did I harm ye?"

"Never. Ye never harmed me. It was a blessed day when first ye smiled at me, Airlee MacMurtray. And each day since."

"'Twas ye who smiled at me. Remember?"

"Ye were swimmin' in the sea, the bunch o' ye lads." She dimpled. "And had taken off all yer clothes. To be sure, I did smile at ye."

"My bonny lass." Da turned fierce eyes on Quarrie, all the tears now burned away. "Ye will look after yer ma? Tak' care of her and o' this clan. I will ha' yer promise."

"I promise to do my best, Da."

"Aye, son, we ha' fought this thing together, but I think the battle is near done."

It ended for him later that same night. He had quieted as if at last his heart had found peace. Both Quarrie and his ma sat with him, Ma holding his hand. The fever burned bright, flushing his skin.

And then the hoarse breaths just stopped. Burned up entirely, his spirit fled his body. Quarrie almost swore he saw it go.

Ma wept tears of weariness and relief.

Quarrie shifted beneath the new weight that descended upon him.

❦

CHAPTER TWENTY-SEVEN

THE SETTLEMENT AT Murtray had become a kind of touchstone for Hulda, a place past which they sailed repeatedly following their various victories. She never paused there. She did not dare. But her longing grew.

She did not understand this longing. One man, just a man. One kiss, just a kiss. She had the world by the tail. Every raid they launched had been wildly successful. The men, despite their youth, fought well and sailed even better. She was one of them, treated as their leader rather than a woman. She'd returned home twice, carrying enough wealth to let her thumb her nose in Faðir's face. The men—her crew—remained eager for more, and said the *Freya* sailed under good enchantment.

Hulda had all she wanted. How dare she want for one more thing?

It was impossible anyway. He was her enemy. His people—if not him personally—had killed her brother.

That thought, even as she entertained it, tweaked something in the back of her mind. As if it had all happened before, long ago.

She concentrated on moving through her days. On her successes. When the men asked why they sailed always past the one Scottish settlement, she said since it was where Jute had died, she paid him tribute.

Forgive me, bróðir, *for the lie.*

Life aboard the cramped ship was not always pleasant. The *Freya* still had her idiosyncrasies with which they all learned to

148

deal. But Hulda had the pleasure of watching her young crew grow and begin to harden. They learned difficult lessons, turned from overeager boys into men. They were learning the price of what they did—the costs of greed. The weight of taking a man's life.

She came to realize she was the eldest among them, at a score and three. The venture should not have gone so well, with a green crew and a patched-together boat, though old Frode had done a good job. They had done a good job working together.

She and Garik, who had always got on well, became fast friends. He and Helje were her second- and third-in-command. She liked Helje full well, but it was to Garik she turned in her rare leisure moments, and to whom she looked to share a laugh.

Often, as when Quarrie MacMurtray had been captive, she shared watch with him.

They were together one such night while the rest of the crew slept, not anchored but sliding through the dark as if, ja, *Freya* could see her own way with her wooden dragon eyes. A rare moment of peace, for these days Hulda's heart rarely stopped questing.

Quietly, barely above a whisper, Garik said, "Can you believe how well we have done? Mayhap it is true—this vessel is spelled for good."

"I never paid for any charms," Hulda returned, "before we left home."

"Some of them may have." Garik jerked his head at the sleepers and grinned. "A superstitious lot."

"Not too superstitious to have a woman aboard."

"I think we have laid that to rest. They do not think of you as a woman." He grinned still more broadly. "No disrespect meant."

She barely *felt* like a woman.

"They adore you," Garik told her. "They would die for you. I hope you know that."

She looked at him, startled. "Nei. Why?"

"You gave them a chance, did you not? Younger sons, many

of them are, and waiting in line for their faðirs' attention."

Even a younger son—or dottir—deserved a chance.

"They are as loyal a crew as you will find."

"I know that, ja." But she thought about it, there in the dark, about the power it gave her. Most members of a crew answered not only to their captain but to the man who backed the venture, often one who remained at home.

They, as a crew, had no one looking over their shoulders. They had an agile boat and a measure of—well, freedom.

Could she use that? Could she use it to return to Quarrie MacMurtray?

"Our targets have all been small ones," she mused aloud. "And have fallen to us easily."

"So far."

"So far," Hulda repeated. "I think it well that we do not reach too far above ourselves. If we have a good season and do not get too greedy, we may be able to afford another boat, in time."

"The men back home," Garik said with some relish, "are talking of us."

"Oh?"

"They have never seen a venture such as ours, where the ownership as well as the wealth is shared. They wait for us to quarrel and fail."

"Mayhap then," Hulda said, gazing into the dark, "mayhap if they hold for us such ill will, *Freya* should cease with going home."

"Eh?" Garik cocked an eye at her.

"What is the goal, Garik? The greater goal?" When he did not answer, she went on, "Land. Land here, where the weather is kinder and we do not need to cover great distances of ocean to get where we need to raid."

"Land? But…us?"

"Why not? Others have done it. In Orkney. In Shetland. Look at York—"

"We are not the powerful jarls who hold sway in York. Far

from it."

"Not yet. We do not need to be. Garik, what if we could offer the men a base here? Not just a share of wealth, but land."

"It is mad," he breathed. "And wonderful."

"Fortune has been on our side so far. What if we tried to deal with the people here? Come to them not in violence but in a desire to bargain."

Garik considered it for a moment. "They would never trust us."

"They have accepted Norse chiefs elsewhere."

"After being conquered, ja. We have not the might for that. And yet…" Garik focused on the stars overhead. "Land. If we could achieve that, we would take a step up on our faðirs, eh?"

"We would."

"That"—Garik gestured to the sleeping crew behind him—"might mean more to this particular lot than any wealth we have taken so far."

"Ja."

"But how?"

"I have been thinking on that." Thinking much. "We cannot hope to conquer by fire, nei—not yet. But by bargaining—ja, mayhap. There is a man here among these lands who owes us for his release. Possibly for his life."

An image of Quarrie MacMurtray burst upon Hulda's mind. A prize more tantalizing than any gold, silver, or lands.

"The Scot you let go."

"Ja. Him."

"You think he would deal with you?"

"I do. Think on it, Garik."

"I am."

"We might return to that isle where we sheltered before. Make it our temporary base."

"And then?"

"I will request to meet and talk with him. He has some authority there. We will bargain."

"Ja, but he and his kind will not want us there on his threshold, hovering like buzzards over a killing field. What is to keep him from murdering you out of hand? You and whoever goes ashore with you. The ruse we used last time will not fly. He will never believe we have a fleet of boats."

"He will not murder me out of hand."

"Why not?" Garik said forthrightly. "In his place, I would."

"He will not murder me," she repeated with absolute certainty. Other words circled her mind. *I will find ye. I will always find ye.*

Nei, but this time it is I who will find you. Wait for me. Wait right where you are.

"It is a risky venture," Garik whispered into the dark. "But so was buying *Freya* in the first place. I will have to speak with Helje."

"Do you think he will agree?"

"I do not know. He is stronger-headed than me. It is possible."

"You must convince him. I have a feeling about this."

"Hulda…" Garik hesitated, and she looked at him. "Is there something between you and this man? This Quarrie Mac-Murtray?"

He was her best friend, was Garik. Surely she could say. Yet something held her back. "How could there be?"

"I do not know. Only—the way you let him go. And the farewell you gave him."

"I did that because I knew without knowing that we would need to deal with him again. Do you not see? We need his goodwill now."

"I am not sure how much goodwill there is. We are Norse and he is Scot."

Ja, there was that. Did it matter? She would not allow it to.

"Convince your brother," she said. "We will take it one step at a time."

CHAPTER TWENTY-EIGHT

THE DAYS SINCE Da's death had been difficult, each and every one of them. The weight Quarrie assumed the moment his father passed only grew heavier, increasing by increments. Everyone expected so much from him.

There had been no chance to recover and precious little time to grieve. The clansfolk assumed he would step into Da's place immediately. In truth, he had been going through the motions of filling that place for a long while. But holding the responsibility for the settlement and everyone in it could not feel more different.

Ma had fallen apart in her grief and made no fit ally. Though he'd known all his life the affection his parents held for each other, he did not think he'd realized till now how much Ma had loved her husband. She wept for days. He could get no sense from her, and he began to worry for her health.

He could not lose her, also.

That particular worry might well pass, so he hoped, as she recovered. His responsibilities would not, never until he himself died.

Those around him made him aware of his responsibilities at every opportunity. At every moment of the day and half the night, people came at him sharing problems and wanting answers. He was not sleeping much, and when he did manage to sleep, he dreamed.

Those same dreams over and over again.

He was with a woman. Not always the same women. Only—
she was the same.

It was as if in his brief moments of sleep he returned to a past he could not remember. A trio of pasts, for she was a woman of varying guises. She stood outside the washing place with him in the sunshine. She walked toward him with a great gray hound at her side. She lay with him in passion while sweet music played upon a harp, somewhere close at hand.

She did not appear to be the same woman, but aye, she was. The smile in her eyes that embraced him was the same. As were the feelings that engulfed him at her presence.

He craved those feelings just as he craved the music he heard in his head. Yet he slept so seldom and had only glimpses of her. Enough to make him ache.

He told himself it was all just fancy, a reaction to his grief and distraction. A means he'd found to escape what he carried.

But the dreams did not feel like dreams so much as—aye— memories. Unlike other dreams, the feelings they evoked did not fade at dawn. He recalled every detail and each one made him tingle, a sensation that, just like his grief, preoccupied him.

Neighboring chiefs both to the north and south heard of Da's death and sent messages with their commiserations. Those messengers also brought terrible tales of Norse attacks all along the shore as far as Anglesea in Wales. A number of churches had been destroyed and smaller settlements burned to the ground. Every chief along the Scottish coast remained on alert.

Which was what took Quarrie up on the walls first thing every morning and last thing every night. Among his other duties, keeping his people—Da's people—safe from attack seemed a most sacred one. But though they did sight sails against the wild blue of the sky from time to time, the boats always passed by.

Until, that was, one sunny morning.

Quarrie had just begun with drilling the men in the field alongside the keep. Indeed, so warm was it that he had stripped down to his kilt, as had many of the men with whom he worked.

They had a number of the younger lads out, those who so often clamored to be allowed to fight, and Quarrie meant to give them a taste of what that meant, now that his ribs had long healed and his bruises were things of the past.

So noisy was it in the field, he nearly missed the cry from the walls above. Men were hollering, lads chirping and exclaiming. Weapons clattering.

Not until someone repeatedly called his name—"Chief Quarrie. Chief Quarrie!" and then, "A sail!"—did he pause and look up.

Those words, *a sail*, captured everything within him.

"Hush!" He held up a hand, and by bits the training field fell silent. He looked up.

Borach it was, straining to catch his attention. "A sail."

Just passing? Quarrie did not pause to ask. His feet already moved, carrying him from the field to the steep stairs with a train of others following.

He never later remembered climbing those stairs. Only the harsh texture of the stone wall under his hands when he reached it and stood leaning out, following Borach's pointing hand.

There.

Aye, it was a boat. Disappointment hit him like a punch to the gut. Not Hulda's ship, the one aboard which he'd been held captive. But...

It might be the other he'd seen sail past, aye, earlier in the season. The one aboard which he'd fancied—*fancied*—he'd spied her.

Had it been but fancy?

This boat was agile, like the other. Light in the water. The dragon at the prow appeared to be staring them down.

That was because the boat was heading in to shore. *Heading in.*

"They are heading in!" Borach called. "Everyone to arms. To arms!"

The men on the wall scrambled. Those below in the bailey, most of whom had followed Quarrie from the training field, including the youngsters, froze and gazed to sea.

Quarrie raised an arm and called, "Halt. Halt!"

This was no attack. The boat came in gracefully without haste, the crew at the oars and not a sword or axe in sight.

Not an attack. Something else.

Men on the shore ran to the place whence the boat headed. As before, when Hulda had come for her answer, it paused just offshore, the boat having a shallow draught.

Quarrie could see figures moving about on deck. He could also see his own men looking up to him for direction.

"Hold!" he called again, and to Borach, "They want to talk."

"Aye, but—" Borach began.

Quarrie, his eyes narrowed against the glare of light on the water, barely heard him. He watched the figures moving about on the boat and fastened on one in particular. He went abruptly light in the head and had to clutch the wall to remain upright.

It was *her*.

She had returned.

To him.

None of those three thoughts made any sense. No more sense than the dreams he'd been having or the sudden conviction that the woman from those dreams would soon stand before him.

Again.

He floated down the stairs and along the lengthy path to the shore, even as she and a single companion leaped over the side of the longboat and splashed through the tide.

They met just where the foam kissed the shingle, two elements that could scarcely differ more coming inevitably together.

"Hulda Elvarsdottir," he said.

He spoke her name, and it sounded like music in Hulda's ears. She had wanted this so long, she'd been more than half convinced that when she saw him again, when he stood before her, it would all come crashing down in bitter disappointment, for naught could match her imaginings.

She'd been wrong.

For he stood here before her whole and alive, and he looked good. Ach, by Freya's heart, better than good. Tall and bare-chested, wearing only a checkered kilt with the sun shining full upon him and turning his brown hair to copper. Her eyes feasted upon the sight of him and her spirit also, something that had all the while been yawning and hungry becoming satisfied.

He was real. He was here. He was all a woman's heart could desire.

Everything else faded away from her. The water at her feet. The boat at her back. Garik at her side. Even the savage Scotsmen glaring at her, most with weapons in their hands.

She might die here and now.

At least she'd laid eyes on him first.

"Quarrie MacMurtray," she returned, and her voice, rather surprisingly, sounded like her own. For she did not feel like herself. She felt like a woman who knew him, who had claimed him, somehow as her own.

Madness.

"I come not to attack," she said, and looked around at all the hostile faces, the hostile postures, even though it hurt to take her eyes from him. "But to talk."

"Talk," he repeated, and even that single word shivered through her.

"Ja. You owe me that." She returned her gaze to him. Did he look surprised?

A man came running up to him, out of breath and heavily armed. Quarrie glanced at him.

"She comes to talk," he said. "No attack. Understand?"

The man gave Hulda a glare out of hard blue eyes but nodded.

"Come," Quarrie said to Hulda, "we will speak together in

the hall."

"Stay here," she told Garik, and to Quarrie, "My man will not come under attack? I have your word?"

"My word on it." Quarrie directed a look of his own at the men and added, "This man's safety is assured, aye?"

No one spoke. No one moved as Hulda and Quarrie walked up the stony path toward the tall stone structure ahead.

How strange it felt, after her summer, to enter a Scot's settlement in peace.

The thought crossed her mind that she might not leave again. She could indeed die here. Felled by a dirk in the back. An arrow. MacMurtray's hand.

Not by MacMurtray's hand. He would not harm her. How she knew that, she could not say. She just did.

She entered the stone structure at Quarrie's side, him meeting every hostile glare with an even stare. She remembered the place, ja, from her last visit—it could not be less like the houses back home, which were long and roofed with thatch or soil and had a central hearth. This had an entryway made of stone and a hall with a timbered roof. A hard place to fight one's way into, or out of again.

A fire burned at the far end of the room. Quarrie led her to this and turned to face her.

After the strong light outside, this seemed very dim. She could not see him as well as she wanted to. His hair—tied back into a tail down his back—looked plain brown. His bare chest no longer gleamed.

It did not matter, because he was close enough that she could reach out and touch him if she wanted to.

She did.

"So…" He spoke softly and it sounded incredibly intimate in that large, empty place. As if whatever words they spoke should be honest ones and would exist only for the two of them. Even if she knew better. Naught in their world could concern but the two of them.

"Will ye sit," he invited her, "before ye say wha' ye will?"

Why did he affect her the way he did, this one man out of the many in the world? Why did the sound of his voice send that shiver through her every time he spoke? Why did the very scent of him—for she stood near enough to catch it—cause her emotions to rise up wild? Longing and an answer to it, all in one.

"Ja, let us sit together and speak."

CHAPTER TWENTY-NINE

QUARRIE GLANCED AT the woman who sat beside the fire in his hall, and had to blink before he could believe his eyes.

She was here.

She had returned.

Why?

The last time he'd been this close to her, she'd kissed him before sending him over the side of her boat to freedom. Aye, she was right—he owed her. A hearing, if naught more.

Was it that truth that kept him from turning her away?

He snagged a flask of ale and two cups from the head table and turned back to her. Stopped cold.

She sat looking as foreign as she could do, here in this familiar place. Still clad from head to foot in men's clothing. In armor. But he knew far better than to take her for a man.

She sat very straight, almost motionless, only her eyes following him as he moved. She had removed her helmet and her hair shone pale in the low light. Long and straight. Beautiful hair.

He had seen the way she looked at him when they were outside, seared him, her gaze flitting everywhere like a touch. Upon his hair, across his bare chest and down his legs. To his lips, and fastening lastly to his eyes, compelling. She looked at him as if she wanted to—

Och, perhaps kiss him again.

He wanted to touch her. Wanted it with such incredibly intensity, he had to catch himself back and make sure he left plenty of space between them when he sat down opposite her. "Will ye drink? 'Tis no' poisoned, I do assure ye, but was left over there from last night."

"I will drink."

He poured both cups, and let her choose one. Her fingers were long, tanned, and roughened by work. The sort of work a crew on board a ship would do.

He had a sudden image of them wrapped around his—

"You will be wondering why I have returned."

"Aye. That is no' the same longboat. A different one."

"Ja, you are right. The boat you were aboard belonged to my faðir. This one belongs to me and my crew. A…venture, it is."

She spoke his language very well, her accent only mildly flavoring the words. The accent was not familiar, nay, but something about sitting here and speaking with her this way was.

"A venture," he repeated.

"Ja. We sail for gain and profit. I do not come to you, this time, seeking revenge. That does not mean I have forgotten my brother or his death. That I will never do."

"You should know—" Quarrie started, then stopped and began again. "You should know that the man who killed your brother is no longer living."

"Is he not?" One pale eyebrow lifted. "You did know his identity, then, when last we met."

"I did. I was protecting him." He gave her a level stare. "He was my father."

"Ah."

"He died by your brother's hand."

"How can that be?"

"He perished not long after you last were here from the wound he took defending this settlement. A wound dealt, in fact, by your brother just before Da killed him."

"Ah," she said again, and swallowed hard. "We are even then. You have lost your faðir and I my bróðir."

"Aye, if ye want to look at it that way."

"There is naught left for which to seek revenge and naught to forgive." She pressed her lips tight. "It seems I made no mistake, then, in returning."

"Why *have* you returned, Mistress Hulda?"

At the sound of her name, her eyes came up and fastened to his. Incredible eyes they were, pale as water and surrounded by brown lashes. Nothing like the eyes of any of the women he'd been seeing in his dreams.

Only they were.

He could not explain it. If he tried, he would have to say there was a thread. A thread running from those women to this one. If he ventured to express that to anyone, they would call him mad.

"Master MacMurtray, mine is a young crew. Out for gain, as I say. To prove ourselves. I have not the might to battle you. So instead, I come to bargain."

"To bargain," he repeated stupidly.

"Ja. Have you influence here in this place?"

"My father was chief. I am chief after him."

"So any agreements made between the two of us will hold strong."

"Any agreements made between the two of us would have to benefit all my people. I live for them."

At that, some emotion flickered in the pale eyes. "You are a selfless man. You gave yourself over to protect your faðir. Now you think of your people rather than your own desire."

"That is so." If he did think of his own desire, he would reach out and touch her. Try to recapture the feelings that had swamped him when they'd kissed. Tell her how often he'd thought of her, almost without ceasing. What a miracle it seemed to be with her again.

"I have for you an offer that is—how would you put it?—of benefit to both of us."

"Mutually beneficial. How can that be?"

"Let me explain. We are a young crew, as I say, and trying to prove ourselves. Most of us are younger sons. You are not a younger son?"

Quarrie shook his head.

"You do not know then what that means."

But he did, instinctively, so it seemed. A younger son had to fight twice as hard for advantages.

"And I," she went on, "am a woman. The wind, so to speak, blows not at our backs but in our faces."

"I understand."

"The season for viking is short."

"Viking?"

"Raiding." She seemed to grope for the word. "And it is a long way home. We would like a base here. Land. A safe harbor."

"Eh?" He could not have heard that right. Aye, the Norse had taken over islands in the north, and there was said to be a sizeable settlement on the east coast of Britain, a place he'd never been. Not here. Not yet.

"Impossible," he said.

"Why?"

"This is our land. Hard held for time out of mind. Fought for. Died for."

"Just so. I suggest to you a cessation in the fighting. Perhaps even the dying."

"I do not understand."

She looked almost apologetic. "I explain it poorly. The language is unwieldy in my mouth. You are familiar with a *hundr*, ja? A—hound?"

"Aye, so."

"A man, he cares for the hound. He feeds it. Gives it a home. It then protects him and his."

"Aye?"

"I ask you to let us—us and the *Freya*—be your hundr."

"Freya?"

"It is the name of our ship."

"I—"

"The bargain I seek is, you will give us room here, a place of harbor, and we will guard you, ja?"

"Guard us."

"Like a hundr."

Quarrie shook his head.

"Chief Quarrie, there are other Norsemen who visit these shores, ja? Some who come in great numbers. Like I pretended to you before, only in truth. They will come. As the season ages they will, for targets will become scarce. A hundr could keep these from your door."

"A hundr could also turn and bite us." Was she truly suggesting what he thought?

"Not a loyal one. It would never bite the hand that feeds it."

"Mistress Hulda, you are suggesting I afford ye a foothold here. On Scottish soil."

"Only a small one."

"From whence I can but assume ye will set out to attack my neighbors to the north and south."

"You have agreements with them?"

"They are Scots. How should I bargain over their safety with a Norsewoman?"

"You must think of your own people first."

She was right in that—he must.

"So you suggest I set a fierce guard dog at my gate that I…what? Loose at the dark of night to maraud against my neighbors?"

She sighed. "Have you heard of—what is it called—Black Pool in Ireland?"

"You mean *Dubh lin.*"

"Dublin in your language, Ja. It started as a Norse enclave. It is now a powerful holding that dominates all eastern Ireland."

Before he could speak, she rushed on. "I do not ask this of you. I will not take your settlement. It is assuredly yours. But it would be enough of an advantage to us, to have a home port from whence we can come and go with—with felicity, that we are willing to keep other marauders, as you call them, from your shore."

"You could do that, could ye?"

"I can. It is a good offer."

It was, in its way. Only his neighbors might well then turn on him, and he would have to cede Scottish land. To a Norsewoman.

"I do not know that my people would agree to such a scheme."

"Do they have to agree? You are chief."

"There is a council. Do you have such a thing, in your world?"

"Ja, surely. But the jarl hears grievances and passes judgment. Here, you are like the jarl, ja?"

"Everyone has a say."

"Ja, everyone has a say. But the jarl overrules them."

Not quite.

He looked her in the eye. "For this agreement to hold, for any of it to hold, I would have to trust you."

"Ja. Ja, you will. As we will have to trust you, that if we take refuge where you afford it to us, we will not be set upon in the night and slain."

She had taken none of her ale. Now she set the cup aside and reached out one hand for him. Laid her fingers across his wrist where it rested upon his knee. No more than that.

Everything within him leaped to attention. Each muscle and sinew. As swiftly as that, his blood caught fire.

"You can trust me, Quarrie MacMurtray."

Cursed if he did not believe her.

CHAPTER THIRTY

A SONG PLAYED in Hulda's head, one from which she could not seem to free herself. It had followed her from that place—MacMurtray's hall—all the way back down to the rocks of the shore. A tune she did not know, yet somehow recognized.

Just like Quarrie himself. She did not know him. Only she did.

She marveled over it even as she rejoined Garik, who looked immeasurably relieved to see her. He stood surrounded by hostile clansmen, all of them armed. None had moved against him, but danger filled the air.

Could it work, this thing she suggested to Quarrie Mac-Murtray?

He had walked her down, she carrying her helm under one arm, the feel of his wrist, his skin still seeming burned into her fingers. Warm. Strong, inexpressibly pleasurable.

A pleasure he was to gaze upon, she thought as she turned to look at him. Even more so to touch.

He had what she would consider a perfect body. Tall, lean, yet well-muscled. Broad in the shoulders and narrow at the hips, with a pattern of red-brown hair on his broad chest. She wanted to feel him. Wanted it with an intensity that shocked her.

How long had it been since she'd had a man? Haakon had been the last, and naught about Haakon had felt like this. How long since she'd let herself feel like a woman?

He made her feel so, from the bones outward. Yet gazing at him now, on this stretch of his shore, she saw uncertainty in his eyes.

"I will need to talk this over with members o' my council," he repeated.

"Ja, good. we will wait where we did before, the inlet of that island. If you need me, you have only to row across. Or"—one corner of her mouth quirked up—"if you choose, you may swim."

THAT MOUTH. IT had once been fastened to Quarrie's. Hot. Hard, yet soft.

He wanted it there again. He wanted more, much more.

This was madness, every bit of it.

And yet…and yet there was reassurance in knowing she would be where he could reach her. If, as she said, he chose.

Her men fairly hung from the longboat not far off in the water. Indeed, one of them clung to the neck of the beast that formed the prow, watching to make sure she returned to them safely.

A hundr.

She turned and, with her man at her side, splashed out. No one on the shore moved. Quarrie could not be sure they breathed.

Hulda and her companion climbed aboard. With undeniable grace, the boat came about, moving lightly on the waves at the direction of the men, who had taken the oars. Not until they were far out did everyone left on the shore turn on Quarrie—all speaking at once.

"Wha' was that?" Borach demanded, loudest because he was right in Quarrie's ear. "Are those the same who captured ye?"

"Some the same. Same commander. Different vessel. Different crew."

"Wha' did she want?"

"Come to the hall. Call others o' the council. I will explain."

Try to explain.

His ma came to the meeting, news of their visitor having reached her. He could only consider that good, for she'd taken little interest in anything since Da's death. She'd only rarely ever sat in on meetings Da held. Did this mean she had no faith in whatever decisions Quarrie might make? Or merely that she sought to represent her husband?

Either way, she sat quiet, face pale, hands clasped in her lap. Quarrie recounted the visit from Hulda, leaving out his own feelings for now. Chaos ensued.

Everyone spoke at once. Protests came thick and fast. *It is madness.* Aye, well, he agreed with that. *Out of the question.* Well, mayhap not so.

"Ye canna trust her," one of Da's old cronies howled.

"I do trust her." From whence had that come? He'd not meant to say it aloud.

"Lad, ye're raving. The pressures o' walkin' in your da's footsteps ha' turned yer mind. They are Norse. Just because she is a woman does no' mak' her less dangerous."

Nay, it did not. More so, perhaps.

"Land!" roared another of the men. "Our land. That which we ha' died to defend. Ye would gi' it over to them?"

"I did no' say that."

He could have her within reach. Where he might see her often. Mayhap every day. Everything inside him yearned toward that, even as his mind agreed with what his advisors were saying.

"They are but a small crew. One boat," Borach said. "We might lure them in and destroy them."

"We could." Quarrie glanced at him. "Wha' good would that do?"

"So many fewer Norse in the world," old Kalen replied. "By God, lad! Will ye even entertain such a scheme?"

Quarrie frowned at the fire. They were not going to agree. These men would not accept any scheme that might keep Hulda near to him.

"Think on it, lad," said old Fergus, who in Quarrie's youth had been their arms master. "She is asking ye to house her that she might prey upon other Scotsmen. Yer neighbors and of Celtic blood."

"Surely," said Borach more softly, "our loyalty is to them."

"I am no' certain about that." Quarrie raised his eyes from the fire and looked at each of them in turn. "My loyalty is to ye, and ye, and every other member o' our clan. Where were our neighbors last year when we came under attack? When our chief was so sore hurt. If I can keep from fighting more such battles as that which stole my father's life, by alliance or otherwise, I will."

They stared back at him, appalled. Angry. Wondering.

He got to his feet. "I ha' heard yer opinions. I need to think."

He went out and drew the blessed air into his lungs. From the front of the keep he could still see the Norse boat, Hulda's boat, moving off with unearthly grace back toward the offshore island. A threat? A promise.

Should there be promises between them, him and this woman who had entered his life from nowhere, and who had somehow been there all the while?

He could not remain standing here. Faces turned toward him and eyes stared. He needed to be alone.

He might go to the burying ground where Da lay in peace or otherwise. Though he'd visited there often enough since Da's death, his father had never yet spoken to him. If he chose to do so now, it would likely be in anger.

Da would not want him to deal with the Norse. No more than Borach or old Fergus did.

He took off walking down to the shore, moving swiftly and then heading northward. He preferred the trail to the south, a good place to be alone and gather his thoughts. Here, the sheds of the fishers and boatbuilders lined the shore along with a few huts that soon petered out into rough gorse and seagrass.

He trudged on, and the rocks lining the shingle grew larger, as if scattered by a giant's hand.

Here, so the old stories told, the hero Adair MacMurtray—an ancestor of Quarrie's hailing from Ireland—had come ashore with his woman to save the settlement, him being a warrior of some renown. Long, long ago that had been. He had taken over the settlement and, if one could believe the scholars and shanachies, led it well.

The man's blood still ran through Quarrie's veins. It made a connection. And a responsibility. Those of his blood had been protecting this place a long while.

Should he be the one to crack open the door and admit an enemy?

He rounded a jut of rock that stuck out into the quiet ocean, and stood looking. Here, around this curve of the headland, lay a narrow inlet not unlike the one on the far island toward which Hulda's boat now headed like a homing gull. Room for one small ship, no more. A rough knoll of land that was not in use, but MacMurtray land. His to lend or gift, if he chose.

He could place them here, the Norse. House them in this wild and disused place like a hound at its master's door.

From here, she could miss nothing that moved up or down the coast. From here she could sally out to do her marauding.

Not his folk, though. She would not harm his own.

How far would a man go to protect what he loved? To be near what he—

But nay. He did not love her. He could not possibly. He was taken by her, aye. Attracted. Fascinated. But...

Och, let him at least be honest about it. He had never wanted anything the way he wanted Hulda. Had never imagined wanting anything so much.

Must he sacrifice a desire so bright to the will of his people? Aye, so. A chief did sacrifice. He had only to look at his da to remember that.

She had been right about one thing, though. As chief, this decision was ultimately his and his alone.

CHAPTER THIRTY-ONE

"A BOAT, MISTRESS! Just rounding the mouth of the inlet."

Hulda narrowed her eyes against the light of the morning. Another glorious day it was, with pale blue skies and a sea as still as a mirror glass.

A boat approached, ja. A very small one. Only one man aboard, and her breath caught in her throat at the flash of auburn in his hair. She knew him even without seeing him clearly.

"I think it is yon chief," Garik said. "The one with whom you went to speak."

Of course it was. She had told him he might row out to see her here, though she had not believed he would.

He had come to her. Just as she had returned to him.

She climbed up on the rail beside Freya's prow, the better to see. He rowed strongly, the lithe grace of his body visible in its movements. She had seen a great deal of him yesterday, when he wore naught but his rough kilt. Sinew and smooth muscle and…

Everything a woman could desire.

This man. *This man.*

He came alone, armed with courage. She stood and watched, barely breathing. It felt as if the whole world moved. As if she stood upon the rim of a wheel that shifted.

The craft was made of wood covered in hide. When he drew near enough, he shipped the oars.

"Mistress Hulda," he called up to her, "come aboard. I ha' somewhat to show ye."

Before Hulda could move, Helje seized her arm. "You had best not go alone."

"There is room in that boat for but two."

"He might kill you."

"I am well armed." She met his gaze. "Do you doubt I can take care of myself?"

He shook his head but exchanged looks with his brother, Garik, who also began to speak.

Hulda forestalled him. "I will go."

Faðir Odin himself could not keep her from that boat.

Quarrie brought the small craft alongside her larger one and watched as she swung down to join him. There was barely room for two after all, and she sat with her legs gathered under her, facing him.

He glanced at the faces hanging over Freya's side. "They worry for ye. There is no need."

"I know."

He would not harm her. He would as soon harm himself.

A buzzing set up in her blood as he rowed away. A feeling of pure rightness.

"Where are we bound?"

"I wish, as I say, to show ye somewhat."

She contented herself with watching him as he rowed. He wore a kilt and a simple tunic open at the throat to reveal a hint of tanned skin and reddish hair. Dampened hide boots. His hair streamed loose over his shoulders and down his back, and his eyes gleamed hazel green.

The best thing ever she had seen.

She wanted to talk to him. Demand words in return. An account of his life. She longed for every detail, but at the same time she wanted to remain silent lest she break the spell of his presence, the sun upon them, the drops of water from his oars and the expression in his eyes.

What did it mean, that expression?

He rowed strongly around the shoulder of the island and

toward the rocky shore, not back to his settlement, *nei*, but headed for a point farther north. No buildings there, just great outcroppings of rock and the sea running fast up onto them.

Not until they neared the place did she see there was a very narrow inlet that led between the rocks to a shallow *vik*, or bay. She could not hide her astonishment.

"I did not know this was here."

"It is difficult to spy from the sea. Do ye think your boat could sail in through here?"

Hulda shot a sharp look at him. "Well, she has a very shallow draught. But it is narrow," she observed as he took them in. A rough, wild place it was, all stone grown over to gorse.

"This is your land?"

"It is. I thought…" He paused, and their eyes met.

"You would give this over to me? To us."

"I must tell ye, my people are against any sort o' alliance."

But he was not. Else why bring her here?

He shipped the oars and they glided up onto the shingle. Hulda leaped out without waiting for an invitation and stood facing the sea, trying to think despite the emotions streaming through her.

He wanted her here. To be sure, he did. Was it not meant that she should stand here beside him? That she should exist in his company at liberty to touch him. Be with him.

"It is a fine place of concealment," she said, even though she no longer thought about the small bay or her intentions. Only of the chance to stand beside him this way, to exist in his company.

An impulse stronger than any she had ever known.

"Will it work for your purposes?"

Hulda pretended to measure the little inlet with her eyes. It would allow her to stay near him. "Ja." She drew her gaze from the water and looked at him. Here in the flesh after all her memories of him, all her imaginings. The sunlight turned his skin golden. His eyes held hesitancy, and a gleam of what might be daring. "Do you offer it to me? Over the objections of your people?"

He appeared to think on that, though he must have considered it all the night long before rowing out to her.

To her.

"Aye, but there will need to be a sworn agreement. Between ye and me. That none o' your men will cause harm to me or mine."

"I will not harm you, Quarrie MacMurtray." She faced him fully now, the sea and all it carried at her back. She was a tall woman; only four fingers or so separated them in height. It allowed her to gaze straight into his eyes.

"Or mine."

"Or yours." Was there anything to which she would not agree in order to remain near him? But ja, her young crew—her friends—relied upon her.

She tossed her head. "There will have to be promises between us." Promises as there had been in some past she could not quite recall.

"Promises," he repeated.

"Sacred ones," she told him.

His eyebrows lifted. "Can that be, when I doubt very much we believe in the same gods?"

"I meant sacred to you and me." Hulda pressed a hand to her heart. "I will trust in you, Quarrie MacMurtray."

He drew a breath that expanded his chest. A new light appeared in his eyes. "And I in ye."

"I will not betray you—that is my promise. If you afford me and my crew room here upon your land, I will be your watch hundr and raise nei weapons against you or yours."

"And I will no' betray ye, and will keep my own fro' raising a blade to ye and yours."

"Ja, so. It is a promise given. Shall we then seal it?"

Any such agreement in the worlds either of them knew would be affirmed with a gripping of hands, palm to palm or more likely forearm to forearm, weaponless.

Instead, Hulda stepped into his arms.

As natural as breathing the action was, and as impossible to prevent as the waves striding to the shore. She had wanted this since the last time she'd touched him. The last time she'd kissed him. She felt awakened by the desire, more alive than she had ever been.

Their mouths met, both open and reaching. His essence, his being, flooded upon her even his lips molded to hers with an inexpressible hunger, and the taste of him poured into her.

She had wanted this, precisely this, all her life.

He made a sound in his throat—desire, perhaps it was, or claiming. Because ja, he claimed all of her in that kiss, from the damp skin inside her boots to the thinnest strand of hair on the top of her head.

She wound her arms around his neck and pressed her body to his. He felt good, hard, right, and somehow familiar. His hair, wild and tangled, twined between her fingers. She coaxed and wooed his tongue with hers, and drew it into her mouth.

Never had she kissed a man so or dreamed she might, a message that she wanted him inside her. But no one could see them here save the gulls and the sun and the gods, whatever of the last may look upon them.

"Hulda, lass," he marveled when at last their lips parted and they breathed raggedly.

Was she a lass? Of late, since Jute's death, she had not felt like one. But she was *his* lass, ja. She was his.

From the distance of a mere breath, she gazed into his eyes. A true hazel, for they carried flecks of gold also, and brown. Thick brown lashes. Freckles beneath the tan of his skin. She liked the strength of his nose, and the reddish hair on his jaw, and the way his brows lifted over those steady eyes.

Perfect, was her man.

"It is a promise," she told him. "Given and sworn."

"Let us swear it again."

He dove for her lips. This time he wooed her, his tongue

caressing hers in a manner that made her knees go weak. No matter that, for he drew her to him with such strength, her feet left the shingle.

She wanted to remain thus forever. Tasting him. Feeling him.

How long that kiss lasted, she never later knew. An eternity, mayhap. Not long enough.

When her feet again met the ground, she had to clutch hold of him for strength, for orientation. A smile gleamed in his eyes.

"Now," she breathed unsteadily, "that is a promise."

"Not to be broken," he agreed. "Yet we maun discuss the details."

Were there details? Was there anything in all the world besides standing here with him? Feeling the warmth of him. This inestimable sense of belonging.

He let go of her. But before she could protest, he grasped both her hands. One after the other, he lifted them and dropped kisses into her palms. Planted a kiss at either side of her mouth and on both cheeks in turn. Blessed her with another kiss on her brow.

So beautiful was it, she wanted to weep.

"Stay here, Hulda Elvarsdottir, where I might be near to ye, whatever comes."

"I will stay with you, Quarrie MacMurtray."

Always.

CHAPTER THIRTY-TWO

W HEN QUARRIE ROWED Hulda back to the island, her men still half hung off the dragon boat, some with weapons in their hands. She waved an arm at them, gesturing them back, her eyes narrowed against the light.

Incredible eyes hers were, pale as the mist and so full of emotions he could not begin to name them. He did not have to. He could feel them in his own heart.

One of the men leaned out from the rear of the vessel and called to Hulda in her own language.

She replied to him in Gaelic. "All is well, Helje." She turned back to Quarrie and prepared to disembark. "I will have to speak to my crew, make sure they agree. This boat, it is owned by all of us who have a share."

He studied her, noting the strength in her face and the determination in those clear eyes. "You think they will agree?"

"We spoke of it beforehand, so ja. And you—you must convince your folk."

"I will have the much harder task, I fear."

"Be strong." She did not add *for me*, but he heard the words in his mind.

She swarmed aboard the dragon boat and he moved off, still under the stares of her crew. He was growing heartily sick of the oars, but he'd better get used to it, if he wanted to see her.

He did want to see her. More, he wanted her in his life. Part of the weave and weft of it, a mere hand's reach from him at all times. Whether or not that might be possible, he could not say.

For the life of him, he could not see how he might make it happen.

A number of men waited for him on the shore when he reached the settlement and pulled the small craft in.

Borach, conspicuous among them, asked, "Is all well?"

Hulda's crew might well have asked the same thing.

"Aye," Quarrie said shortly. "Summon back the members o' the council. I ha' news."

He must present it to them as such, he told himself as he trudged up to the keep. A decision made, and naught left open to discussion. He was not, in an ordinary way, a man to throw his weight around. Anyone who had followed Da—a force to be reckoned with in his own right—did not. He'd been a good son. An obedient and dutiful one, always in his place and fulfilling the tasks set before him, for the benefit of all.

Now he must become the chief. Seize the power available to him. This he had not done since Da's death. Aye, he had stepped into Da's boots. He had not walked far in them.

He maun make his own path. It was bound to be a stony one. But since holding Hulda in his arms, since kissing her—och, God, the way they had kissed—he did not think there was a force on earth that could turn him from it.

He needed to see her again. Needed—not wanted—to gaze into her eyes. To touch her. To lie with her the way a man lay with a woman, needed it the way he needed to breathe.

He could not let anything, *anything* get in the way of that.

He made the announcement starkly, once the council had gathered, his ma again present among them. He left no room for quibbling or quarreling. The thing was done.

"I ha' forged an alliance wi' the leader o' the Norse band. They will be sheltering at the inlet north o' here, given their boat will tak' so shallow a berth. I ha' pledged we will no' harass or worry them while they are there."

Staring faces met his announcement. A sweeping glance on

Quarrie's part showed him shock, disbelief, and some anger.

"But—" old Morchan began.

"The decision is made. There will be no further discussion o' it."

Borald, who had come straight from the shore, narrowed his eyes. "Wha' do we get in return?"

"Safety from attack by their—"

"We do no' need safety fro' them!" exploded an old warrior. "We could defeat so small a band wi' one hand bound behind our backs."

"—and fo' any other marauding bands that come fro' the north. Mistress Hulda has assured me they will interfere wi' any o' her countrymen who do threaten us."

"Mistress Hulda!" someone hissed.

"It costs us naught but a temporary lend o' a bit o' land we are no' using," Quarrie concluded.

"*Our* land," Morchan objected, "given over to those savages."

"Wha' if they will no' leave again?" asked another of Da's friends. "Wha' if they call in others o' their kind and destroy us? Tak' the whole settlement. They ha' strongholds in the east, ye ken. And in Ireland."

"That will no' happen."

A number of voices howled, "How d'ye ken?"

"I trust her. I trust Hulda Elvarsdottir."

That surprised them so much, they actually fell silent. For a few short moments.

"Trust her?" Borald exclaimed then.

"Trust her?" Kalen roared. "The Norse are a scourge upon the world. Upon our land. And ye would afford them house room? Wha' when they sally forth and attack our neighbors? Wha' then?"

"I mean to further negotiate with Mistress Elvarsdottir to spare those wi' whom we ha' alliances."

"And be damned to the rest o' Scotland? Where is your conscience, man?"

"Ye maun go back and tell this woman ye ha' changed yer mind," said Morchan.

Quarrie looked him in the eye. "That will no' happen. I ha' given my word. The alliance is made."

"Then ye maun be mad—"

Quarrie surged to his feet. "I am yer chief. Ye ha' sworn fealty to me. If ye ha' a problem wi' that"—he narrowed his eyes—"ye are free to tak' up yer possessions and go."

Absolute silence met his words. A few of the men exchanged looks. No one accepted his offer.

"Then there is naught more to be said," declared Morchan at last. "No doubt 'twill all end in sorrow."

The men filed out, Borald leaving last and looking as if he wanted to speak to Quarrie, though he did not. It bothered Quarrie more than it should. Besides being his master at arms, Borach was his friend. He did not want a break between them.

When only Ma remained behind, Quarrie took a turn about the hall. The place felt big and too empty with everyone gone. With his da's presence missing. Da had possessed such a grand personality and had been so much a part of this place, it seemed he must linger still.

What would he say to this alliance Quarrie had made with the Norse? Quarrie shuddered to think.

"They are no' happy," Ma said gently.

"They will ha' to grow accustomed to the agreement. 'Tis best for the clan."

Was it, though? Or best for him? Either way, he could not let Hulda go.

"Sit wi' me." Ma came and perched on a bench beside him. "Talk to me."

"I ha' had enough o' talking."

"Still and all." She captured his hand. When he lowered himself beside her, she studied him with wise eyes. "Tell me o' this woman, this Hulda Elvarsdottir."

Why should she ask him to do that?

"I think," Ma said very gently indeed, "there is more in it than a mere alliance."

Ah, so Ma's instincts were all up and howling, were they?

When he did not speak, she went on, "I did see her down there on the shore. Quite…unusual, I suppose I should say, for a woman to assume a man's place the way she has."

Hulda was all woman, though, beneath that rough clothing. Her body supple and willing. Her very spirit calling to his, seducing him.

"Son, are ye attracted to her?"

That made Quarrie look into his mother's eyes. A good woman she was, a soft spirit every bit as steady as his own, fiercely loyal and generous to those she loved. She must have felt a great attraction to Da.

Softly still, she said, "I ha' never much believed in love at first sight. I ha' no need to. I knew yer father all my life, fro' the time he was an annoying wee laddie onward. And by God, he was annoying. He used to pull my hair. No' till much later did I see somewhat in his smile that went beyond teasing."

"Ye had a good marriage," Quarrie offered.

"A fine, braw one. It seems now like a dream. I ask myself constantly, how can he be gone fro' me, and my heart still beating? Quarrie, I understand love. If ye—"

He cut her off with a lift of his brows. "I am no' in love with Hulda Elvarsdottir." Did he lie to his ma? But nay, what he felt for the woman could not go by so ordinary a name as *love*.

"Attracted to her, then."

Aye, he was wildly attracted. Her mouth hot on his. His hands upon her. An attraction like nothing he'd ever imagined. Madness. Surely it was a form of madness.

"If I am," he told his mother, "it has no bearing on the agreement."

"Are ye certain? For aye, though this decision lies wi' ye, the men are right. Ye ha' invited a fierce wolf in among our beasts."

"The wolf may bite, but will no' turn on us."

"How d'ye ken ye can trust her?"

"She has given her word to me."

Ma seemed flummoxed by that. Her lips pressed together tight before she said, "Son—she is a Norsewoman. She may be lying."

"Anyone may lie, Ma. I might. I may ha' lied to her also. I could call up a force o' men and fall upon her company once they are ashore on the bit o' land I ha' afforded them. But I will no', because I ha' given her my promise also."

"Aye, well." Clearly not happy about it, Ma laid a hand to Quarrie's cheek. "A promise is a sacred thing. I only hope we will no' pay dear for this one."

A promise was, aye, sacred. Trust even more so. He believed in Hulda. And that reached deepest of all.

$$\textit{\textbf{CHAPTER THIRTY-THREE}}$$

CHAPTER THIRTY-THREE

THE *FREYA* BARELY negotiated the passage into the small bay. Indeed, it took all Garik's skill to get her through, and he swore they would never make the passage at low tide.

A forlorn sort of place, one of the men declared it. But they were young, Hulda's crew, and still looked upon everything they did as an adventure. They adapted quickly and soon had a camp set up above the rocky shore.

"'Tis a good hiding place," Helje declared, as they stood watching *Freya* ride the still waters. "Even better than the island. No one will know we are here."

"Save for that great settlement of fierce Scots," said Varg, rolling his eyes. "What is to keep them from creeping through the thistles and killing us in the night?"

"The word of their chief," Hulda replied. She must trust Quarrie. Else she might get all these lads killed.

Varg snorted.

An experienced crew, so Hulda reflected, an older one, would never have agreed with this scheme. She herself had to hope Loki had no hand in it.

But nei. She did trust Quarrie. Just as she ached to see him again. *To lie with him.*

She had been with only one man in her life, besides Haakon, who had taken those rights as given. Olaf had been his name, and a handsome, tall boy he had been. She'd possessed no real feelings for him and had accepted him mainly out of curiosity, to discover what all the furor was about. Because she was much in the company of men, and they spoke about rutting almost constantly.

It had been quick, with much fumbling, and not overly pleasant for her, though Olaf had seemed to enjoy himself. He was dead now, having fallen in a battle far north of here, and would never tell.

Things with Haakon had been quite different. He it was who had taught her the means of pleasure, and though he had expected her to spend her passion on him far more than ever he had troubled to please her, she had tasted what could be and learned that she was a woman beneath it all.

But ja, she knew the ins and outs of it, so to speak. The prospect of those ins and outs when it came to Quarrie flushed her with heat.

A very different proposition from Olaf or even Haakon, for she sensed that with this man, everything would be deeper and more immediate. She would consume Quarrie. Her body would, and her spirit.

She must make it happen.

Yet she felt as if she walked a rope line strung high above the sea. She wanted to reach the end so badly, but the way was perilous and she could take only one step at a time.

Those kisses they had shared, though—those had been a leap. She had never known a man, a mere man, could taste so good.

Since Haakon, with her heart bruised, her body satisfied and mayhap thwarted, she'd wanted little to do with another mating. In the company of men too often, no doubt.

Now she felt starved for Quarrie.

Ja, she would have him. It must be soon.

"We shall set a strong guard tonight," she told Helje. "And every night we are here."

"And then we will go out raiding?" He looked anxious.

"Ja, sure. Are we not perfectly set for it?"

Another of the crew came up to join them. "Mistress, do you think you could trade with yon chief, Murtray, for some supplies?

If we are to stay here, that is."

Hulda smiled. "I just might." Any excuse made a good excuse to tramp over the stones and the headland to see Quarrie.

SHE WENT ALONE, though both Helje and Garik clamored to accompany her. She wore her sword, with no less than three knives secreted about her person.

"Let us test the waters," she told the men. "You understand I can take care of myself."

"Ja, sure." They rolled their eyes. She did not doubt they would follow partway and keep watch.

Again, an older crew would never have let her walk away on her own. A woman less a fool would not have gone.

She smelled the settlement before she saw it. Clouds had moved in overnight, and smoke from all the morning fires hung heavy in the air. The sea was the color of a newly forged sword blade, and Hulda felt a tremor of foreboding, lost, almost, in her anticipation.

There were men on the shore, workers as well as guards on watch, for they knew full well what lay around the curve of the headland. They all came to attention when Hulda's foot hit their stretch of shingle.

She felt their sharp gazes like the points of so many spears. Did they breathe, for watching her? As she began to pass them by, she wondered how to handle such hostility.

Staring into the face of the nearest man, she gave him a bold "Good morning." Head high and pace steady, she continued past them, scattering the greeting every so often.

Not one man replied.

When she reached the path that led up from the sea to the stronghold, she saw Quarrie just emerging from the building. Someone had run to inform him of her approach.

He came charging down to meet her, surprise in his eyes and alarm in every line of him. He'd not paused to braid his hair, and it flowed over his shoulders in a red-brown curtain. His gaze captured hers and did not waver.

Her pulse accelerated. She wanted to run to him but could not possibly do so, pinned here by so many eyes. Yet at sight of him, the world seemed to change color, the very air to brighten.

They met halfway down the slope, a well-populated spot devoid of privacy.

"Mistress Hulda? Is there some difficulty?" Before she could reply, he added with a frown, "Is there a problem wi' the landing place?"

"Nei. My navigator managed to guide *Freya* in." He would have had spies to tell him so. "We passed a quiet night. Indeed"—she shifted on the balls of her feet—"I came in hope to trade."

"Aye, so?"

By Odin's eye, she liked his voice. The sound of it in her ears was like singing, a music finer than any bard's.

"We are in need of some supplies. Basic things." She patted the purse that hung at her side. "I can pay."

"Ah. Come along, then. I will introduce ye to my steward who keeps our stores. Will ye tak' a bit o' breakfast first? I was just about to sit down."

So ordinary a thing, to take breakfast with him. To sit as two civilized people might, as two friends might, they that were born mortal enemies. His people had killed Jute, right down there on that shore.

Was it wrong of her, then, to desire him?

"I have broken my fast," she said. "I am sorry to delay you."

"It does no' matter." He said it easily, without rancor. "In a place like this, I am constantly being called awa' from one duty to another. Come."

He took her through the main gate into a narrow yard turfed in green and around the side of the stone building where lay a whole gathering of small houses. Stables, these must be, and what looked to be a blacksmith's forge. Workplaces—perhaps an armory. Other structures. A bustling sort of place, yet once again each and every man or woman froze as they passed—froze and stared—as if a spell was cast by Hulda's very presence.

A man came hurrying out from one low building and Quarrie addressed him. "Kalen, this is Mistress Hulda Elvarsdottir. She wishes to bargain for some supplies."

The man, of middle years, balding but with enough bristle on his chin to make up for it, goggled at Hulda as he might at a monster that had emerged from the sea.

"Aye, Chief Quarrie."

"Mistress Hulda, what d'ye need?"

"Some basic things, only." She recited the list she had made in her mind. "Small measures, all." She would ask for more later, if this agreement held.

If she got away from here alive. For she sensed—heard and felt—people edging up behind her, closing in a circle to listen. If she so much as breathed wrong, she'd be cut down before she could blink.

Yet Quarrie stood firm as an oak beside her. And she trusted him, did she not?

Ja.

Part of her bargained for stores with the man called Kalen while part kept track of the enemies behind her, and still another part remained so aware of the man at her side that her skin fairly vibrated.

When the supplies had been gathered, when she'd paid for them in silver, Quarrie said, "Ye canna carry all that yoursel'."

"It is not so much." She gave him a smile. "I am stronger than I look." To Kalen she said, "Pray, put it all in one sack I may carry."

"I will send someone wi' ye," Quarrie said, overruling her, and as swiftly decided, "'Tis I will accompany ye."

With that, she would not argue. Whether he meant it as a gesture of accord, whether he sought to return her act of boldness in coming here with one of its equal, she did not know, nor did she care. It meant a few more moments in his company.

Though the chief of this stronghold was surely not meant to fetch and carry for her, no one objected as they both took up a share of the supplies and started back down the slope to the sea.

The people—his people—continued to stare. They would be talking of this for days, no doubt, how the Norsewoman, and she dressed as a man of all things, had walked boldly in among them and away again.

A couple of guards came running up, concern in their faces. Quarrie nodded them off again.

In a low tone meant for his ears alone, Hulda said, "I do regret causing all this fuss, and interrupting your breakfast."

"Och, I can eat anytime." Implying it was a fair, rarer thing, and hence more desirable, to be in her company? So it was.

"They do stare."

"They ha' never seen the like o' ye. And they marvel ye should have such—er—courage, being a woman and all."

"I learned long ago, it does not do to have a man act on my behalf when I can act on my own."

"Ye will ha' made an impression, and no mistake."

They walked on in silence, she savoring his presence, the soft, damp air of the morning gathering around them. Not until they cleared the settlement did she breathe out a measure of tension and speak again.

"I must see you. Later today? Is it possible?"

He slanted a look at her, a curious sort of glance that glinted with hazel green. "Ye wish for a meeting?"

"I do. Just the two of us. Alone." She gazed straight into his eyes so he would take her meaning. Saw it when he did.

I want more kisses. I want more than kisses.

"I do no' see how that might be arranged. A private meeting, that is."

"It must be arranged. *It must be.*"

"There are eyes everywhere."

"I can see that. Do you tell me in this great holding of yours there is nowhere?"

He thought about that. She could feel his thoughts moving. When he spoke again, it was not to agree or disagree.

"Mistress Hulda, this that ye suggest—it may no' be wise. Indeed, it might prove a verra risky thing."

"I understand very well it may not be wise," she shot back at him. Her voice softened when she added, "It may also be the very best of things."

They had reached the point of the headland and stopped walking. He faced her and she him. Her camp lay just ahead. Her men, as well as his, could be watching.

Somehow, she held his gaze. She had offered herself to him, as good as. Had she mistaken him? Did he not desire her in the way she desired him?

She remembered his kisses. Nei, she had not been mistaken.

A storm filled his eyes. His voice, though, remained low and calm when he said, "I can think of no place—"

"There must be."

"—where eyes will no' see." She said nothing, but he must have sensed her agony, for he hurried on, "Gi' me some time to think on it. 'Twill no' be today."

She strove to master her disappointment. "But it will be?"

"It will be."

"You do promise?"

He did not hesitate. "I do."

And she trusted in his promises, did she not?

She took the sack from him and shouldered it with hers.

"Do not follow from here," she told him, and trudged off to the camp.

Obedient, he did not follow.

CHAPTER THIRTY-FOUR

QUARRIE SPENT THE rest of the day striving not to think about what Hulda had suggested. Not that she'd come right out and suggested it, but he could not mistake it, for the invitation—and the desire—had stood clear in her pale eyes. Impossible to dismiss, no matter the tasks he performed, the people he saw, or the complaints to which he listened. She and her request remained there in his mind.

She wanted to lie with him. He had not misunderstood that, had he?

Nay, he had not misunderstood. Her desire had not only lain stark in her eyes but vibrated in the air between them. He might mistake any number of things, and had done in the past. Not that.

When he should have been concerning himself with other matters—not the least with the camp of bloodthirsty marauders lying on his threshold—he could think only of her. Of those kisses they had shared and what it would be like to have her naked in his arms. To spend himself in her welcoming heat.

He maun make it happen.

But how? Eyes were everywhere, as he had told her, and all of them watching avidly. Were there places where he could take her to be alone? Painfully few, but having been born here, he could surely come up with somewhere.

If he thought of a place, so might his men.

Naught would prevent them following him. And if they caught him making love with the dangerous Norsewoman?

He should not take the chance. He dared not.

Yet he had made the woman another promise. What was it about her that drew promises from him?

The folk with whom he came in contact throughout that day had to repeat what they said to him and fight hard for his attention. His thoughts persisted in straying.

How would her skin feel when he got that rough clothing off her? She lived her life as a man, yet he bet she'd be soft and yielding to him as to no one else. All woman.

How would she taste? If the rest of her pleased his tongue half as much as had her kisses, he could be naught but satisfied.

Nay, he was not himself, not all that day. Rain moved in and he had no chance to get away on his own to scout likely places—or unlikely ones. Night drew down amid pounding rain and he thought he would go mad.

What if he walked along the shore and around the headland? Walked there through the rain while everyone else took shelter.

Might they slip away alone?

In the end, he did not go. He took his father's old seat in the great hall—the first time he had done so since Da's death—and heard the complaints that came to him. Many complaints, most of them concerning the Norse.

At last he, who considered himself by and large a patient man, wedded to his duty, had had enough of it.

When yet another clansman came complaining that his old mother could not sleep for fear the Norse would come in the night and slit her throat, he rose from his chair.

"Where are they, then? Where were they last night, that they did no' attack? Their leader has given her word we are safe fro' them."

"A woman," his applicant said nervously. "A woman wi' a sword."

"As if our own women ha' no' picked up a blade a time or two, to defend their homes. List to me, all o' ye." He gazed round at his audience. "Even if the Norse do break their word and come attacking, they are few enough in number that we can fall upon them and leave their blood on the rocks. *Our* rocks," he added deliberately. "'Tis an alliance, like any other."

"No' like any other, chief," one of the guardsmen said. "Our other alliances are wi' Scotsmen, no' our enemies."

"Aye, Lohr, but it has no' always been so. In the past we ha' had alliances wi' other Gaels who wanted to take our land, and we ha' fought against them also. We ha' had alliances wi' the Pictish in the old days. Most o' those ha' proved advantageous. I hope this will also."

An uneasy silence fell. They did not agree with him, but they would not push it. God help him if their Norse guests did put a foot wrong.

IT RAINED FOR three days straight, the waves of moisture blowing in across the sea in every possible guise, from a fine mist that gathered on the hair and skin to fierce pounding. No one heard further from the Norse. Indeed, no one would know they were still there had spies not gone stealing through the soaking gorse and bracken to take a look.

On the afternoon of the third day, Quarrie could endure it no longer. With all his immediate tasks seen to, he donned his good cloak and weapons and walked up the shore.

He would be followed, as he well knew. But the watchers would have to keep to a distance, for he made sure to glance back often in order to keep them honest.

The Norse had forsaken their longboat, which rode at anchor with mist gathered in her rigging, for a camp on the shore. It looked wet and miserable, with a number of skin tents set up in a rough circle and a fire in the middle, which smoked badly.

Hulda had indeed set a guard. Two men came loping toward Quarrie as soon as he rounded the headland, weapons on prominent display. One was fair and one darker, but they gazed at him with identical hard expressions.

"Chief Murtray?" said the fairer uncertainly.

"That is right. I would ha' words wi' yer leader, Hulda Elvarsdottir." He would see her, touch her pale hair, breathe in her essence.

They exchanged glances. "Ja, come."

By the time they reached the circle of tents, Hulda was climbing out into the rain. She wore no armor, and her slender form looked more feminine than he'd ever seen it, even if clad in a man's tunic and leggings.

She gave him a blazing look from her pale-gray eyes.

"Chief Murtray. Is something amiss?"

"I need words wi' ye, mistress."

"Ja, well, come in out of the wet." She shot a look at her men, all of whom now gathered. "Back on guard, ja?" She added words in her own tongue.

"Come," she said to Quarrie, and ducked back into the tent.

A small space, poorly lit, that smelled of her. She would have slept here on the furs in the center of the floor. Her weapons lay close at hand, a sword and two good knives. She wore a third knife in her boot, as he saw from the corner of his eye.

She pulled the tent flap closed behind him. He expected her to invite him to sit. Instead, her task done, she stepped up to him where he stood and gazed into his face, a storm in her eyes.

Before he could draw breath to speak, she seized hold of the front of his cloak and kissed him. Her lips claimed his and her body slammed into his, all heat. All heat and desperation.

For several endless moments, he lost his mind. He forgot where he was and who he was. A number of bright images tumbled through his head. A golden-haired girl standing in bright sunlight leaning to him in order to kiss him just so. A brown-haired beauty claiming him with her lips and her soul. He had done this before, not counting those other kisses they had shared out on the longboat, on the shore.

"Hulda," he said into her mouth.

She returned to him a word, or perhaps it was a sob. Her arms clenched him so tight it hurt. "So long," she said against his lips. "It has been so long."

It certainly seemed so. An age, those three days.

"I had to see ye," he told her, failing to regain any of the sense that had flown. He cradled her head between his hands and gazed into her eyes. "I ha' nay excuse, though."

"You need none. No excuse to see me." She kissed him again, so hungrily it rocked him back on his heels. "Have you thought of a place?"

"Aye. Mayhap. But 'twill no' be easy to get there unseen, wi'out a reason."

"Think of some reason." She sucked one of his lips and then the other. "Soon. *Now.*"

"Aye. I could say I am showing ye a good hunting ground. But why would we go alone? And in the rain?"

"Because I say so?"

"Hulda, we walk dangerous ground."

"You think I do not know it?" She narrowed her eyes on his. "I do not care. I *need.* You. I need to have you."

"Aye." He could but agree. She made him weak in the knees and at once strong enough to accomplish anything. "Put on your cloak," he told her. "And mak' your excuses to your men."

She did as he bade her. But she paused first, for one more kiss.

CHAPTER THIRTY-FIVE

THE RAIN PICKED up as they climbed the rise of land and headed away from the sea. Hulda felt glad of it, for it provided some cover from those who followed. Certain ones of her men would follow. This she knew as she knew her own name.

They would do so in order to protect her, so they would say. But she and Quarrie would have to lose them, if what she needed so desperately were to take place. If it did not take place, she would surely burn up to ash.

As it was, she dared not touch Quarrie along the way. Even a simple clasping of hands would tell too much, if her men were watching.

She asked him, "Where are we bound?"

"There are two places."

"The nearest," she chose promptly.

"The nearest may no' be the best."

She had to swallow back her words in an attempt to control her emotions. She did not know herself. Calm, she usually was, controlled, and not prey to this kind of madness.

"By Freya's heart," she whispered, "we had better get there soon."

Did he laugh? A flash of white teeth said so, but she could not hear him over the rain.

Wherever they were bound, she trusted him to lead her. That might be the worst sort of folly, for he could lead her off and leave her dead where none of her men might find her.

She trusted him.

He looked back several times as if determining whether they were followed, but in the end it rained so hard a silver curtain shrouded them from sight.

They came to a half-ruined structure. Stone sides it had, tumbled at one end.

"This place used to be for hunting parties," he told her as they ducked inside. "Shelter from bad weather long ago. So ye see, ye will no' be lying to yer men."

The place lay empty, the end still boasting a roof mostly dry. It smelled of ancient thatch and vermin.

Quarrie looked at her doubtfully. "If this is no' good enough, we can continue on—"

"It is good enough." She turned to face him. "Touch me."

He lit a rushlight that he had brought, keeping it dry somehow beneath his cloak. The poor light barely illuminated the place. He laid his hands upon her, big hands that were nevertheless gentle, and the sensation went through her like pain. She closed her eyes.

"Hulda." He dropped kisses on both her eyelids and something inside her melted. Her desire became no less fierce, yet it blended with softer feeling.

"Let us get out of this wet clothing."

"I am soaked to the skin," he agreed.

"I want to lick the moisture from you. All over."

Desire leaped in his eyes. "Do ye, then?"

"Ah, ja. Then I want to do all those things I have been imagining for the past three days."

"I should no' wish to hamper ye." He helped her off with her cloak.

She took it from him and spread it on the dirty floor. Removed her boots, one of which held the knife. Laid aside her other weapons that she'd donned before they left. "Help me off with this."

Her tunic proved difficult to remove, it being wet, as did her leggings, the strips of leather that bound them tightened by the wet. He stood and watched as her body came to his view, and she could not tell what he thought.

Matter-of-factly, she said, "I am not a—a buxom kind of woman. I have no spare flesh. I work too hard for it. And I have no hips to speak of." Her breasts, now peaking in the cool air, were firm and high. "Whatever I am, Quarrie MacMurtray, I am yours for this night." *Forever.*

"Ye be perfect." His gaze alone touched her, from the tumbled hair on her head to that below, and on down her legs. "Never doubt it."

"Good. That is good."

He shed his own cloak and, just as she had, the clothing beneath it. His body, long and lean, showed corded with muscle and rough with hair darker than that on his head.

When he caught her watching him, he slanted an amused look at her. "I am what I am, also."

"Do you hear me complaining?"

A smile curved his lips. "I would no' want ye to be disappointed after three days' wondering."

For answer, she moved into his arms. Placed her mouth against his wet shoulder and sucked off the rain. He drew in a breath, and just like that, desire came alive in the lowly place. No need at all for frivolous questions, or further wondering.

"Come," he whispered. "Lie wi' me."

They had done this before, Hulda thought dreamily as he stretched out upon her cloak and drew her down atop him, pulling his cloak over them both, as she—keeping her promise— moved her mouth over him from the hollow of his throat, over the rippled muscles of his chest and stomach. The taste of him was familiar. More than that, it was just as she'd imagined it to be. The scent of him, as she moved ever lower, brought back memories. *Memories.*

She kept her eyes shut against the intense pleasure of it, and feeling him, he might have been another man. One with a mane of dark-blond hair and sea-blue-green eyes. A name appeared unbidden in her mind. *Deathan.*

Whatever his name, he was the man she adored above all others.

An interesting dilemma, but as she traversed his body and made her way to something far more distracting, all other thoughts fled. He stood proud for her, did this man she desired.

Only for her. For her, always.

Unabashedly, as if she had done so a hundred times, she took him in her mouth.

He began to speak, what sounded like praying. Music to her ears. His hands closed around her head, fingers entwined in her hair, and he drew her from him.

"No' yet. No' yet."

He pulled her up his body and she kissed his mouth. Her blood began to hum. A perfect state of being, this was. His mouth joined to hers. His flesh at her fingertips. She could ask no more because there was naught more to be had.

His fingers, rough with calluses, yet still incredibly gentle, found her breasts. Men were seldom gentle with her, she who lived and worked with them as an equal. It undid her, that he should touch her so.

She broke the kiss only to guide his mouth to her breast, a gesture of silent supplication.

No man owned Hulda Elvarsdottir, but she gave herself completely to this one.

And who could have convinced her, ever, that such sharp and beautiful bliss existed? That every part of her—blood, sinew, muscle—would want so intensely to be part of him that she could lose every restriction, could very nearly lose her words?

Because it happened that she could only manage to say, "Inside me. Now." She had forgotten all other means of speaking in her tongue or his.

They moved together like one person, a beautiful being, a

song. Sweet and effortless. Blinding. When at the last instant he would have withdrawn from her, she locked her heels at his back and held him fast.

I want all of you. She did not say it aloud, not in any language. Did not have to.

He gave to her. All of him.

After, she lay with his weight clutched to her, eyes tight shut. She could hear the rain striking the floor at the other end of the hut, but it might have been happening anywhere, and any-when. She did not know who he was, or who she was. Only that they were together.

Love. She spoke in his ear. She had to struggle for it in his language. "I have forgotten how to speak to you."

"No need to speak." He lay sprawled atop her, his hips cradled between her thighs. Now he rose to his elbows and peered into her eyes. "Are ye weepin'?"

Was she? It could not still be rain that wet her cheeks.

"Ja."

"The grand warrior-maiden, Hulda Elvarsdottir, shedding tears?" A smile warmed his voice. Hearing it gave her such pleasure, it curled her toes.

In ordinary life, she might seek to command her feelings, to hide her emotions, to appear harder than she was. With him, there could be only honesty. "It was so beautiful."

"It was," he agreed. "But I would no' ha' ye weep."

"Good tears. Lie here. Hold me. Talk to me, Quarrie Mac-Murtray. I love the sound of your voice."

"Do ye?"

"It is like music. Like singing."

He murmured softly, his lips a mere breath from her ear, and told her of his childhood and his life here. What came through was his deep attachment to this place, belonging that stretched back many generations in blood, his value for his ancestors. His love.

He loved hard and completely, did this man of hers.

That he was her man, she had no doubt. She did not quite understand how, out of a world of men, she had found him. Yet she had, and she did not intend to leave go of him, not ever again.

CHAPTER THIRTY-SIX

QUARRIE WOULD NEVER have believed that lying in a filthy, ruined hut in the pouring rain could feel so comfortable or so right. Yet it did. The comfort reached deep and stemmed from something other than his physical location.

It came from the woman in his arms.

He'd known even before she shed her clothing and they lay down here together, she was perfection. Perfect for him. The taste of her. The feel.

The feel.

By *feel* he did not mean only the slide of her skin beneath his hands or even the heat of her mouth, but her spirit entwining with his. Enfolding him. Welcoming him like one long lost and returning home.

And when he entered her—naught else had existed.

Sanity returned to him slowly and very much against his will. They *did* lie in a filthy hut, he and this woman who should be his enemy.

Who belonged with him as did no one else.

They *did* have a world of difficulty and conflict before them.

He closed his eyes. Mayhap he could keep that world at bay a few moments longer.

"What does it mean," he breathed at her, "that word ye spoke to me?"

"Word?"

"*Àst.*" He repeated it carefully.

Her breath caught in her chest. "Love. *Ást min* means *my love*."

An endearment spoken in the heat of the moment, mayhap.

In keeping with the honesty that held them, as fundamental as the sense of belonging, he asked, "Am I yer love?"

"It seems so." She stirred a little beneath him. "Does it not?"

"Aye." He kissed her because he could do nothing else, and fell into her again. The one place he wanted to remain.

Struggling for words after the kiss ended, with a lingering tug of lips on lips, he said, "Ye do no' feel like a stranger."

"Nei." She touched his cheek, and the tenderness of the gesture near undid him again. "Can you explain this?"

"I do no' ken. But, Hulda, since we met I ha' been having a wealth o' dreams. Dreams in which I am with particular women. Women I adore. Only they are no' *other* women. Somehow, they are all *ye*."

It should have made no sense to her. Indeed, she blinked up at him with those pale, luminous eyes.

"I too had this sensation when we were making love. With my eyes closed, I could not be certain who you were. Only, you were *you*. And you belonged to me."

"A curious sort o' thing," he breathed. "And a powerful one."

"Very powerful."

His thoughts raced. "The ancients—my ancestors—believed we live not one life but many. They said we come into the world through the cauldron o' rebirth. I ne'er gave much thought to it before—"

"One would not." She blinked at him again. "Unless caught in such a situation as ours."

"But 'tis madness."

"As mad as us meeting out o' a world of strangers and feeling"—she brushed her fingers across his cheek—"this?"

"I do no' ken. I canna say." In a way, it terrified him, that memories from a past he could not recall might come rushing at him. Overtake him in this way.

Yet there was the familiarity of it. The staggering rightness.

"My people," she whispered, "we hope for a valiant life that we may enter Valhalla when we die, and remain ever young. Me—I can imagine hoping for no more than *this*."

"Hulda." He kissed her, and the rest of it, the questions and the wondering, ebbed away to the back of his mind.

She drew his hand to her breast. "I want you here, ja? And I want you inside me."

And Quarrie, a man who attended always to his duty, surrendered the world and everything else in it.

IT RAINED. A fury of the gods it was, perhaps sent by the great Thor himself to help conceal this haven in which Hulda and Quarrie lay. It rained while they ran their hands and their mouths over each other. While she memorized this body of his that, ja, housed a spirit all too wonderfully familiar.

It rained while he came inside her, and she lost count of how many times. While their cloaks dried because they lay so long. While he became so much a part of her, she could not conceive of parting from him.

Yet she must. That thought lingered at the back of her mind, that this time out of time must end. That she would have to surrender him from her arms and return to the world.

This that she felt for him, though—it was boundless, bottomless. Just like her desire.

What would her men say when she returned after so long away? Would they wonder what she had done alone with the Scotsman? Would they be able to tell?

"Quarrie." She spoke his name just because she liked the feel of it on her tongue. "How long till morning?"

"Who can tell?" The light he'd brought had long since guttered out.

"We need to go back."

"Aye." He ran his lips across her cheek to her mouth, and fires that should be well quenched flared again.

"Once more, mayhap, first?" she suggested.

He laughed. Ach, by all the holy gods, she loved it when he laughed. Above all the other things she loved about him.

Ja, he was her ást. Her love.

"Lass, ye ha' wrung me dry."

"I do not think so."

It proved she was right. Sometime later, when she came to herself once more, she realized morning light filtered through the broken roof and allowed her to see him. He lay with his eyes closed, brown lashes making two fans.

"By the gods," she groaned. "We are late."

"Ye ha' fair killed me. I am too weak to rise."

"Fool." She kissed him fiercely, which opened his eyes. He smiled at her, and she near lost herself in him again.

Yet when they got to their feet and began to dress, it was she who felt weak and light in the head.

They held on to one another like two children.

"It has stopped raining," he observed.

"Has it?" Was there still a world out there?

"Wha' will ye tell your men?"

"That we waited out the rain, I suppose. That you have given us leave to use these hunting grounds. Do you give us permission to hunt here, Chief Murtray?"

"Aye so, but I would keep well north o' the settlement if I were ye. Armed men meeting other armed men out in the wild canna be safe."

She thought about that. "Any excuse to loose an arrow, eh?"

"That is what I am thinking."

They ducked out of the half-ruined building, a haven it now seemed to Hulda, into the gray morning light. The entire world had changed, though it had not. She had changed, as had the very color of all she saw.

She turned to him. "Do I look like a woman who has taken off all her clothing and put it on again?"

He smiled. "A bit, aye."

Ach, but she loved it when he smiled that way, with his head thrown back and the light in his eyes.

"Come," he told her.

They went hand in hand like two lovers till they left the trees and the sea came into view. A glorious sight it was, the sky still lowering but with early light showing through in ladders, combers raking the shore far below.

"We maun part here," he said with regret.

Nei. Her heart cried it. But she was a grown woman, a leader of men. She had learned, had she not, better than to whine and moan at the unbearable?

She had to go back to her camp and he to his settlement. Even now, eyes might be watching. She should not, could not touch him.

"When will I see you again, Quarrie MacMurtray?"

"I do not know."

Not an answer she could accept.

"I must see you."

"Aye, so."

"I must lie with you again."

He did not look at her now but gazed away toward the sea, giving her his profile, which was very fine. Strong nose with a slight hook to the bridge. The beard curling along his jaw looked red. She loved everything about this man.

Loved.

"Aye," he said so softly that she barely caught the word. "But we maun be careful, lass."

Ja, they must. Difficult to tell her heart so, for it already missed him.

He looked at her then, his eyes sparkling with green in the morning light. "We will find a way."

She wanted him to promise. But she had wrung promises

enough from him, had she not? And nei, she was not a child.

She turned northward even as he must head south.

"*Ást min,*" she branded him in parting.

CHAPTER THIRTY-SEVEN

A NY NUMBER OF eyes located and followed Hulda long before she reached camp. Ja, they had been watching for her, had her men, and several came forward through the morning to meet her, Garik among them.

He examined her with concern, head to boots and back again. She strove to appear calm, as if naught much had happened last night, even though her very world had changed.

"Hulda!" he called. "Where were you? We had begun to worry."

"That the Scot had killed you," said Helje, who followed him.

She tossed her head in a vain attempt to seem casual. "Ach, nei. We walked too far and took shelter in a ruined hut from the rain. Thought it best to wait for daylight. But we have a good hunting ground. I can show you today."

Helje lifted his eyebrows. "It is well. I will tell the others." He loped off toward camp.

Garik did not move. Again, his gaze prodded her. "Is that what truly happened?"

"Ja, sure."

"You did not spend the night with the Scot?"

"I just said we sheltered together."

"Hulda, do not lie to me. I saw you with him back on the boat, when you let him go. I see the way you look at him. And your tunic is not tied properly."

Her fingers flew to the laces and arrested there.

Softly, Garik added, "I ask as your friend as well as your fellow viking."

"We spent the night together, ja—as you suppose."

Garik swore, addressing Loki grievously.

"I understand it is unwise. I could not help it."

"Hulda." Garik seemed to grope for words. "I like you. I admire and respect you. I would not be here on this venture if I did not. But I have to say—"

"It is madness? I know."

"He could well have throttled you. You are strong, ja, but he is stronger."

"He would never harm me." Gentle, callused hands moving over her skin. Touching her everywhere.

"You cannot be certain of that. I understand the flesh wants what it wants—"

"It is not just the flesh involved, Garik, but my heart."

"That is worse." He gazed at her, troubled. "A woman—or a man, for that—directed by her heart may be led astray. Could this man, this stranger—for he is that—be using your feelings against you?"

"You think because I am a woman, I toss away all good sense?"

"I think anyone in your place might."

Hulda sighed. "I do not think he takes advantage of me."

Garik said nothing.

They had been walking as they spoke and now drew near the camp. Hulda could see everyone milling about.

"List to me," she said. "We are in a goodly position. It is a haven here. We can go hunting today. We can go out raiding if we wish. Where is the disadvantage?"

He shook his head. "I feel trouble. In my bones."

Trouble might well be coming, but Hulda could not feel it. Only the desire.

"I ask you, Hulda, to keep the welfare of your crew in mind."

"Would I do aught else?"

Again, he did not answer. But ja, she felt his doubt.

They did go hunting that day, once the weather cleared. Hulda herself led a small group in order to show them the range they'd been granted, though she would have much preferred to hang back.

She wanted time to herself. A chance to sort out her thoughts and her emotions. Her body felt sore. Ja, Quarrie had been gentle with her, tender. Yet they had joined frequently and she was not accustomed to such activity.

How could she want him again so soon? It was the memory of the tenderness, she decided, that would prove her undoing. The way he kissed her. The way he suckled at her breast. The care with which he entered her.

She kept her hunting party well away from the half-ruined hut in the forest. She wanted no one to know of its exact location, save the two of them.

"WHERE WERE YE?" Quarrie's mother unknowingly echoed Garik's words to Hulda almost exactly. "I was worried half to death."

Quarrie put aside his weapons as he entered the hall and made his way to the fire. He had already run the gamut outside—the guards down on the shore and more at the gate. Borald waylaying him with concern in his eyes.

"We were about to send out a party for ye," Borald had said.

Aye, he had been inconsiderate. Incautious. And, given the opportunity, he would be again.

"Were ye at the Norse camp all night?" Ma asked. "We nearly went there to ask."

"Nay." He did not look at his mother as he replied. "I ha' given the Norse leave to some land for hunting. 'Tis well north of our usual tract. I will tell the men—"

"Quarrie!" she interrupted him.

He had to face her then. He could see worry in her eyes that mirrored Borald's, and more distress than he liked. He never wished to cause this woman distress.

"Son, what are ye about? This is no' like ye."

Nay, it was not. He was steady, reliable. Predictable. Folk always knew where he was, usually tending to his duty. He did not disappear off on wild nights with a woman he barely knew, who had unaccountably got inside him.

But och, he *did* know her.

In their discovery of each other last night, there had been an undeniable wealth of remembering. It was as he'd told her—the ancients had believed their souls might return to this world again and again. Given that, one might—almost—expect to meet someone known before.

Had the cauldron of rebirth—if, aye, such a wonder existed—spat him and Hulda out and woven their fates together so that, having known each other in the past, they might meet once again?

Difficult to believe otherwise. This ancient song, sung again, might be meant for her. For him.

Could he explain any of that to the worried woman standing before him? Nay. She had lost her love. She was hurt and wounded and uncertain.

"Forgive me, Ma. I did no' mean to worry ye."

"Quarrie, I do no' ken what to mak' o' this. Land granted to the Norse and—"

"Ye must try to trust me."

"I do, son. I do. But can ye no' see? Ye have invited a wolf to sleep on our very doorstep."

Aye, Hulda was a wolf of sorts. A she-wolf, with her pale-gray eyes and fierce spirit. And if anyone else had done as he had, he would denounce them for foolishness, or worse.

Patiently he said, "For years uncounted, Ma, we have watched the horizon for dark sails. Lived life always on guard.

Met every spring and summer with the threat of attack and destruction. We can, aye, go on fighting and dying." As Da had. As Hulda's brother had. "Or we can try another way. If we hold to this alliance I ha' made, we may win a season o' peace."

"Do ye truly believe that? Even if this woman—this Hulda—holds to her agreement, there is a whole sea of other invaders out there. And wha' of our neighbors? Ye toss them to the wolves like carrion, do ye?"

"Nay. I mean to negotiate with Hulda for the welfare o' the others wi' whom we hold alliances."

"And ye think she will agree?"

"I do no' ken. But I do believe we must be welcoming to her group. Lower our barriers and cease hostilities wi' them."

"And if they break the agreement and attack?"

He shrugged. "If that happens, we will crush them. We ha' the greater numbers."

"I do no' like it. Yer father would no' ha' liked it."

Quarrie closed his eyes for a moment, fighting back the pain of those words. "I am sorry. But I believe we ha' an opportunity here. One that reaches beyond killing and dying. I would tak' advantage o' it."

His mother, a gentle woman with a compliant nature not unlike his own, said nothing. But he had rarely seen her look so mutinous.

"I suggest," he said softly, knowing full well she would not like the prospect, "we arrange a feast for the Norse. A kind of welcome. A chance, mayhap, for our folk to see they are people no' unlike ourselves."

She stared at him as if his head had fallen off and rolled across the floor.

"Food, drink, and entertainment. Music." He reflected on it. "Limited drink, mayhap. We do no' wish for tempers to rise. Will ye help me to arrange it?"

"Ye ha' gone mad. Yer father's death has unhinged yer mind. Grief has. And the responsibilities ye have assumed."

"I am no' mad."

"Ye maun be, to invite those beasts into our hall. Ask our folk to sit down beside them, that ha' killed their brothers and sons and even their wives—"

"Ye will arrange it," he insisted softly, the gentle tone covering iron.

"Mad," she whispered again.

But nay, he was not mad. Merely in love.

━━━◆━━━

CHAPTER THIRTY-EIGHT

QUARRIE WENT TO visit the harper, Danoch, once he'd taken a meal and something to drink. His body wanted sleep, but he could not make an excuse for it, and anyway, he was much too unsettled to find rest.

He could feel the physical effects of a night's long lovemaking. Indeed, at random moments he could still feel Hulda's mouth, her fingers upon him, to devastating effect. But the spiritual effects reached far deeper. The longing deepest of all.

He received a lot of pushback on his decision to feast the Norse, first from Ma, then from the seneschal, who came to him nearly in tears as soon as he heard of it.

"Chief Murtray, ye ask me to spend our stores to celebrate our mortal enemies?"

"Nay, but only to celebrate an alliance wi' them that will prevent more dyin'."

"I maun say"—Kalen had to fight for the words—"I do no' like it."

A sentiment shared by everyone else Quarrie met. Such word traveled swiftly in an enclosed community. Even before he went to see Danoch, folk approached him to protest.

As calmly and kindly as he could manage, he heard them out and turned them away.

Old Danoch lived with his daughter, a widow whose husband had been slain fighting other Norsemen. Quarrie had always liked Danoch, whom Da had taken on after years of traveling bards had come and gone. A slender man who did not look his years, with a charming tongue and a quick smile, Quarrie liked his music even better.

This one, quiet household, so it seemed, had not heard of his perfidy in choosing his guests. Danoch's daughter, Raisa, invited him in with courtesy and visible surprise.

"Chief Murtray. Father, 'tis himself come calling." She addressed the old man sitting by the fire.

Danoch greeted Quarrie warmly. Quarrie sat while Raisa fussed around them for a time, providing hospitality. Not until she withdrew did Quarrie speak.

"Master Danoch, I ha' come to ask your advice."

"Have ye, then?" Danoch's hair had once been black and his eyes were still bright blue.

"Aye. Ye ha' traveled much during your time on the road, ha' ye not? In yer role o' shanachie."

"Och, that I have. In my youth, before I came here to your father, I was all over Scotland and Ireland, and much o' Wales also. On foot that was, mostly. I carried all I owned on my back, and the main o' that my clarsach."

The instrument in question stood not far away, another presence there in the room.

"A fascinating life that must ha' been." Quarrie found himself distracted for the moment from his purpose.

"Aye, so it was. And often a difficult one. But I lived for the music, ye see. And och, but I collected some songs and stories."

"And we ha' benefited from those." Quarrie could not help but smile. "Wha' made ye settle here?"

"I ha' Murtray blood, way back. And I would come here often on my yearly rounds. Your father always made me most welcome."

A bard provided wondrous entertainment, and a chief could not always afford to keep one of his own. They tended to move with the seasons.

Danoch smiled. "On one such visit, I fell in love wi' a Murtray lass. Raisa was born not long after. Eventually, your father was good enough to offer me a place and a home here. He was a fine man, yer da."

"He was," Quarrie replied gravely. "Tell me, wha' d'ye ken o' the Norse?"

The enthusiasm in Danoch's eyes cooled a mite. "Ye mean, besides the fact that they love to wet their swords and axes wi' Scottish blood?"

Quarrie's lips tightened. "Besides that, aye."

"Back in the days when I traveled, I saw the damage they did in Ireland as well as here in Scotland. Families broken and folk taken for slaves. I was nearly captured myself, once. The Norse chief decided he wanted a bard o' his own. I barely escaped wi' my clarsach."

"Ye ken a little o' their ways, then?"

Danoch gave him a long look. "In Dublin, they ha' established a kingdom and hold sway there. Wexford and Waterford also. They ha' their own culture, one o' boasting and drinking, mainly."

"And music?"

"And music," Danoch replied.

"I would like for ye to help me. I ha' decided to feast the band o' Norsemen that ha' taken up the wee bay to the north o' here. I ha' made an alliance wi' their leader"—and had given her his heart—"and wish to celebrate that agreement. I thought wi' all ye had seen, ye would best know how to honor them."

The old man blinked at him. He took so long before answering, Quarrie began to wonder if he would.

At last he spoke. "Honor them, ye say?"

"Aye."

"Chief Murtray, even if ye invite a wolf in beside yer fire, 'tis still a wolf."

"I understand that." He had heard almost the selfsame warning from his mother.

"I am no certain—wi' all respect—ye do."

"For generations, as ye say, there has been killing. I seek to change that."

Danoch sighed. "Since coming here to settle, I ha' learned much o' the history of Clan Murtray. 'Twas my duty to do so, and to sing wha' I know in honor and respect. A chief likes to hear his ancestors praised."

"Aye."

"Did ye know yer heritage goes back all the way to Ireland? To the great Ardahl MacCormac himsel'?"

"I did know that, aye." Quarrie wondered what this had to do with the Norse.

"He was a warrior wi'out compare, back in those ancient days."

"So they do say."

"His clan would ne'er ha' survived wi'out his sword. And later, after your ancestors came here to Scotland—it was called Alba then—they had to fight for this land. Fight for what became dearer to them than their ancestral Irish lands."

The old man had fallen into a storytelling rhythm now, his rich voice taking up the cadence of the tale.

"So I ha' heard."

"They fought each other, clan against clan, and the Caledonians also."

"And one o' them wed a Caledonian princess, did he no'?" Quarrie added deliberately, "To end the fighting." Why could that not happen again? Love and war. Which might prove the stronger?

"Aye so, that is true, and there is Caledonian blood in yer veins. My point is, all these who came before ye were warriors. I would caution ye about laying yer sword aside too quickly or too soon."

"I do no' intend to lay my sword aside. Just, mayhap, be sure I do no' need to use it before times. The Norse leader has promised that in exchange for a berth here, there will be no conflict between us."

"And ye believe him, do ye?"

"Her. I believe her, I do."

Danoch's gaze sharpened. "The Norse leader is a woman? This had no' come to my ears. I must be getting old."

"I wish to honor this alliance—to mark it with a feast. I thought ye might best know how."

"Aye well, as I ha' said. Food, drink, music."

"Will ye play for them?"

The old man did not hesitate. "My music is meant for all. I will no' withhold it. But, Chief Murtray, I maun urge caution. Trust may be misplaced. And ye ha' yer people to think upon."

"So I do. So I am." Was that true? Or did Quarrie think of himself and his longing for Hulda? His need for her.

"If ye give these wolves a den, might they no' invite others o' their kind? Enough to rend us limb from limb."

"Should that happen—should I see any hint o' other Norse moving in—the alliance will break. Then will I tak' up my sword."

And what would such an act cost him, in breaking with Hulda?

He leaned toward the old man. "Tell me this, Master Danoch. Ye say ye ha' traveled far and heard many a story."

"So I ha'."

"Wha' do ye ken o' the cauldron o' rebirth?"

Danoch's gaze returned to his. It held a spark. "An old tale, that." Again his voice assumed a cadence. "Our ancestors believed that life was but a wheel, one that never stops turning. We are born to our place upon that wheel, and as it turns we meet the successive occurrences of our lives—including death." Danoch gave a rueful smile. "When we die, our spirit flies awa' to feast and celebrate. But eventually—or so they said—it finds itsel' in the cauldron o' blood and pain and hope that is rebirth. We are once more born into yet another place on the wheel, to struggle and learn, and so become the beings the gods wish us to be."

"And," Quarrie asked carefully, "should such a thing prove

true, is it possible we should meet other souls upon that wheel o' life, those we ha' known before?"

"It seems, does it no', that we must do. For do we no' learn from one another more than any other way?"

Old wisdom. Ancient as a song only half remembered. "And," Quarrie pressed, "that being so, will we know these people, remember them from before? Would we recognize them?"

Danoch's gaze prodded his kindly, yet with wondering. "We do no', lad. No' in the ordinary way. For surely therein would lie madness."

CHAPTER THIRTY-NINE

THE MESSENGER ARRIVED amid a knot of guards, all of them heavily armed. Their appearance along the shore had Hulda's entire company up and bristling, more than ready for a fight.

She had to bellow at them. "Nei! This is an envoy, not a war party."

To her disappointment, Quarrie did not make a member of the group. Two full days had passed since she had seen him, touched him, and the ache grew to unbearable proportions. The time had also given her young crew an opportunity to think. Inactivity was not good for them. They felt exposed and vulnerable here, and began to reconsider the wisdom of the alliance.

She'd been just about to suggest a foray out to raid when the Scots party was sighted. She ran out with Garik at her side.

The Scots came walking up as if they owned the place, which in truth they did. Wariness and a good measure of hostility filled their eyes. The messenger, whom the guards surrounded, was a young man surely no older than her own crew.

"I am looking for Hulda Elvarsdottir."

Hulda stepped forward. "I am she."

The young man examined her closely. "I ha' for ye a message fro' my chief."

Quarrie. Her pulse leaped.

"He bids ye welcome at a feast in his hall this night."

"What?" Hulda blinked. She could not have heard that right.

"A feast o' welcome. In his hall this evening."

The men behind Hulda stared. Most of them could not understand Gaelic beyond a few simple words and commands. Some, like Garik, could. He shot her a sharp look.

"A feast," she repeated. "Of welcome." And she said it over in Norse.

What was he about, her braw Scots lover? Was it an excuse to see her? Or something more? If he ached for her one part as fiercely as she ached for him, he might well do near anything to arrange an encounter. But *this*?

From the sour expressions on the Scots' faces, they did not approve. From the muttered comments behind her, neither did her men.

She lifted her chin. "Pray tell Chief Murtray we shall be honored to accept."

An explosion of mutters from both sides. Had the Scots been hoping she would refuse?

The messenger inclined his head. They turned and left with all due speed, several looking back over their shoulders, presumably to see if the Norse chased after them.

Hulda's men closed around her.

"What does it mean?"

"A trap, you think?"

"It has to be a trap."

"He lures us there to fall upon us and cut our throats."

"Hulda." Garik touched her arm. "Why did you agree? It must be a trap."

Ja, to be sure, that was what they would think. Madness, with just under a score of them to go walking into an enemy's hall. Unlike her, they did not trust Quarrie MacMurtray. Ach, how she wished she could speak with him for just a few moments. Ask what he was about. But he chose to do this thing properly with a messenger and a certain amount of ceremony.

"Do not worry," she told Garik. "All will be well. We will go hunting today, that we might bring a contribution to the feast." It would be Quarrie's own game, but that was neither here nor there.

Helje muttered disagreeably, "A last feast before dying, it may well be."

SOMETIME LATER, HULDA stood in her tent struggling to get a glimpse of her image in—of all things—the blade of her sword before giving it up as a bad bet. Seldom had she wished to be other than what she was—a woman striving to succeed in a man's world. She gave little thought to her appearance and was comfortable in her skin.

Until now. For she went to attend a feast given by the man she loved. Ach, ja, she could not deny that she did love him. Her love for Quarrie seemed to have come to her like a memory full blown. It felt as natural and as ancient as her existence, or nearly so.

Much to her surprise, she wanted to look beautiful for him. He had called her beautiful during their night together. At least, she thought that was what he'd said in passionate whispers. *Bonny hair. Bonny breasts.*

She had braided her hair, and could scarce go to him now with the other attributes he'd admired on display. She had nothing to wear better than her rough tunic and leggings. Her sword.

There had been a sharp argument over the wearing of arms to the feast. She had suggested they lay aside their swords, if not their knives. Her men had objected vociferously. The men had won.

They went armed in a visible effort to prove they might defend themselves. Though if MacMurtray and all his warriors turned on them there in his hall, they were as good as dead.

And her men knew it. A wonder they were willing to accompanied her.

They trudged southward in a ragged band while the sun was still high in the sky. The days lengthened as the season stretched out. At home there would be very little other than daylight, as opposed to the dark winter when men were confined and tempers grew ugly.

Midsummer may well have come and gone. She had lost track of the days.

Guards had been stationed to keep watch for them and soon went running. Her men began to grumble again.

"It is a death trap," Helje declared. "We walk to our doom."

"How foolish of us," Varg agreed with the dark humor that marked Norsemen, "to make it so easy for them."

"When the fight begins," said Brynjar, "I want the Scots chief's head."

"There will be no taking of heads." Hulda spoke as if to children. "We are guests. Have you no manners?"

She had to admit, a chill ran up her spine when they entered the settlement and started up the slope that led from the shore to the keep. The staring eyes unsettled her, as did the similarity of expression on every face: fear mingled with hostility.

Then she saw Quarrie standing at the gate waiting to greet them, and she forgot everything else.

Ach, but he looked fine. Dressed richly, as she was not, in a grand cloak that swirled around his tall, lean form, his hair flowing upon his shoulders.

She had buried her face in that hair. Breathed its essence while he came inside her.

She needed to touch him, a desire so intense it near overwhelmed her. She could not, but had to act composed and dignified, as if he meant naught to her beyond a fellow leader.

Quarrie stood where he was till her small band reached him, an undeniable advantage in position. She could feel the uneasiness of her men shifting behind her. It would not take much to cause a massacre here. Just one man drawing his weapon.

Only she—and possibly Quarrie—could prevent such a disaster.

She lifted her head high and said clearly, in Gaelic, "Chief Murtray, thank you for calling us here to feast. We are honored."

He nodded in a very formal, lordly fashion. "We welcome ye here in peace."

No one smiled. The faces of the people grouped around Quarrie, a woman close beside him and an elder who might be an advisor, remained wooden. A veritable cluster of guards.

Hulda could feel her men vibrating with tension. But Quarrie held out his hand to her.

That hand—broad and callused in the palm with long, supple fingers—had touched her breast. Had slid up the inside of her thigh. Ach, how was she to behave like a sane woman?

She took his hand, and his fingers tightened on hers in a sudden squeeze. Did he seek to lend her reassurance?

They entered the keep. She could hear her men chattering behind her, no more than a few muffled words. Usually when they entered such a place it was with weapons raised and throats howling.

The great hall lay directly ahead, and it had been prepared lavishly for them. Torches flared on every hand, and the tables had been laid with food and drink.

"Mistress Hulda, I hope ye and your principals will sit at the high table wi' me and my lady mother."

He indicated the woman who had kept pace on his other side. Clad well if somberly, she had the look of him about the eyes. She nodded at Hulda, but still gave no hint of a smile.

"Ja," Hulda responded. "Garik, Helje, with me."

"The rest of your men may have the first of the side tables. I thought they would be most comfortable together."

"That is considerate." And wise. Why strain tensions to the point where something had to break?

Quarrie escorted her to the high table. Her men all rolled

their eyes at her as they filed past.

She sat with Quarrie on one side of her and his mother on her other. Garik sat beyond that lady and Helje beside a younger woman, farther on.

Hulda looked out upon a sea, a veritable ocean, of hostile faces, wondering what she had done.

If they got out of this alive, it would be by the grace of Father Odin, alone.

❖

CHAPTER FORTY

T HE GREAT HALL fairly vibrated with tension, as if the very
stones of the place strained to cast out the unwanted
intruders. Quarrie, gazing about with a sudden rush of misgiving,
wondered if everyone who had opposed this move on his part
had been right, and he had been terribly wrong.

Yet…Hulda sat beside him, so near he could reach out and
touch her any time he chose. He dared not do so, but the
certainty that he could provided some satisfaction.

The table set aside for her crew lay to their right as they faced
the room. Turning his gaze there, Quarrie could see that her men
looked dangerously on edge, repeatedly putting their heads
together and talking in their own tongue.

Quarrie calculated it would take naught more than a disdain-
ful look to set them off. The place was filled to the rafters with
disdain.

Servers began hurrying about pouring ale and passing loaded
platters. Quarrie had himself chosen the individuals to serve at
the Norse table. Intrepid fellows, the both of them. No lasses.

Ma, seated on Hulda's far side, gave him a desperate look. He
rose.

He had planned every word of what he meant to say. Calming words, so he hoped, and suitable ones. He could not control
how they fell upon the ears of his listeners. If they wanted to
remain angry or outraged or offended, they would. Yet he felt he
took the leadership of the clan into his hands firmly for the first

time. This was not what his father would have done, nor anyone he knew.

He would either sail upon the strength of it, or sink spectacularly.

"Welcome to our guests, whom we receive wi' honor." He did not know how many of the Norse could understand his words. Enough, so he hoped, to translate for the others. "We are here to feast the alliance that has been made between mysel' and the Norse leader, Hulda Elvarsdottir. In the past, we ha' known much of killing and strife and mistrust in facing one another. Members o' both our families ha' perished. We can continue on inviting more death, or we can agree here tonight, in this very hall, that among us, at least, there will be nay more o' it."

Mutters from the throats of his own people greeted his words, while the Norse crew stared as if trying to decide the best way to dismember him. The hostility brought despair to his heart. He'd been mad to attempt this thing. Everyone had told him so. He'd been mad to hope there might ever exist between him and Hulda anything more than a fleeting passion.

Yet somewhat more *did* exist.

He went on steadily, "Let us prove wi' this night o' gathering together that more than hate can exist between us, that we might someday achieve not only an alliance, but a peace."

At the Norse table, one of the men was busy translating for the others. Would Quarrie's words make them decide he was weak? Did talk of peace represent, to such men, an invitation to violence?

His own people looked as if they wanted to shout him down. Only loyalty and their unwillingness to betray their vows of fealty before the strangers kept them from it.

He sat down, dismay and doubt hitting him in waves. The room fell silent apart from the Norseman's hurried catch-up.

Slowly, Hulda rose in turn.

All eyes flew to her. A curiosity she was, for many reasons. A Norse warrior here in their hall, and a woman, no less. Tall, strong, and composed. Far more composed, Quarrie thought, than he.

Into the silence she spoke with her heavily accented Gaelic.

"We are honored by our reception here in your hall this night, and honored by Chief Murtray's words of *velkomin*. There is bad blood between us, ja. There are grievances old and recent, yet we lay them aside. In return for the place we have been granted upon your shore, we agree to wet our blades no more with your blood. Further, we pledge to stand with you in times of trouble. We will help you to defend this place."

Deliberately, she gazed about the near-silent chamber, her pale-gray eyes touching on the faces of the listening Scots and those of her own men.

She concluded, "If only between your clan and my crew, let us found a new age."

She sat down again to only faint coughs and mutters. Would it work? Quarrie doubted it. He fully expected that, come morning, there would be protests from his folk and hers. Fight alongside the Scots? Why should they? Trust the Norse? How could they?

For tonight, at least, there was feasting, and Quarrie hoped a realization that strangers were not necessarily monsters. He gestured to the servers, who once more began circulating. Conversation at the tables rose.

Under the cover of the table, Hulda's fingers brushed his. Only a glancing touch, but it brought his whole body to life.

She inclined her head toward his. He expected her to speak of what had been said or the reactions of their audience to it.

Instead she murmured, "I must see you again."

His very blood leaped. She did not speak of *seeing* him. He understood completely what she meant.

"Aye, but how?"

"The same place, mayhap. Tomorrow?"

Tomorrow. Tomorrow would be a morass of arguments and protestations. Of people waylaying him to voice their complaints and their fears. He would be constantly in sight of someone or other.

"I do no' doubt tomorrow will be spent in meetings o' council and hearings wi' my folk. Do ye realize wha' we ha' done?"

"Ja. It is a step of which my faðir, back home, would not approve."

"Nor mine."

"Yet we move on through life, eh? The wheel of time refuses to stand still."

The wheel of time.

They ate, though whether the fare was good or otherwise, Quarrie could not have told. He failed to taste it, too busy watching the room and the reactions of those within it.

The Norse, whatever their opinions, ate heartily. Opportunists, he supposed, who would take food—or aught else to benefit them—where offered. Even though he had limited the amount of drink, Hulda's crew grew louder as the evening wended on.

If they all got out of this without drawn swords, it would be a wonder.

That was his last thought before Danoch arose. The harper had been afforded a place at the end of the head table as, Quarrie believed, he richly deserved. Now he took up his instrument and moved to the cleared space beside the fire.

Would the Norse quiet to listen to him? Or would they be rude enough to keep up a racket?

To Quarrie's surprise, it was Hulda's right-hand man, Garik, who leaned forward from his place beside Ma and barked a single word in Norse. *Listen,* it might have been.

Young men all, they shot Garik startled looks and obeyed.

The music began. Only it was not just music. Here in this tumultuous place, Danoch gave them ripples of sound as calming as rivulets playing on the hillsides or waves kissing the shore. Wisely, he did not, as was his want, begin with a tale that their guests might not be able to follow. He gave them instead the magic of ancient songs, which no man could fail to heed.

He wove memory with his old hands, and longing. The tears of loss and the laughter of reunion. If the Norsemen had a place in their hearts where warmth resided, the tunes surely found it.

When Danoch lifted his voice in words, there was not another sound to be heard. He gave them an old, old tune of praise. Not for any gods, but the things all men must love. The song of birds and the softness of the south wind. The blessing of sunlight. The gift of a new morn.

Down between them, Hulda's hand brushed Quarrie's again. Her pinky—only that—hooked his and held tight. Very nearly enough.

For he could almost—*almost*—hear what she was thinking. As if the music, and the tremor in Danoch's voice that was somehow both old and young, conveyed it.

I love you.

Did she? With everything in him, he longed to gaze into her eyes, to behold the truth there. Instead he kept staring straight ahead, listening to the music and pretending his whole being did not hang on the answer, connected to her by her finger twined through his.

While Danoch played, the servers quietly took away the dregs of the ale and began removing the scraps of food. When the aged harper arose at last, to stomps of wild approval from the Norse—apparently not too drunk to appreciate his playing—Hulda rose also.

"We thank you for your warm welcome this night, Chief Murtray, and for the wonderful playing of your harper. We go now in peace." She looked at her men. "Ja?"

They rose with a clatter, as did Garik and Helje from the head table. Suddenly everyone was on his or her feet.

This would be the moment, with the peace of Danoch's harping shattered, when trouble would break out. But Hulda moved down the length of the hall, gathering her men the way a hen might her chicks.

Quarrie hurried after.

At the top of the outer stairs, she paused and turned to him. "I think that went well."

"Better than I expected."

"Ja, sure. I much enjoyed your harper and would like to hear him again. Much as—" She caught herself and lowered her voice. "When? Where?" She repeated her earlier suggestion: "The same place?"

"'Tis dangerous," he said with reluctance.

"Ach, by Odin's eye, I must—" Again she caught herself.

"If this alliance holds," he told her very softly indeed, "we may be able to see one another more often."

She gave him a tight smile, just visible in the flaring torchlight. "And here I thought you acted on behalf of your people."

"I do." And, so he prayed, his own.

She left him. He stayed at the top of the stairs and watched her go at the head of her men, off into the endless dark.

CHAPTER FORTY-ONE

HULDA'S MEN WERE full of questions. All the way back to their camp, the path lit by moonlight, they spewed those questions while barely giving her leave to answer.

Most of the queries, as she determined, came down to one.

Why did you tell them we would stand with them in a fight?

Even Garik, who walked close beside Hulda, seemed invested. He did not say as much as the others, but she could feel his uneasiness.

Not till they reached camp did Hulda gesture them to gather around the firepit, where she gave answers.

"Among these people, it is the nature of such an alliance as I have made to offer one another support at arms in time of war."

Helje spoke. "But yet who would these folk fight, save others like us? Do you mean for us to stand with them against others of our own blood?"

"Other Norsemen," she corrected him. "Mayhap not of our blood."

"And are we to ask them about their lineage before we cut their throats? Pardon me, but who are your cousins?"

"And what"—it was Garik who asked this—"of the service we have sworn to our own jarls?"

"List to me," Hulda said as calmly as she could. "Have our men not in the past hired out their swords? On countless occasions, we have."

"Ja, but that was for payment."

"Think of our leave to hold this place as our payment." Hulda lifted her hands. "A fine place, this is, from whence to go raiding."

"Then let us go raiding!" cried Sven, one of their youngest men. "I have had my fill of sitting here with naught to do."

"Ja, we will do that."

The men turned away, only half satisfied. But when she would have followed, Garik laid a hand on Hulda's arm.

"I would have thought," he said, "you would consult with me and Helje before pledging our swords. We are the three of us in this together from the start, nei?"

She met his angry gaze. "You are right. I am sorry. You object?"

"It is too late for that, is it not? You have given our agreement and I stand with you. But ja, I object."

"Forgive me. I thought the advantages outweighed the price."

"Advantages to whom?"

He did not give her a chance to answer that but stalked away after the other men.

So she took them raiding the next morning, when they still had sore heads from Quarrie MacMurtray's heather ale. They loosed *Freya* upon the morning tide, threading the needle of the passage, and struck away southward.

That took them past the settlement where Quarrie's men, out on watch, called and pointed. The keep, up on its rise, looked formidable and impenetrable. It made Hulda wonder. Had Loki been whispering in her ear when she made that agreement with Quarrie?

Yet such agreements must eventually be formed. Warring could not go on forever. The men who had settled at Dublin, at Wexford, at Waterford, and at York must have made similar agreements on a march larger scale, or they would all have slaughtered one another by now.

As Quarrie's settlement slipped out of sight, she near convulsed with longing for him. Yet she looked at it fairly. She and he might never have an opportunity to be together again.

Their campaign proved a vicious and a bloody one. Her instincts still for Quarrie's welfare, Hulda made sure to sail far enough south to avoid his immediate neighbors before striking, but her crew, young and hungry, showed little mercy to their prey.

They returned north after more than a sennight sated with goods and gore, Hulda thinking there could not possibly be an attainable future between herself and any man of Scots blood.

The same blood that stained their swords and axes.

What had she been thinking?

At least the crew, well satisfied, seemed inclined to rest at their home base for the time. They boasted to one another of their exploits, the wealth they would eventually take home to Norge, and of improving the camp.

Turning it into a settlement with proper huts, perhaps. Even though they spoke of going home.

If they left, might Hulda stay behind?

Ordinarily at the end of the raiding season, the Norse sailed home. Settled in for the winter, their boats safely moored in the fjord. Set about marrying and begetting children.

No matter how successful their season, her crew would likely want that. No true place for them on this bleak shore.

She tried to talk with Garik about it, him being closest to her among the men. She took him walking one clear morning, northward along the shore.

"What would you think, Garik, of us overwintering here?"

He rolled his eyes at her. "Here?"

She had sensed a difference in him since the night of the feast at Murtray when he had showed her his anger. Ja, on the surface things were much the same. They joked and teased. Underneath, not so much the same.

"Out of the question."

She had expected him to say that but still felt disappointed. "Why?"

"There is nothing here for us. As soon as the season for raiding ends, the men will want to go home."

"But—"

"List to me, Hulda." He gave her a dark look. "There is nothing here for us. For you, it may be different. You have feelings for the Murtray."

"Ja." Why try to deny it?

"The rest of us are not besotted."

She caught her breath. Why try to deny that too? She could not fairly define what *besotted* meant. What she felt for Quarrie was far, far more than mere attraction. Something deeper than the infatuation she'd observed affecting her friends. Though what she felt for Quarrie might include that kind of physical attraction, it reached deeper, and ja, she was convinced it had existed even before she first set eyes on him.

She said nothing. Garik glanced at her again, perhaps a bit less fiercely this time.

"I do not blame you, Hulda. As my old móðir told me, one cannot help where one bestows the heart. Men fall in love too."

"Do they, indeed?"

"Ja, though I will admit we are much more likely to take what we need where we find it, for as long as we can. No man wants a halter around his neck."

"I do not wish to put a halter around his neck." Far from it. She thought Quarrie fine and strong and able to make his own way in the world without her help. What she wanted was to stand beside him, fight along with him and for him, if need be, and be with him for as long as she could.

Because she knew instinctively that in life, there were meetings and partings. Having met him, she wanted to put off the necessity for parting as long as possible.

Whatever that took from her.

So if her men wanted to winter at home, to make nests for themselves at Avoldsborg for a season, she did not know that she could go with them.

Yet to stay here alone? Among strangers? Unthinkable.

"I was in love once," Garik said out of nowhere as he paused and gazed across the sea.

"Were you?"

"Ja. It was while we were busy preparing *Freya*. I let the feeling pass and it went away. Mayhap, Hulda, you should do the same. Once you go home, you will forget the man exists."

She would not. The longing for Quarrie was like a fever now, always with her. Though she had not seen him for days.

If it was somehow so that they had known one another before, just as Quarrie speculated, if the gods had sent them, reborn, to find one another again, then ja, it must be true that she had forgotten him once upon a time. Or even twice, however many times they had come through the ordeals of death and rebirth.

As a babe, had he been in her mind? As a young girl? While growing? When Jute taught her to fight and when she went on her first raids?

What made a woman the person she was? The events of her raising, that shaped her knowledge of the world, or something far deeper that endured from life to life?

Perhaps she was a mingling of both. As was he. Thence, even though in their youths they had not known each other, something within had been waiting.

That *something* inside Hulda had now been brought to life. Freed, she did not think it would lie down again.

Yet staying here could cost her everything.

"Hulda, you will be careful? Sensible. I always thought you such a sensible woman, like a man, almost."

That made Hulda snort. "Men are no more sensible than women. Less, I am sure."

"How so?"

"Women think about practical things. Birth and death and keeping people fed. While men run about boasting of their deeds and how strong they are beneath the blankets."

That made him laugh as he used to do. "Men boast about

how they provide so their women can keep people fed. Hulda"—again he grew serious—"you will have a care?"

"I always do."

He hesitated before he disagreed, "Not always. If I have noticed the way you look at Murtray, others may also. Our men may not like it—some among them are still convinced he had a hand in Jute's death, and you know how well liked was your brother."

"Ja, but Murtray did not—"

"Do not bother telling it to me. Whether or not you avenge Jute is for your heart to decide. But if our men may not like it, the Scots might not either. If they scent something between you and Murtray, it could prove dangerous to you. It could cost your life."

Could it?

She did not speak those words aloud, yet Garik went on anyway. "The Scots do not want their chief—their strong new chief—forming that sort of alliance with one who has spilt their blood. Do you not see? The very thought of staying here is madness."

Madness, ja.

But what would leaving Quarrie do to her heart?

CHAPTER FORTY-TWO

QUARRIE WAS ON the walls with Borald discussing the assignment of the guard when a cry rang out. Both he and the guardsman looked up with instant attention.

A glorious day it was, the sort that Scotland offered up so rarely even in summer. Great, white billows of cloud sailed in a sky of deep blue, chased by a soft and kindly wind. The entire world seemed to glitter from the tops of the playful, wee waves that raced to shore, to each trembling stalk of bracken and heather on the slope above them. Colors stood out bright and true.

Och, for a wealth of such days! Upon rising, Quarrie had thought only one thing could make such a day better.

And now here she came walking down the shore.

Borald made a muffled sound in his throat, one that indicated dismay before he spoke. "Och, it is that accursed Norsewoman."

Aye, so it was. Quarrie narrowed his eyes against the strong light. She came boldly and steadily, as if unafraid even though she moved among enemies, all of whom now focused upon her.

She came alone.

Where were her men? And why would she take the dangerous step of visiting among them when only an admittedly unpopular alliance shielded her?

Why indeed, save to see him?

They had not laid eyes on each other since the feast, at least not to speak. He'd caught glimpses of movement up the shore and they had seen *Freya* sail past, southward. She had not returned for some time.

But it had been days since, aye, they had been spied returning, and no word from Hulda.

No glimpse of other Norse sails either, though his men kept vigilant watch.

"I will go and see what it is she wants." Not waiting for a reply from Borald, Quarrie ran down the steps from the walls and out through the gate. He met Hulda just as she turned to begin the climb up from the shore.

Some of the men who had been at work there, along the shingle, had followed her in. Others now gathered as she prepared to enter the settlement proper. The expressions on their faces sent a quiver down Quarrie's spine.

It would take so little to fell this woman who meant so much to him. A dirk in the back. A blade at the throat. A stone aimed at her head. Only the existence of an alliance upon which he'd insisted protected her.

"Mistress Hulda, good afternoon." She looked well—beautiful, if that could be said of a woman wearing men's clothing, her hair tightly braided and with a sword at her side. A warrior she looked, aye. A bonny one.

Her pale eyes met his, wary and calculating as might a warrior's be. Another emotion lay beneath all that.

Desire? Longing. Aye, the same as he felt. Had felt for days.

"Chief Murtray."

"Wha' can I do for ye?" He could not quite hide his surprise at finding her here. And they stood amid a circle of his people. Men watched from the walls and the shore.

"A word only, if that is possible." In a voice meant for his ears alone, she whispered, "We must speak."

"Aye, so. Will ye come awa' in?"

She nodded.

Was there somewhat wrong? His thoughts raced as he led her into the silence of the great hall. A few servants worked there, but they fled at a gesture from him. On such a fine day as this, the hearth fire had been allowed to burn low. The chamber felt cool.

"Will ye tak' some ale?" A pitcher was always left with some cups on the head table. When Quarrie would have crossed to it, Hulda laid her fingers on his arm.

"Nei. Not that. I need nothing but to see you."

"Hush." He barely breathed the word. "There are eyes and ears everywhere." It may not seem as if anyone watched. That did not mean they went unobserved.

"Some ale then, ja." A desperate light shone in Hulda's eyes.

"Then we will sit. Talk. Ye wish to speak o' the alliance?"

"That, ja."

Now that she was here with him, now that he stood close to her, he could feel the turbulence beneath her calm and confident surface. Like the currents beneath that bonny ocean outside.

He poured two cups of ale and led her to sit beside the fire. At the center of the room, they had less chance of being overheard.

"I had to see you," she said again, as if she could not hold the words in. "It has been so long."

"It has." Too long. Wanting her had been like a sickness inside him, always on the simmer while he fulfilled the duties of his life. Seeing her now—well, it brought everything to the fore.

They gazed at one another. He wondered if the hunger in her eyes, now unleashed, reflected his own. He hoped not. Because aye, if anyone spied upon them…

"Wha' is it I can do for ye, Mistress Hulda?" A foolish question, for he knew. He could take her somewhere that they might be quite alone. Free her from that restrictive clothing she wore. Remove every braid from her glorious hair. Run his hand up her leg all the way to the thigh. Plant his mouth at her breast.

She drew a long, quivering breath, one he felt. "I wish to discuss the details of our agreement."

"Aye, so. The alliance still stands between us, does it no'?"

"It does. Everything still stands between us."

Her feelings had not changed. The desire, the longing.

"I have been contemplating the end of the season."

"The season?"

"The season for raiding, when my men will wish to go home."

Oh.

"And"—he said it very softly so that, indeed, any straining ears would not hear—"ye mean to go wi' them?"

She did not answer at once. She toyed with her cup of ale. She frowned at it.

Even when she did speak, her words skirted his question. "I have discussed it with Garik, who has heard from the crew that they do not wish to overwinter here."

"Ah. Was there a possibility of that?" He should have thought. He should have realized that to be sure, the season would come to an end. She would go away with her men. They would not have forever together. He should have insisted on making the most of every moment, of being often in her company even if they did not lie together.

"Not truly, nei. These voyages we go upon, well, the men see them as adventures."

Murdering and destroying were adventures. Could they be more different?

"With their adventures complete, they want to go home. To…to boast and flaunt their gains, to visit with their families and perhaps—be with women."

"I see."

"I wished to discuss with you—"

"When?" He could not prevent the question. "How soon will ye go?"

"It will be a while yet. The end of summer or longer, if the raiding holds good."

So if she kept on slaughtering his fellow countrymen, he might have the chance to see her. It was insupportable. Unbearable.

She resumed what she'd begun to say. "I wished to discuss

with you the duration of our alliance. Did you intend it for but this season? Or will it last into the next?"

Might she return, she meant. Could she sail back to him after the long, unendurable winter and once more take up residence upon that patch of land he'd allotted her?

He gazed into her eyes. "Hulda, so far as I am concerned, our alliance—what lies between us—is forever. Forever, do ye understand? No end, between us."

He saw it then, the emotion blazing suddenly in her eyes as if the sun had burst through rain clouds. Did tears follow that light? Hard to tell, for she ducked her head over her ale cup.

"That is how I feel also. You will be waiting, if I return?"

If. She could not promise. Naught was certain.

"I will be waiting, Hulda. It feels as if I have always been waiting. Now that I ha' found ye—touched ye—I will continue to wait as long as need be." Constancy, he offered her, the constancy of love eternal.

"I wanted you to know, no matter how long the winter, I will not forget. And I wanted to say—" She broke off.

"We canna waste any more time," he finished for her. "'Tis far too precious." Now it was he who drew a breath. "I maun be wi' ye."

"And I with you. That, above all, is what I came to say."

"The same place?"

"Ja. When?"

"'Twill prove difficult. There are eyes everywhere. Men constantly on watch."

"Ja."

He did not see how he might slip away. If he had, he would have striven to arrange it already, so fiercely did he ache for her. Yet, rashly, he said, "Soon. *Soon.*"

"I will assign my men to some repairs on *Freya*. Keep them occupied. I will say I must meet with you here. You do the same, saying you meet me at my camp. We will meet instead at the ruined hut."

Like two children, Quarrie thought ruefully, weaving stories to deceive their parents. But he nodded. "Ye remember how to find the place?"

"I have walked there a score of times, in my mind. Tonight?"

"Nay. Tomorrow night."

"If I can wait so long."

"Hulda." He wanted to touch her but still did not know whether anyone watched them.

"I will tell my crew we meet to discuss terms for next year."

"Aye."

She rose to leave, setting her ale cup aside. Not looking at him, she turned for the doorway.

"Ást min," she whispered, barely above a breath.

He remained her love.

It would have to hold him till they met again.

CHAPTER FORTY-THREE

Dark arrived very late at this time of year, if it came at all. On a clear night, the gloaming might hover in the sky till dawn. Just like at home, where a kind of madness sometimes set in due to the surfeit or lack of light.

It was mad for Hulda to go walking off now, after lying to her men about having another meeting with Quarrie.

We may speak together long, she'd told them. *Do not expect me back till late.*

Only Garik had looked askance, and he was too tired to object. She'd kept all of them working hard on overhauling *Freya,* the whole day long. They would sleep well and hopefully forget about her.

Once she veered from the path that led south to the settlement and climbed into the trees, she appreciated the lingering light, even though this night was not a clear one. Soft clouds gathered and obscured the blade of the moon. It might rain by dawn.

The last time she and Quarrie had been together, it had rained. If it did so again, did it mean the very world wept for them? That their love was doomed?

Anyone but a fool of a woman who had lost her heart would know it was. Apart from stolen moments and those hard come by, how could they ever be together?

She reached the half-ruined hut ahead of him and began to fret. He had changed his mind—he was not coming after all. He did not love her.

Then a shadow moved among the trees that had grown up around the hut. The great bound of her heart told her who it was even before he spoke.

"Hulda, love?"

Love. Ach, ja, well she had told him she loved him. Should he not do the same? Should there be anything the one of them withheld from the other?

She went to him, pressed close into his arms, which closed to embrace her fiercely. The rightness of it, sharp as pain, stole her words and closed her throat.

They did not speak. Did not need to. She inhaled his scent while a confusing series of images tumbled through her mind.

A tall young man standing over a washbasin, but half clad in the bright sunshine. Auburn hair and hazel eyes—not Quarrie's eyes, but those eyes regarded her the same way Quarrie's did, with love. He was, and yet he was not Quarrie.

A fair-haired man with gray-green eyes, rowing a tiny boat across the far ocean. Her name on his lips. *Bradana.*

Another young man with light-brown hair, riding on the back of a pony, racing—racing her with his eyes alight and a smile on his face.

The memories twisted together and convulsed her heart. All of these were the man in her arms who had loved her, and loved her, and loved her again.

How could they do anything except love each other now?

She lifted her face to his. "Kiss me." She spoke, unthinkingly, in Norse, but he understood her anyway and his lips took hers. They molded together, bodies, mouth, tongues, spirits, and her heart steadied, perhaps beating in time with his, while desire rose in a staggering wave.

"Love me," she begged, even as she had long, long ago.

They moved to the sheltered end of the hut, where Hulda spread her cloak. Undressed themselves and each other.

Before they lay down, he turned her to face him. Beautiful he looked, standing there in the filtered light of the gloaming, holding her, holding her with his gaze. Deliberately, he lifted each of her hands in turn to his lips and dropped fervent kisses into the palms. He kissed both corners of her mouth, each cheek. He left a lingering kiss on her brow.

"Myself I do give to ye, Hulda. For all time."

"Ja, and I—forever."

They fell onto her cloak and wrapped themselves in each other. As it had been before, the joining seemed familiar yet new, a discovery of an old memory, an ancient song Hulda's heart had never forgotten.

No beginning to how she loved this man, and no end. She withheld nothing of herself from him and they became, in truth, one being with one flesh.

I love you.

She whispered it to him over and over again, in two languages. Or mayhap he said it to her. Who could tell? Hulda knew only that she existed in this moment with him, and nothing else might be desired.

Time ceased to pass. If there was a wheel upon which the lives of men and women turned, it ground to a blessed halt and let them be.

"I love you," one of them whispered again before, upon Quarrie's chest, Hulda fell asleep.

QUARRIE DREAMED. WHILE the woman he loved slept close in his arms, he did. He was in a chariot behind a team of wild-headed ponies. His best friend—a yellow-headed lad with a bright, crooked grin—was beside him, handling the traces. On their way into battle, they were. Secure in their friendship. Secure in their lives.

His friend turned to him. "When I die, will ye take good care o' my sister?"

The scene changed, tumbled and fogged with smoke and flame. He ran toward another battle with a sword in his hand. This land he knew—it was his own stretch of shore, his own settlement. But it did not look the same. No keep stood on the knoll, only a roundhouse—a dun—and the dead lay everywhere. He stepped over them to reach his opponent.

The dream tumbled again. He saw a man, black hair streaked with gray, a cruel sneer on his face. He would fight that man to the death if he must in order to free the woman he loved.

Hulda stirred in his arms. Whimpered. It brought Quarrie from the dream.

"Hush, love. Wha' is it?" He cradled her against him, precious to him as his own life.

"I dreamed—" Her lashes fluttered desperately. He could see her clearly. Morning must be almost come. "You were going off to fight. Ready to die for me." She gulped back a sob. "Die. *For me.*"

"Aye." Had they, after sharing so much, also shared the same dreams?

She began to fight her way free of his arms. "No man need ever fight for me. I fight on my own behalf."

"Aye, love. Aye."

"You were a warrior, you were always a warrior, and you tried to sacrifice yourself for me again and again." She sat up and began to weep, this woman who, Quarrie imagined, very rarely shed a tear. She wept as if heartbroken.

"Love." He seized her hands and tried to reason with her. "Ye canna keep a man fro' fighting for what he loves."

"I can. I can!"

"'Tis his God-given right, that."

"I will never let you die for me, not again. I will stand for myself. Fight for myself."

"Aye, so ye can."

She cradled his face between her hands. "I do not want you to be a warrior. Not ever again."

"My love, I am what I am, who I am. I was raised to fight in defense of this land." Against those such as she, though he did not say so. "If ye love me, ye maun accept—"

"I can never accept your dying for my sake."

"List. List. I am no' dying. Am I no' here wi' ye now? Hush. Hush."

He drew her back against him, seeking to comfort her. The jumble of images from his dreams still filled his mind. Had she dreamed somewhat else more terrible? Had she dreamed his death?

She kissed him, pouring herself into the caress, into him. Before Quarrie knew it, they were making love again, flesh to flesh and soul to soul, even as the sun grew strong in the sky.

It had not rained after all. The night had been kind to them, allowed them a magical span of time to share themselves with one another.

He had done that, completely. Quarrie dragged his eyes open as the thought occurred to him. During the night past, might he not have given her his child?

Best not to mention that, just like past losses, or future partings.

"It is late." He roused her. "We maun go home."

"I do not wish to part with you. I fear if I do, I will not see you again."

"Aye, but ye will. The end o' summer is a while off yet."

"And much, much can happen to separate a woman from the man she loves. I know that. I am not a fool."

She *feared*. Since they had found one another, she'd feared losing him even though he doubted she feared much else. Quarrie thought of the glimpses he'd had in those dreams—of other lives? Ones in which she might well have lost him, for he'd, aye, been a warrior. So now she worried about losing him again.

Life made no promises. Like her, he was no fool and faced that squarely. That meant he could make her no false promises either. Only that he would never stop loving her.

That was truth.

"Hulda, love, against all likelihood we ha' been given the gift o' meeting one another. We may also ha' been given glimpses o' a past or many pasts full o' risk and danger. We canna change the past by worrying for it."

"You are right." She strove visibly to gain control of her emotions, drew herself up, and tossed back her mane of hair, the same he'd loosened from its plaits with his own hands. "I am with you now. It is more—more than anything for which I ever thought to hope."

"Aye." Yet he could feel the pain inside her, even as he could feel the love.

"Tell me we will be together here again before I sail for home."

Dangerous to chance it when each meeting exposed them to possible discovery. Yet he did not possess the strength to deny her. "Aye."

"When? Tomorrow night?"

"Nay, too soon. 'Twill arouse suspicion."

She made a sound of protest before she said, "I will try to be patient. But being with you, Quarrie—it is more than desire I feel, eh? It is *need*. Do you understand?"

"I do." All too well. And if he had to watch *Freya*'s sail disappear over the northern horizon, it would half kill him.

Do not think about that yet.

"Come." He rose and pulled her to her feet, stood for an instant gazing upon her. Naked, beautiful, withholding nothing from him.

He wished he could tell her what he felt in that moment. What he believed. That if destiny had gone to all the trouble of bringing them together this way, there must be a powerful reason for it. A life-changing one.

Instead he told her softly, "We maun hurry. 'Tis already growing light." He picked up her garments and handed them to her. The two of them dressed as unashamedly as a wedded couple, rushing now.

He said to her before they took their separate paths, "Ye will be strong? Be strong for me."

"I will."

But the pain in her eyes when she left him matched his own.

CHAPTER FORTY-FOUR

"THE NORSE HA' gone off raiding again." Borald greeted Quarrie with those words when he climbed the steps to pace the walls, some days later. "We saw them sail past just after dawn."

Quarrie narrowed his eyes upon the sea, even though *Freya* would be long gone. He'd been waylaid en route here by half a score of people wishing to state their complaints.

About the Norse.

When are they going to leave? Will they hold our lands forever? 'Tis good hunting ground to which ye ha' given them leave.

And, *Why do they come here so often? Can they no' keep to their own camp?*

How long will they use our lands to prey upon our neighbors?

He had but few answers for his folk, who clearly were not happy with him.

The Norse did come to the settlement frequently, mostly to trade, a familiar if unwelcome sight. They paid well for the goods they bought, the ugly truth being that they price they offered had blood upon it. Scottish blood.

The three Norse leaders—the man called Garik, the one named Helje who Hulda said was Garik's brother, and Hulda herself—came most often. Indeed, Garik had become…not friendly, for it was far from that, but garrulous with some of their folk. He, like Hulda, possessed a working knowledge of their tongue. A good-looking young man, he also possessed a measure of charm, and Quarrie had seen him more than once talking with their young women.

His men did not like it, and more than one had told Quarrie so. Indeed, he tired of hearing about the Norse.

If the complaints were the price he must pay in order to see Hulda, however, aye, he was willing to pay it.

He had seen her in passing, though they had been alone together only once more. A night of bliss that had been, for they had sated themselves in one another, mating in every way a man and woman could, and then some. His Hulda, it proved, was both imaginative and uninhibited. Despite her having left him utterly spent, however, the desire for her continued to gnaw at him after.

Which just went to prove that whatever he had of her could not be enough.

"They will be leaving soon," he told Borald. "Off back to Norway."

Borald's gaze flew to him. "Is that what she told ye, the woman warrior?"

Quarrie hesitated. The whole clan knew he and Hulda met to talk. He could only pray they suspected naught more. Yet he swore he caught a gleam of knowing in Borald's blue eyes.

"They will go home for winter, aye."

That made Borald snort. "Winter is a long way off, curse them."

It was not, not truly. On days like this one, clear, far-reaching days with a brisk wind off the sea, Quarrie could almost smell autumn.

His chances to see Hulda, talk with her, lie with her, dwindled. And these days might be all he would ever have.

She did love him, aye. He could not doubt that. Yet their situation was all but impossible.

Their alliance, however, had helped to keep the settlement safe. He had no doubt of that either. For during these days, *Freya*'s sails were not the only ones the Scots keeping watch had sighted. One afternoon, a group of three longboats had appeared out in the waters just past Oileán Iur. Defenses had scrambled, men racing for arms, women gathering their children and fearing the worst.

Before any attack could come, however, *Freya*—in readiness for a voyage of her own—had sailed out to meet the incomers.

Hulda had herself related what passed between them, during the night they shared that came soon after.

"I told their leader, a man I did not know, for he is not from my home *vik*, that these are our waters. He agreed to turn away."

She had done as she'd promised, acted as a fierce hound on Quarrie's behalf. That did not mean others would not come, after she had gone.

"Keep good watch," he told Borald now. "Wi' them awa', we are more open to danger."

Borald snorted again. "Wi' all respect, chief, d'ye no' think we can look after oursel's? 'Tis what we did long before that lot came."

"And plenty died for it, aye? I say only, we ha' an alliance. Why no' mak'the most o' it?"

"And I say we better no' rely too heavily on such an untrustworthy set o' allies."

The man was right. Yet so tangled were Quarrie's thoughts and emotions, he could scarcely think straight.

"I do no' trust them," Borald stated plainly. "And I do no' like their men comin' here so often to trade. Speaking to our women. That fair-haired one now—"

"Garik." Hulda's second-in-command.

"Him, aye." Loathing entered Borald's voice. "He has been speaking wi' Morag."

"Has he, then?" Quarrie fixed his friend with a sharp eye. They were close enough that he knew Morag for the young woman Borald had himself been courting for nearly two years without much success.

"Aye." Sourly, Borald added, "I do no' understand how she can gi' him her time, and him with Scottish blood on his hands."

"Does she give him her time?" Quarrie asked, surprised.

"Och, aye." For an instant, despair looked at Quarrie from Borald's eyes. "As much or more than she ever ga' me."

Aye, that was a problem. Quarrie's men might—just barely—tolerate an alliance with hated members of the race that beleaguered them. Allowing them to poach their women? Never.

Yet men were men and women were women, and attraction would spring up where it may. He could hardly argue with that.

But he could not say so to Borald.

"Ye meet wi' yon Hulda often enough," Borald said unhappily. "Tell me they do no' mean to come back in the spring."

"We ha' spoken, aye, about the alliance enduring for next season. But who can tell wha' will happen by then? Many things may change over the course o' a winter."

"I can only hope so. I will be happy if I ne'er see them again—any o' them."

And Quarrie's heart would shatter into a thousand pieces, were that so.

"HULDA—THE MEN WANT to go home." Garik, having handed the tiller over to another crew member, chose the moment they sailed back into their borrowed Scottish harbor to deliver the news. They came flush with plunder following yet another series of successful raids farther south. That being so, Hulda could not imagine what reason the men had to complain. Had her bargain with Quarrie not given them a canny berth from which to operate?

She eyed Garik closely. "Are they not happy with what they have earned?"

"Ja. No one can say he is not."

"Then why withdraw before times?"

"They tire of the rough camp. Of the hostility that lurks just out of sight."

"They would be hostile too, toward folk who so often laid a blade to their throats."

Garik hesitated. "They grow tired of what they see between you and the Murtray."

Alarm raced through Hulda like fire. "What do they see?"

Garik gave her a speaking look. "Do not insult them, Hulda. They see what I saw long ago. You want him. For all I know, you have likely had him. Those *meetings* you keep arranging that last the whole night long..."

Dismayed, Hulda said nothing.

"It is none of my business, with whom you lie down." Garik, though, still sounded uneasy. "A woman wants to rut as does a man, so I suppose."

"Ach, does she?"

"Ja."

"That is generous of you."

"Do not grow annoyed with me. Believe me, I understand. There is a little woman among the Scots at the settlement—"

"Is there, now?"

"She is in charge of trading their food supplies. We have been bargaining. And talking."

Surprised, Hulda said nothing.

"She is among the loveliest women I have ever seen. We have grown...not friendly, nei, but perhaps comfortable talking with one another. I once even made her laugh."

Garik, at his best, could make most anyone laugh.

"So—so though I perhaps did not before, when we spoke, I do understand it. And me, I would not mind coming back next spring. But the men..."

"What is her name, this Scots lass?"

"Morag." Garik stared away over the rail with a look in his eyes such as Hulda had never before seen there. "She is able to understand my garbled command of their tongue, which is why the head o' stores put her on to dealing with me. They are not so different from us," he reflected, "once you stop with slitting their throats."

Hulda had no response to that.

"So as I say, Hulda, I understand. And a promise to return—one I could perhaps give to Morag—would not go amiss with me. To be honest, I do not know how many others among the crew will be eager for a return voyage."

"Despite what they have gained?"

"The alliance with the Scots makes them uncomfortable. Your attitude toward the Murtray does."

She had heard the mutterings, aye. *Freya* and, indeed, the camp was not large enough for her to miss overhearing. But Norsemen were by and large a practical breed. She had hoped avarice alone might bring them back.

"Well, then." She puffed out a breath. "We will find another crew, come spring."

Garik scoffed. "Not if they tell everyone you have gone making alliances with the Scots, instead of killing them."

"It is done in Dublin. In—"

"I know, I know. It is done there by powerful jarls and commanders. Not by such as we."

Hulda frowned. The fear that seemed to have become lodged inside her, all tangled up with her love for Quarrie, stirred and unsheathed its claws.

She must return. Leaving would be hard. Near impossible. She could not do it, were she not certain she could return.

"We will find another crew," she insisted with certainty she did not feel. "You may tell your Morag you will be coming back to her."

"She is not my Morag." But he would like her to be. "And she has said nothing to make me think she would welcome me back. There are many, far too many difficulties between us." He leveled a stare upon Hulda. "I doubt such a joining would ever work."

"Ja." Hulda had to admit it. There was a surfeit of doubt in the world, and far too little certainty.

CHAPTER FORTY-FIVE

"MY MEN WANT to go home." Hulda whispered the words but a breath from Quarrie's lips, having just finished kissing him. She had not meant to speak them—not here, not now when his body lay naked beneath hers, in this time apart. The words merely came on their own.

His eyes, which had closed against the pleasure of her kiss, opened. By Freya's heart, she loved his eyes. That rare hazel sparked with green, they contained all she would ever need of the world. Nei, they contained a world of their own.

His thick brown lashes swept up and down and his gaze narrowed on hers when he said, "Do they, now?" He slid his palms down her back to her naked buttocks and drew her closer in a gesture that had become wonderfully familiar. It brought desire and comfort in equal measures. He fitted her, he did. She belonged with him and *to* him. No need for further questioning.

They had met again at the ruined stone hut, even though it was surely unwise to do so, for they might well be discovered by her men or his people. Hulda had delivered the message when she and Brynjar had gone for supplies, Garik having made up an excuse to stay away, that Quarrie should come here to her this night.

Now she wondered. Did Garik not wish to see his Morag? Ach, he was stronger, then, than she.

She felt as if she had spun out her endurance for being without Quarrie as long as she could, without dying. And now, when they'd made love once, when she knew she could have him again, she reached to satisfy the even deeper need of confiding in him.

"Ja. And Garik thinks… He thinks most of them will not be interested in returning, come spring."

He drew a quick breath, one she felt through her whole body, which told her he comprehended the implications. When she sailed away from here at the end of the season, it would cost both of them dear, but knowing she would not return…

"Garik says he would be willing to come, and as the navigator, he is vital to me. I can try to get another crew. But *Freya* is one boat alone. She is not large. I was able to gather this crew because they were young and largely unproven."

"That is not so, now."

"Nei, it is not."

"Surely"—his gaze held hers—"they feel some loyalty to ye."

"They should, ja." Hulda frowned over it. "I did give them a chance. And they will sail home with a measure of riches. But they have not liked all that has happened here."

"Our alliance, ye mean."

"And," she concluded bitterly, "there is little glory in sailing for a woman."

His hands traveled to her waist and cradled her. Grief showed in his eyes.

She reiterated, "I will do my best to hire another crew. But I—I cannot promise. Without a crew, I cannot return."

Emotions flickered through his eyes like light on water. That grief. Protest. Terror. Love. Hulda understood them all because she also experienced them all.

"I wish," she said, "I wish I could promise to return."

"I wish," he whispered just as softly, "ye could stay."

"Stay when the rest of them leave, you mean?" Her heart began to pound as she considered it. It would mean surrendering her life. All she had been. Spending the remainder of it among people who feared and despised her.

Not that she would refuse to do so, for him.

"Are you asking me to stay with you?"

"I am. Become my wife."

All the breath left Hulda's body in a rush. She fought to regain it, along with her thoughts. "Your folk would never accept it." A Norsewoman standing at their head? The mother of their future chief?

"I ha' lived my entire life for this clan and will live for it every day I ha' to come. May I no' ha' this one thing?"

This one thing he needed, he meant. This fundamental thing that they both needed.

But people, as Hulda well knew, were selfish. They wanted what they wanted. Her crew did even though, ja, they owed her for this chance she'd offered them.

Just as, in a way, she owed them.

With regret, she shook her head. "I want to. I want nothing more than to be your wife. But I cannot give you that promise, either. For me not to return home—well, my faðir has already lost his son; my móðir has. Should they lose their dottir also without explanation? Faðir—he is a powerful man. He is capable of sending a force to attack this place out of revenge. Out of spite."

"He would do that? If your crew, if Garik told him ye chose to stay?"

"So that I might wed with the man who killed his son?"

"My father did that, not me."

"No better." A wry smile twisted her lips and she shook her head again. "Nei, I must go home. Talk to him, and to Móðir. See if I can make explanations and get her on my side. Faðir listens to her, sometimes."

"Then it seems I maun let ye sail awa' from me."

It would be a long winter, unbearably long. And when she returned to Norge, would all this seem like a dream? As if it had never truly happened. Like those other dreams she'd had of Quarrie when he wore another man's face and body—different yet the same. But that *was* real. It was a past truth.

"I maun let ye go," he repeated. "And doing so, I maun ha' faith. I canna believe fate brought ye to me for this moment in time, only so we might be parted again, forever."

"Not forever." A sob rose to her throat. "But ja, perhaps for this life." She did not want to admit that, did not even want to think it, but it might well be so.

"Then—then, Hulda, we will meet again in the next life. This I do promise ye."

"Love me," she beseeched him. "Love me now."

And he did.

Time, so Hulda decided as she sheltered there in his arms, as she took him inside her, was a fickle commodity. It flew when she was with him. Dragged when she was not. Terrified her when she thought of the span of it before spring.

Became unimaginable when she considered the remainder of her life. She was not yet a score and four years old. How would she live the many years without him?

He was right—she had to *try* to believe. Believe in something beyond the reach of her own intentions, in the same destiny that, out of a world of men, had brought her to him.

This love they shared was wondrous. It was also terrifying. Could she trust that it had a power of its own?

They lay lost in loving till dawn, when they rose and dressed without words, the cold of the outside world stealing in with the morning light.

Not until they prepared to part, he to take one path through the woodland and she another, did he catch both her hands in his and ask, "Hulda, how many days do we have left?"

"I do not know. If I take *Freya* out for a few more raids, that may keep the men content and make them willing to linger yet a while."

The corners of Quarrie's mouth tightened. He hated it when she went raiding—the price of keeping her near to him.

"Even that takes ye awa' from me."

"Ja."

"Time has become verra precious."

The tears in Hulda's eyes blurred his face. She blinked them away. "Quarrie, we must be together as oft as we can before I take *Freya* home."

Once more, she saw the emotions flicker in his eyes. Doubt. Protest. A weighing of risk against desire.

He said only, "Aye."

"Tonight."

His fingers tightened on hers. He should refuse, as a sensible man would. Instead he said again, "Aye."

Very well, then. She could live another day. Stave off the thoughts and the dread that accompanied them.

They kissed goodbye, a lingering of lips on lips, a clinging of soul to soul.

"Tonight," she whispered in parting.

But before the night came, a message arrived in camp brought by one of Quarrie's guards. The man asked to speak with Hulda alone, and delivered his message with narrowed eyes.

"Chief Quarrie bade me let ye know there is trouble at hand. A fleet o' longships has been sighted movin' in fro' the outer islands."

Hulda's heart fell. *He would not be able to come.* That was her first thought before she focused on what the man had said.

"Longboats?"

"Aye. We see to our defenses."

Hulda knew what that meant. The gates guarded. Every man armed. The women and children quite possibly sent off to shelter in the forest.

She could not go to him. He would not want to see her now, nor would his folk.

This—this was the reality of their situation. When the monsters arrived from the ocean, she would be seen as one of them.

"I understand," she told the man, and he went pelting off as if a howling horde pursued him.

As it did.

CHAPTER FORTY-SIX

IT HAD TAKEN nearly all summer. Most of the killing season, anyway. It had been a time apart, aye. A time of dreams. From the moment Quarrie first spied Hulda's sail on the horizon, his life had acquired a mystical quality that defied the ugly truth of his world.

Truly, so he thought as he stood on the wall above the keep, staring out across the sea, he should have known better.

Life was all about ugliness, endurance, loss, and dying. Had his da not perished so in ugly agony after months of suffering? Had Quarrie not lost his own brother and countless childhood companions, grown into fine warriors, in these years just past? Was he not himself first and foremost a warrior?

Standing there with his eyes narrowed against the descent of the afternoon sun, he no longer knew quite who he was.

The man who'd been born for this place, who would likely die in defense of it? Or the man who lived to be in Hulda's arms? The two had become so twisted, as had the emotions of loyalty and desire, that he could no longer tell them apart.

But with the appearance of dark sails on the horizon, Hulda had once more become the enemy. No more, for his folk, of an imposed alliance. No more the uneasy tolerance of Norsemen, and one woman, in their settlement. They knew death when they saw it coming.

As did he.

The Norse had been clever, coming out from the distant

islands when the glare of the westering sun would be in the defenders' eyes. Four ships, there were. *Four.*

Could they defend against so many? And would the Norse attack now, or wait for morning? The gloaming would last long enough, as the men aboard those boats well knew, to afford a battle straight away.

Such a battle, against so many invaders, would be crippling. They might well lose.

Someone pressed into place at the rampart beside him. His mother, it was.

"Ma, ye should no' be up here."

"Nay? Where should I be?" Without giving him a chance to answer, she asked, "How many?"

Too many. "Four ships."

"By God!"

"If ye want to be o' help, go organize the women. Get them ready to flee for the hills."

For the briefest instant her eyes met his, and he beheld her distress. She had seen her beloved husband take his mortal wound in just such a battle as would now come. And, Quarrie reflected, if there could be one thing worse than fighting such a battle, it would be standing by and watching, as good as helpless.

"Already underway," she told him. "I am sending three o' the older men wi' them along wi' the harper. He is far too precious for us to lose."

Quarrie's head swam. This too seemed familiar. Had it all happened long ago? Aye, it had, all his life fighting against the Norse. He should not have a moment to think of Hulda, not at such a time, yet she held a place in his mind. What would she do when the settlement came under attack?

He could not worry about that now. He could not worry about her.

He could not seem to do anything else.

But aye, he thought of that as, leaving the ramparts in Borald's hands, he ran down the stairs with Ma at his heels into the confusion. Men hurried everywhere, bristling with arms. Women and children flooded the bailey, many of the bairns crying and the women trying to find their men to speak a farewell.

He was not the only one who risked losing his love.

That was why they fought, was it not? Not for greed or power, but for love.

Someone ran up to him and seized him by the arm. Blinking fiercely, he saw it was Norah. As before when he'd encountered her, she had her wee babe on her shoulder and she looked frantic.

"Wha' is happening?" she barked at Quarrie. "Tell me."

Surely she had heard, the foolish lass. "The Norse are attacking. Headed in for shore."

"How many?"

"Four sails."

"Where is Corban? I canna find him. I maun find him!"

Quarrie tried to rein in his impatience, wondering in that moment what he'd ever seen in the lass. She was bonny, aye. But she was not Hulda.

What if he'd wed with her and only met Hulda after? What would have become of his heart?

He told Norah as calmly as he could, "There is no' time for that now."

"Ye will no' let him die, Quarrie MacMurtray. Do no' let my man die!"

She loved Corban truly, Quarrie thought, and that took away any remaining sting. If any had endured the light that was Hulda.

"Get yer bairn safe awa'," he told her shortly, and pressed on.

Down to the shore. Here would be their first line of defense, and every man there knew it. This was the attack they had dreaded all season. For which they'd prepared and drilled. Against which they'd prayed.

The longboats looked more threatening from down here at the water. And closer. Bigger than *Freya* and somehow finer. They no doubt belonged to some great jarl or warlord who had been raking the coast all season long.

Like a shoal of sharks, they were. And like sharks, not much could stand before them.

He must. He'd been born to do so. He must now step firmly into his father's boots, stand as bravely as Da had ever done.

Even if the cost be the same.

"They are moving in," said someone beside him. Borald had come down from the walls. He had drawn his sword and taken a shield from two lads handing them out. "No doubt about their intentions."

"Nay," Quarrie agreed.

"They are comin' for us."

Dread and doubt and certainty made a horrible soup in Quarrie's gut. He could not fail.

"Form up!" he bellowed to his men, these that were his friends and neighbors, that he would have to watch die. He could not let himself think of that, only of the settlement at his back.

Let none through. That was what Da had said to him before his first battle against a Norse raiding party, when Quarrie had taken the place at Da's side. And Quarrie had thought then, *Aye, how hard is that? I need no' let anyone past me.*

It had been hard. He had killed his first opponents on that day and watched friends perish.

But no one had got past.

The same today. Only that.

The quartet of Norse boats drew closer. They would anchor offshore, where the water began to grow shallow, and come pouring over into the ocean, weapons raised and howling.

He lifted his voice. "A line! A line! Shoulder to shoulder." He repeated Da's words. "Let no one through. Ye ken for what we fight."

They fought for love. But what of the other love in his heart?

The men on the shore began to yell. At first Quarrie thought it was in response to his words. Then Borald, beside him, squawked, "Look. *Look!*"

Quarrie did, trying to push back his fear, to disregard the

confusion still pouring from the keep behind him.

He looked and nearly failed to believe.

Another longboat sailed out into the water, driven by half a score pairs of oars, streaking from the northern shore and on a direct course to intercept the Norse ships.

Freya, it was.

A cry was going up all down the line of defenders. Men did not know what to make of this. Aye, Hulda had intervened for them before, earlier in the season. Acted as their hound. But this, here, would be a large-scale battle. Did she mean to fight for or against them?

He could see the men aboard, Hulda's men, pulling hard at the oars. He could see Hulda standing near the prow, tall and straight, dressed in her armor. From this distance, she looked like another warrior.

"Wha' are they doing?" asked Kenneth, the man standing on Quarrie's other side.

"Betraying us!" someone else bellowed. "They are goin' out to join their fellows in the attack!"

Nay, that could not be it, Quarrie thought. Surely Hulda would not betray him. But what of her men?

A silence fell then, one so complete that Quarrie could hear the hiss and gurgle of the waves at his feet. Even the noise from the keep seemed to dampen. The defenders on the walls had seen.

The *Freya* looked small and weather-worn as it approached the four proud vessels. Across the water, Quarrie heard Hulda's voice as she called a command to her men.

He heard her voice.

They shipped their oars.

She hailed the men on the nearest of the Norse ships.

CHAPTER FORTY-SEVEN

Panic stirred in Hulda's heart. Fear lodged deeper down in her gut, possessed of sharp claws. She acted now not by thought but by pure instinct. A woman defended what she loved.

He—her love—would be there on the rocky shore, one in the ragged line of defenders she could already see standing, taking their places to withstand the opposing storm.

The thing about storms was, not all of them could be outlasted.

Her men—her crew—had been reluctant to obey her in this instance. She'd been forced to shout at them, bully them, and remind them that at the beginning of this voyage they had pledged their loyalty to her. Well, to her and Garik and Helje.

Helje—well, he had protested. Garik, eyeing her, had said naught, but he had gestured the men aboard *Freya*, wasting no time.

Might Faðir Odin bless him for it.

Now, as *Freya* drew near the foremost of the invading ships, Hulda strained to see who was aboard. She might know them, or she might not. Raiders came from many places in the northern realm. These could well be fierce and hungry strangers.

And yet…something looked familiar about the lead boat. She had seen it before. At home, in Avoldsborg.

She stepped as far forward as she could as *Freya* slid in alongside the larger boat. Men aboard that vessel had rushed to the rail, as curious about her as she was about them.

Ja, she knew some of them.

Face after face turned to her, more than one she recognized. A man with dark-brown hair shoved several others aside in order to face her.

Her heart plummeted.

"Master Ivor," she called.

Her men, behind her, had gone silent. Garik, who must have handed the tiller over to one of the other men, stepped up to her side.

Ivor Larsson, well clad for war with his helmet already in place, leaned forward to stare at her.

"Hulda Elvarsdottir?" He appeared surprised. "You, here?" He gave a bark of laughter. "We thought you and your wreck of a boat would be at the bottom of the sea by now."

His scorn made her crew bristle. She called back, "As you can see, we are still asea and thriving. You are in our waters."

"What?" That made him and every man aboard the lead longboat stare. In truth, it made her crew stare also. "You have no holdings here. And we are raiding."

"You are wrong," she called back as boldly as she dared. "I do have holdings here. *We* do."

Muttering broke out on the larger boat.

Ivor called back, "Impossible. There is a fine prize sitting at your back, girl, and we mean to take it." A sly sort of smile stretched his lips. "And mayhap avenge your brother, as you were unwilling or unable to do."

"I have an alliance with the chief of this place, who has granted us rights here. We cannot allow you to attack."

That forced another laugh from him. "You think to stop me? With your handful of boy-warriors?"

"Along with those men ranged upon the shore. We will join them in the defense, if we must."

Dead silence fell. Hulda did not think any member of her crew was breathing.

"You are not in earnest," Ivor said at last. "This is one of your games. Get out of our way, little girl."

"I will not. I have an alliance, I say, and I will stand by it."

"Then we will kill you all and fire your boat."

Hulda drew her sword. Either a courageous action or a mad one. "Try for it. We are the sons—and dottir—of warriors."

"You are a poor excuse for a crew sailing a poor excuse for a boat. The dregs o' poor families back home."

"Are we?" Helje stepped up, strong pride apparently making him forget his differences with Hulda. "Then why have we had a successful season?"

"Consorting with the natives?" Ivor's sneer was plain to see. "So much for the worth of a female commander."

Hulda felt her crew bristle. No one behind her spoke, but ja, she could feel. They had proved themselves during this season. Would they accept this arrogant man's disdain?

Ivor, apparently thinking they would, went over Hulda's head and called to her crew, "Your mistress is a fool. Get this tub out of my way."

No one behind Hulda moved.

Ivor began to look seriously annoyed.

"Move this boat, I say, or we will board and do it for you."

The wrong tack to take. *Freya* might be aged and humble, but each of the crew had a stake in her repairing, and sailing her. She was *theirs*.

A silent consensus passed from man to man before Garik spoke.

"Will you kill all of us, Ivor? Will you slay your neighbors' sons and then go home with your spoils from yon settlement and tell everyone there what befell us?"

"I would not want to bring your families such shame. Dealing with the Scots—"

"We do what we must to get ahead. What our people have always done. We have made an alliance to our advantage, and possess the honor needed to keep to it."

Men now crowded the rail of Ivor's boat and the other three

vessels as men strained to hear. The line of defenders on the shore must also wonder what was happening.

Quarrie.

Hulda called to Ivor loudly, "There are targets enough for you to attack further along the coast. This one is under our protection."

"Yours," Ivor repeated, as if he yet could not believe it.

"Ours! Take yourself elsewhere."

The men aboard Ivor's boat clustered around him as they discussed it. This could go either way, Hulda conceded. Ivor's pride could refuse to lie down. He could go through *Freya* to reach the shore. But it would hurt him.

It would harm the *Freya* and her crew more.

It took a while for Ivor to decide. Raised voices could be heard, and the cluster of four dragon boats rose and fell on the swells as if time itself suspended for them. The gloaming began to fade as night came in from the east.

Freya floated, a small hound standing against a pack of wolves.

"They will never agree," Helje muttered. "We are all going to die."

At last, Ivor returned to the rail. He wore a sour expression.

"The commanders of the other boats do not wish to go home and explain why we have killed you all. Though I think doing so because you seek to defend the very people who killed your brother makes a fine reason!"

Hulda, holding her breath, said nothing.

"We will move on. There are some others of us who wanted to raid in Ireland before we turn for home."

Some others. Not him. It had been his idea, his desire to strike here, where Jute had died.

"We will move off," Ivor told her. "But prepare for great dishonor when you reach home."

Still no one behind Hulda spoke a word. The *Freya* held her place, broadside to the shore, while the Norse boats scrambled.

While orders were shouted and they began to move off one by one.

Ivor's boat was the last to leave.

What would her faðir say? What, if Ivor returned to Avoldsborg ahead of them and talked her down?

Faðir would never forgive her.

Yet she had done the right thing, holding to a promise. And her men had stood with her.

Not until Ivor's boat had come about and headed westward, slipping into the lingering light of the day like a dream, did Hulda become aware of a ruckus on the shore. Raised voices, some calling out. Some cheering.

She looked there and saw the man she loved standing.

He had waded out into the water, far out, as if he reached for her. As she watched, he thrust his sword back into its scabbard.

"Take us about," she told Garik. "We will patrol here a while. Make certain they do not return."

"They will not," Garik said. "The other commanders want no part of killing us and taking word of it back home."

"They would far rather take the news that we are traitors," Helje said bitterly.

Hulda turned and faced her men. "Thank you. Thank you all for standing with me. For keeping to the alliance."

"We could not let that bastard get the better of us, could we?" asked Varg, who usually made light of everything.

But mayhap they already had.

CHAPTER FORTY-EIGHT

THEY MET ON the path that led between the settlement and the camping place Quarrie had lent to the Norse visitors. A fitting place, so Quarrie could but think. The two of them came together as if by mutual agreement. As if by inner knowing.

Emotions fought their way up inside him and through him. He had watched what happened out upon the ocean. All the men had watched.

Now, face to face with Hulda, he did not know what to say to her. He wanted to reach for her hands but knew eyes could still be on them, critical eyes even though all the settlement celebrated.

She spoke first. "I told you I would be your hundr and would defend you as best I might."

"We owe much to ye and to your men. How did ye manage it? How did ye turn them awa'?"

"We knew them. The man in the lead boat was Ivor, with whom I sailed here before."

"Was it?" Quarrie grunted. He remembered Ivor all too well.

"Ja. He had come back to avenge Jute, or perhaps he but used that as an excuse to kill and plunder."

"Then I maun thank ye once and thank ye over again."

"I am glad it did not come to a fight. Even with our help, I am not sure you could have defended against so many."

"Ye would ha' stood wi' us?"

"I told Ivor so."

Quarrie lifted his brows. "And your men, would they have gone along wi' that?"

"They are an honorable lot." She smiled wryly. "For Norsemen."

"We will feast them. No' tonight, for we are still holding a strong guard and keeping watch, bringing the women and bairns who fled back into the settlement. But tomorrow. Bring your men and we shall feast them in gratitude all day long."

Dare he hope this might begin a new age between them? A chance, mayhap, for them to be together at some time in the future. Man and woman rather than Scot and Norse.

But Hulda shook her head. "We cannot."

"To be sure, ye will be welcome. We all, there on the shore, saw—"

"And I would be grateful if your people are made aware that it was my men speaking up that convinced the others to turn away."

"So I will—"

"But now"—she raised her voice slightly to speak over him—"my men have decided to go home."

"What?"

"They wish to return home, and after the way they stood behind me, I cannot refuse them."

"Nay, the season is no' over. Hulda, we ha' time yet."

"The season is old. My crew discussed it while we patrolled the waters. They want to reach Avoldsborg before Ivor's ship does so we might ward off some of the harm he intends."

"Harm?"

"He will label us traitors. For seeking to defend those who killed Jute. My faðir will not want to hear it of us. None of their families"—she jerked her head back toward the camp—"will."

"Oh."

It felt like a knife to the gut. But even here in the soft dark— as dark as ever it got at this time of year—he could see the determination in her eyes.

Among other emotions.

He did not know what to say. He could try to persuade her to talk her men round. To keep raiding yet a while and increase the wealth they'd already gained. But what sort of man would he be to unleash a longboat on his fellow countrymen just so he might be with this woman a wee while longer?

A man in love.

The feelings tore through him, and he did not try to hide them from her. She must be able to see all in his eyes.

He had no right to ask her to stay. Only that given by a devoted heart.

He said aloud, hoarsely, "I ha' no right to ask ye to stay."

"Quarrie." Her head came up even as she spoke his name. There was pride in this woman he loved. "I would stay with you if I could."

"Ye could remain behind, lass. Let the rest o' them go home."

Slowly, as if considering it, she shook her head. "I must try to salvage the pieces of my life back in Avoldsborg, before Ivor ruins me. It may not matter to you, who I am there, who I have been, but it does matter to me. I owe explanations to my faðir, whether or not he will accept those explanations. I owe comfort to my móðir."

Something inside Quarrie died. She would leave him. He could scarce believe it. Despite all the troubles and the differences between them, in his heart he had thought she would not be able to do that when it came to it—leave him.

He took a step forward and reached for her hands. A curse upon anyone who watched them and saw. He had to touch her.

"Tell me ye will return. Once ye ha' made your explanations at home and salvaged your reputation."

Her gaze burned on his, even in the dim light. Aye, a thousand things he saw there, the foremost among them regret.

"I cannot come by myself. *Freya* is not mine alone." She wet her lips. "Mayhap in the spring."

The spring? The whole of a winter to get through, then.

Without seeing her, without touching her. Without the promise that ever he would again. He would not survive it.

He drew a breath that snagged against his pain. "Och, Hulda. How d'ye expect me to endure?"

"Quarrie, I do not know how either of us may endure this." She shook her head. And her regret, that same he'd seen in her eyes, swamped him. "I should have known better. From the first, I should. How could it ever end well between us?"

He did not know. He did not know, but at the same time he never could have refuted what existed between them.

"Could ye ha' denied me, lass? Could I ha' denied ye? I knew ye before ever I met ye in this life."

His fingers tightened on hers convulsively. He drew her nearer, defiant of anyone spying upon them.

"It is true," she allowed, "and I will not try to say I ever could have denied what lies between us. Misguided," she added swiftly. "Star-crossed. The product, mayhap, of Loki's twisted intentions."

"Do no' say so. Say, rather, ye will return to me. I care no' how long I ha' to wait. If ye do no' return, Hulda, love, I will find a way to come to ye, if I ha' to search the very earth."

"Do not come to me. Do not try. For you to come to Avoldsborg—it is certain death. And I could not bear—"

Her voice broke despite her hard-held control.

But, Quarrie thought in distress and confusion, he had promised to follow her always, to find her always. Long, long ago he had.

"Not every love is meant," she told him with deliberation. "No matter how beautiful. I am glad—glad I had a chance to know you. But not every tale spun by the bards, or the gods, can be a happy one."

"Tell me but one thing, Hulda. Ye will *try* to return." He could not live, if he did not have that promise.

"I will, ja, try."

He drew her into his arms, wrapped her tight. This might be the last time he held her. The last time he would experience the perfection of having her in his arms, the need answered, her soul coming to anchor alongside his own.

"When?" he whispered. "When do ye go?"

"At first light."

And so, after dreading the sight of sails on the horizon all his life, he would now have to stand and watch one slip off through the morning, knowing it tore away the better part of him.

She murmured against his neck, "I wish I could make you understand. I have obligations to my men. To my family back home. To…to myself. It does not mean I love you one whit less. I cannot imagine loving anyone the way I love you, Quarrie MacMurtray. And ja, I will return to you—if only in some other life. One we cannot yet see."

She drew away from him, pulled out of his arms. At the last, he refused to surrender her hands.

She had tears on her cheeks, this strong and determined woman. She had a world to which she must return, one that did not have any place for him. That, that was what she tried to tell him.

"I will never love anyone as ye, Hulda. And I will wait as long as I must. Till the life after this, if need be. Or the one after that. Aye?"

"Aye," she echoed softly.

He raised her hands to his lips, one after the other. Dropped fervent, burning kisses into the palms. Leaned forward to tenderly kiss either side of her mouth, her cheeks one at a time. Her brow.

Only then did he leave go of her.

"Forgive me," she said, and turned and ran. This woman who scarce ever ran from anything. She ran now from him.

He stood until she disappeared amid the bracken and the darkness, out of his sight.

⚜

CHAPTER FORTY-NINE

Q UARRIE'S KISSES BURNED in the palms of Hulda's hands, on her lips, cheeks, and at her brow. She could still feel them, livid as a brand, when *Freya* moved off northward the next morning out of the narrow slip between the rocks and away.

A beautiful morning for it, and no mistake. The ocean, calm as glass, spread before them in a path lit by morning light. To the west, fair-weather clouds clothed the horizon.

The men were in high spirits. Despite the dubious encounter with their countrymen and the stance they had taken to defend the Scots settlement, one that might very well damage them back home, they were happy to be going. They had gathered their belongings eagerly from the camp where they'd spent most the summer and departed with scarcely a backward look.

To a man, they wanted to reach home before Ivor and his contingent arrived. To brag of their exploits, of which they were justifiably proud, and make their explanations before Ivor could arrive and besmirch them.

As he would no doubt take great pleasure in doing.

Hulda—Hulda was the only member of *Freya*'s crew who did not want to leave. The only one who looked back longingly as *Freya* pulled away under the oar, with no wind at her back.

The others chatted excitedly. Of the wealth they had gained. Of what they would do first when they reached home. No one mentioned what had happened the day before, though Hulda did not for an instant doubt it was on everybody's mind. They may well feel, upon reflection, that they had made a dreadful mistake in standing with her.

Which meant she owed them this, a return home on their terms.

But ach, not until they sailed away from that rocky Scottish shore did she realize what a great and terrible part of her she left behind.

The whole of her heart. Could a woman live without her heart?

He had said he would wait for her. Forever, if need be.

Or till their next life together.

And if such an opportunity did not come? If, ja, they were born into new lives after these ended but in the wide, wide world they never more met one another?

Ach, what had she *done*?

She felt ill, physically as well as emotionally. She'd not expected that, yet spent the best part of their departure at the rail, fighting back nausea.

She had not been nauseated aboard a boat since the age of three.

To comfort herself—and in order to keep drawing breath—she began to imagine ways and means to return. Because now, once away, it seemed evident how vital to her a return would be.

No one could endure such loss, such mortal pain for long.

She, like her crew, had gained some wealth during this season. Not an enormous amount, but sufficient. Enough to allow her to buy out *Freya* from her companions? Nei, they would never part with the aging boat that represented their first venture, and as such held a measure of sentimental value. Could she commission a boat of her own? Nei, she had not the wealth for that, and anyway, she would still need a crew.

This crew, preferably, who were free to make up their own minds.

She paced the deck, and when she came near Garik, he looked up at her. "Hulda? Are you well?"

She was not. Sick to the heart. Sick beyond the heart.

She perched beside him where he sat at the tiller. "Are we doing the right thing going home?" They could still turn back, even though out further among the islands they had picked up a fair wind and the men had shipped their oars.

"Ach, ja, without question." He swept her with another glance before looking away. "You are not so sure?"

"I am not so sure." Could she confide in him? No question but that she felt closest to Garik of all those here. And he already knew some of what she felt for Quarrie.

Quarrie.

Even Garik might not understand that she had pulled her bleeding heart from her chest and left it in the Scotsman's hands.

"You have heard what the men are saying," she said quietly. "Do they regret what happened back there? Standing with me against Ivor?"

He pursed his lips. "I do not know that they regret. You gave them a chance no one else would, and they are loyal hearts. Let us say the ramifications are setting in. Ivor—"

"He is not a man with whom anyone wishes to be at odds."

"He is not. One way or another, he will make us pay."

That statement hung between them.

"I am sorry," Hulda said then.

"Do not be." Garik shrugged. "You are an honest woman. One cannot deny one's own heart."

A longer silence ensued.

"I feel," Hulda said then, "as if Loki has turned his eyes on me. A cruel joke, this is. An irony."

Garik gave her a still more perceptive look. "You had better hope he has not. Do you remember when my sister, Astrid, lay down with that Irish slave to whom she took such a fancy?"

"How could I fail to remember?" A scandal, it had been, and Garik's faðir had wound up ordering the slave killed.

"I remember how my sister looked that autumn, how ill she appeared when she was carrying her lover's child." Garik looked away from Hulda quite deliberately.

"Nei," Hulda breathed. It could not be. Frantically she tried to tot up the days in her mind. When had been her last monthly? Ach, it could not have been that long ago.

Nei, and nei.

"I am only saying, are you sure?" Garik asked.

She could not go home to her faðir carrying potential disgrace and a Scottish child.

And yet how wondrous it would be. She thought of all she and Quarrie had shared together, how surely they had joined.

What if she took something away with her, in exchange for her heart?

BY THE TIME they arrived in Avoldsborg, Hulda was certain she carried Quarrie's child. She had all the signs that she—admittedly vaguely—recalled hearing about from married friends. Sickness in the morning, an aversion to even the smell of food, and bone-deep weariness such as she'd never known.

Loki had indeed turned his eyes upon her. Could there be a more ironic outcome? She, set upon living her life as a man, becoming a móðir. Móðir to a faðirless child.

Nei, but her babe was not faðirless. But so far as her own faðir would be concerned…

The crew was happy to see home, especially as there'd been no sign yet of Ivor or his fleet. They anchored *Freya* in the main harbor and went off to their families, eager to boast of their season and try to smooth the waters ahead of the approaching storm.

To Hulda's surprise, Garik hugged her when they parted. "Will you tell your faðir?"

"Tell him what?" asked Helje, who stood by.

"About our defense of the Scots settlement," Hulda said

quickly. "Ja, sure. I will have to tell him."

Her gaze met Garik's for an instant. "Better perhaps to tell your móðir," he suggested. "Móðirs are often more sympathetic."

Good advice, as Hulda decided when she got home, especially as she found Faðir away at a council meeting.

She thew herself on Móðir's mercy and told her all. Well, nearly all, since there was no real way to explain what she felt for Quarrie.

It did not help to see, as she spoke, the growing horror in Móðir's eyes.

"Ach, Hulda! What have you done? That was most unwise."

"Mayhap so. But Móðir, surely you understand that a woman cannot always choose to whom she loses her heart."

"Her heart!" Móðir had been seated beside the fire when Hulda began her accounting. Now she got to her feet and turned away. "We are surely talking about something far more vulgar. You were tempted. By, of all things, one of *them*."

"Nei, it was not that way."

Móðir stormed on. "I thought when you went off with a boat full of young men, it would be one of them to seduce you. I mean, one woman among so many. Bad enough for you to come home with a Norse babe in your belly." She whirled and eyed Hulda starkly. "But *that?*"

Hulda's throat went dry and her heart began to pound. She had hoped, ja, for some understanding. It seemed she would not receive it.

"My babe will be a babe like to any other." Indeed, despite her best efforts during the voyage home, she'd already begun picturing the child. Male or female, she did not care. Would it have its faðir's eyes? His hair? Ach, by Freya's heart, his smile? Wee freckles on its skin?

A maternal sort of woman or not, she already loved this child near as much as its faðir, if only because it was his.

Móðir, completely out of character, raged on. "Is it not enough we have lost your bróðir? The son of whom your faðir was so proud. Left with a dottir. And now you bring us disgrace."

Disgrace. "Móðir." Hulda tried to calm herself by drawing a breath. "This happens all the time. It is not such a disgrace to come up with a babe outside an official joining."

"Not some…some Scots mongrel! Your faðir will never stand for it. Thanks be to Freya he is not here now." Móðir glared at Hulda, her eyes wild. "There is only one thing to be done."

Hulda, who had also sprung to her feet and now stood trembling, lifted her chin. "What is that?"

"You must go and see old Roskva. At once. At once! Before your faðir finds out."

"Roskva?"

"She will know how to get rid of it. She has—has ways, Hulda."

Hulda believed it. Old Roskva was a witch, a powerful woman among the members of the community. An aged hag of whom Hulda had been terrified when she was young. Perhaps she was terrified of her still.

"I am not about to let her touch me."

"Unfortunate, ja, but you must."

"She will kill my child." *Quarrie's child.*

"Ja. You are very early, so it will not be too bad. Best to take care of it now."

"I am not letting her kill my child." She would, with everything in her, protect this babe. Just as she would have protected its faðir.

"Then what?" Móðir challenged her. "You will not be able to go viking again with a babe at your breast, and no one will agree to look after it for you. If you think your faðir will have it here—"

Cold settled over Hulda, a deep chill that penetrated to the bone.

"I will not allow anyone to harm this child."

Móðir tossed her hands in the air. "Then may Freya help you, dottir. No one else will."

CHAPTER FIFTY

HULDA LAY HUDDLED down in the furs of her sleeping place, a refuge she had known all her life, and waited for the axe to fall.

After her outburst and her condemnation, Móðir had calmed down a little. Offered Hulda something to eat. Told her with some asperity to await her faðir's arrival.

Which was what she did now.

Her mind insisted on chasing itself, running over all the things she had done wrong. The things her society would insist she'd done wrong.

For in truth, she regretted naught of what she'd done. Taking up a sword and begging Jute to teach her how to use it. Sailing with Faðir and, ja, with Jute after. Acquiring her own boat and hiring her own crew.

Falling deep, deep into love with Quarrie MacMurtray.

But that last—ja, it proved she was a woman after all. As did this babe in her belly, the product of their love.

She folded her arms over that belly in a gesture of protection and stared at the wooden slats overhead. She did not see them. Instead she saw a stretch of rocky shore and Quarrie with his hair blowing in the breeze, his gaze fixed on her in that look he gave to her alone.

The other half of her being. Of her heart.

Ach, it must indeed be an act of Loki, all of it. How ironic that she'd left Quarrie only in an effort to repay her crew for their loyalty and mayhap avert some of the disgrace Ivor was likely to level upon them. She'd brought disgrace instead.

What had she done wrong, besides love?

Love the wrong man.

And yet…and yet he was the right man, the one man, the only man. She might live a hundred lifetimes only to find him.

She battled—rightfully or no—because it was the way she was made. She would ask no man to sacrifice his life for her. Better to make her own way.

Only, she could not see a way now. The season drew swiftly to a close. Her crew, even if she could persuade them, would not want to venture out again till spring.

By spring she would be great with child. Able to sail? If so, not a man among them would countenance taking her.

She heard a ruckus at the far end of the longhouse, and voices raised. Faðir was home.

She got to her feet and girded herself for a battle she dared not lose.

SOMETIMES HER FAÐIR listened to her quietly. When she could present a reasoned argument, one that appealed to the practical— or even better, the avaricious—side of him, he might hear her out and even, as when she'd first asked to go viking with him, lay aside his own misgivings in favor of her wishes.

Not so this time.

Móðir had reached him first, getting to him and pouring her version of the tale into his ears as soon as he arrived home. No chance at all for Hulda to apply reason.

By the time she went out to join him and Móðir beside the hearth, he was spitting flame.

Indeed, all the household but Móðir's own serving woman fled. She, at least, had enough loyalty to stay and, having been with Móðir since her marriage, had heard enough arguments to withstand this one.

Hulda shot the woman a look as she joined her parents. Any sympathy there? For ja, Rota would have heard already what this concerned. But Hulda saw no sympathy, only a face kept carefully blank.

"There she is!" Faðir roared as Hulda stepped up. "The dottir who has betrayed me."

How? How had she betrayed him? By loving?

"Faðir," she began steadily, "let us come to terms over this."

"Terms?" His eyebrows jerked up violently. "As if we bargain over plunder? There will be no bargaining, Hulda. Your móðir has told me what you've done."

Hulda drew breath to speak. Before she could, he raged on.

"Bad enough you should come home with a babe in your belly." He made a gesture with his hand, like an axe falling. "But a Scots brat? Nei, and nei. It is not acceptable."

"Yet the child exists." Safe within her. Cherished.

"How could you be so foolish, Hulda? How could you lie down with one of those...*swine*? Did he force you? Tell me he forced you and I will send five longboats back there to take his head."

Hulda went hot and cold in turns, because she knew he meant it. He had the wealth and he had the might. Come spring...

"He did not force me," she said quietly. "I lay down with him because—" Could she mention the word *love* while Faðir ranted at her? "Because I wanted to. As a free woman, I chose to."

"A free woman," he repeated, staring as if he had never seen her before. "You might have the pick of any man, and you choose *that*? I quite see where I have gone wrong."

"Where?"

"I have spoiled you, dottir. Overindulged you. I take responsibility for that, but, by Odin's eye, it will be difficult to hold up my head if that child is born."

"It happens, Faðir. Between our people and slaves—"

"Not in my home! Not to me!"

"I am sorry for bringing you shame. I never meant to." Quite the opposite.

"Who knows of this? Your crew?"

"Only Garik."

"He is a clever lad. He will not speak. The gift of a heavy pouch will assure it."

"You have no need to bribe Garik. He is a friend and loyal to me."

Faðir eyed her. "Will he marry you? Take the brat as his?"

"Nei. I do not want—"

"Hulda, do you not see I no longer care what you want?"

"I do, Faðir, ja."

"That is what got us to this dreadful place. If you will not take Garik for husband—"

"I will not."

"—then I see we have but two choices. I can beat the brat out of you. You are not far along. It should not be difficult."

"Nei." Hulda shifted her feet. She should like to see him try.

"Or you can go to see Roskva, as your móðir has suggested."

Móðir had wasted no time telling him that, had she? Hulda turned accusing eyes on her móðir, who looked away.

"Faðir, I will not do that. I want this child."

"Impossible. Not under my roof."

"Then"—Hulda drew another breath—"I will not remain under your roof."

"And where will you go?"

She did not know. She purely did not. Certainly not to the warriors' quarters where she'd been before, not carrying a child. She might stay a while with a friend, mayhap. Though the disgrace would follow her soon enough.

As if he heard her thoughts, Faðir said, "And how will it remove the disgrace, having you wandering the settlement?"

She must find a way back to Scotland, to Quarrie. But how?

Ach, if she'd known she carried his child, naught could have persuaded her to leave him.

"It will not, and I regret that, Faðir." She repeated, "I never intended to bring shame upon you."

"You should have thought of that before you spread your legs for a Scots savage. Will you go to Roskva?"

"Nei."

"Then get out of my sight."

"I will."

Hulda looked at her móðir, who said nothing. Stiffly she turned and went back to her sleeping place, where she gathered her belongings into a bundle. Clothing. The wealth she had earned. Her weapons she would have to carry separately.

It made a staggering armful, but she wanted to take it all. She would not be coming back here.

"Farewell," she said to the little haven of her childhood, and walked out.

She would not cry. *She would not.* She was too angry to cry. But she did hope at the last, when he saw she meant it, Faðir would change his mind. Call her back.

He did not.

With her belongings clutched in her arms, she stepped out into the wide world. Night had fallen.

Night, and she had nowhere to go.

◆━━━◇◆◇━━━◆

CHAPTER FIFTY-ONE

QUARRIE WAS NO longer himself. He knew that very well. He had become another man, one who was short with his ma and with Borald. Brusque with the other members of the guard. With the folk who, in an ordinary way, came to him.

He carried a load of hurt impossible to bear.

How could he miss her so terribly, a woman he had not known at the beginning of the summer? A woman who now seemed almost like a dream, or would if he did not remember her so well.

He did remember, every detail.

The way she turned her head, the fair hair flying out. The smile in her eyes when she looked at him. The strength of her body, slim and lithe beneath his own. The taste of her on his lips and on his tongue. She haunted him like the tune of some exquisite song.

He still could not believe she had gone from him. That the strength of what lay between them had not kept her close at his heart. The ease and familiarity of it, the sheer comfort—not just of touching her, but of being in her company.

They had been together before in the past times he glimpsed in dreams.

They might not be together again.

He tried to tell himself, as he went through his days biting off the heads of those around him, that at least he'd known her for a while. Better than not at all. But the hurt would not ease. He did not know what to do with such pain.

Danger lay still off shore and over the horizon. The season had not yet ended, and he had to remain vigilant. Keep watch for sails. The Norse who had been raiding farther south must pass by on their way to their home fjords.

Those whom Hulda had sent off could well return.

So, aye, he haunted the walls and the shore, never admitting even to himself that he hoped for a glimpse of *Freya*'s sail. People began to avoid him, if they could. If they could not, they approached him with a caution he hated to see.

This was not him. Patient, he was. Tolerant. Welcoming to those who needed him.

Willing always to put the needs of the clan ahead of his own.

He slept little and walked for hours upon the shore. He hiked to the place where the Norse had camped. He did not know why, for there was little of them there but a few cast-off items and the burned patch where their fire had been.

Once, on a dreary, rainy afternoon, he even trudged up to the half-ruined hut where he and Hulda had been together, and then wished he had not. Because the memories that lingered there were so sweet, immediate, and painful that he could not bear them.

Would she have stayed if things had ended differently? If he had put it to her properly.

Asked her again to be his wife.

Och, and what would the clan have said to that?

Would she have stayed if the threat from the four Norse ships had not existed? She had sacrificed herself for him; he knew that very well. Played the part of the hound, even knowing the hound would have to be off and away after.

At night, in the few short snatches of sleep he did catch, he dreamed of her. Only it was not always her. The women he saw were those of whom he had dreamed before, those who felt like Hulda. Loved him like Hulda. But the love for him shone from different eyes set in other faces.

They were, so he came to accept, the women she had been. Now all lost to him even as she was lost to him.

It made one of the reasons he slept so little.

One morning when he went up on the wall at first light, Borald edged up next to him. The head of the guard had taken up night duty, and Quarrie wondered if he felt as uneasy as Quarrie did.

"All quiet?" Quarrie asked, even though he could see that it was.

Borald eyed him in the way people had begun to do, as if assessing his mood. "Aye, so. And yet"—he narrowed his eyes and flung his gaze out over the sea, which lay smooth as a tarn—"it is not. If ye ken what I mean."

Quarrie did. For days he'd had that feeling, as if something lurked out there unseen. He nodded.

"D'ye think—" Borald hesitated and then asked, "D'ye think they'll come back?"

"The Norse? They always do. We need to be strong enough and ready, when they come."

"I mean that batch. The ones Mistress Hulda helped run off."

"They are awa' to Ireland, eh?" God help the Irish.

"Aye, only—will they stay there?"

A frisson of uneasiness ran up Quarrie's spine. "Ye ha' that feeling, do ye?"

"It has crossed my mind."

"And mine," Quarrie admitted. "If it happens, we will ha' to be prepared to fight. To defend."

Borald shot him another look. All around them, the guard changed, men coming to take the places of those who had been on duty all night. They were as good as alone.

"Chief," Borald said, "is it that, weighing so heavy on ye? The fear that we shall see sails before winter comes?"

The wrong sails, Quarrie thought.

"Or is it her—Mistress Hulda?"

Quarrie turned to his friend. For aye, Borald was that, as well as a trusted defender.

"It matters not," he said. "She is gone."

"There will be other seasons. She may return."

Other seasons. Other lives. Future turns on the wheel of existence that spun them through time.

Hard to wait, to have faith, when his very heart had been torn from him.

He said with no harshness at all, "I maun deal with what is before me, and that is the welfare o' this clan." He gripped Borald's shoulder briefly. "Thank ye for your concern, man."

"I ken fine ye be a braw chief like yer father before ye. But…'tis painful to watch what ye are going through."

"Canna be helped. Thank ye for speaking to me. And if I ha' been difficult—"

"I suppose we are all difficult fro' time to time. We will keep a watch for sails, aye?"

"Aye."

If that conversation was not enough to convince Quarrie he needed to take himself in hand, the one with his ma that came soon after was.

She found him at midafternoon in the armory, assuring himself they had sufficient weapons ready if the worst came, and her breathlessness convinced him she'd spent some effort hunting him down.

"There ye be!"

He looked at her in alarm, as did the young armorer's assistant with whom he'd been counting swords and shields.

"Wha' is it? Sails?"

Ma shook her head. "I wanted a word wi' ye, just. Come, let us walk."

They paced up the shore, one of the old tracks that led to the heights. Long ago, this holding had come to Quarrie's ancestor by marriage, it belonging to the grandfather of a distant ancestress. Well-guarded, it was, over the intervening centuries.

Quarrie knew every rock along this shore. Had run it as a

child. Was prepared to die for it, just like those selfsame ancestors.

"Wha' is it, Ma?"

"People ha' been coming to me, Quarrie. No' wi' complaints," she added quickly before he could speak. "Ne'er that. But wi' concern. They worry for ye, as do I."

Quarrie said nothing. He did not know what to say.

"Is it that woman?" Ma asked. "The Norsewoman?"

Och, and was he that easy to read? First Borald and now Ma. Clear as glass, he must be.

"Does it matter?" he returned. "She is gone."

"And ye walk about here like a man wi' a mortal wound. Quarrie, wha' did it cost ye to see her go?"

"My wounds do no' matter," he told her savagely. "All that matters is the safety o' the clan. Surely Da's sacrifice taught me that."

"Aye, and yet—"

"Hulda's leaving came in exchange for the safety o' the settlement," he told her. And he prayed, even as he paced by his mother's side and sought to reassure her and perhaps himself that the price he and Hulda paid would at least buy the safety of his clan.

It did not, a fact that became evident when sails were sighted beyond Oileán Iur, and not those that in his very soul Quarrie wanted to see.

With a damaged heart, he accepted it and prepared for war.

CHAPTER FIFTY-TWO

WITH NOWHERE ELSE to go, Hulda took refuge on *Freya*. It had the advantage of removing her from the main part of the settlement, the longboat now being anchored back in Frode's small harbor. There she could, perhaps, lick her wounds. Hide for a few days, if she would admit to that desire.

They had returned *Freya* so that the old man could give her a proper overhaul, but he had not yet begun the work, and she stood as she had come in, battered from a season's sailing. By then, Hulda scarcely cared. She stowed her belongings and sought the bed she'd used while aboard, which smelled of salt water and musty furs.

The little bay lay quiet, only a single plume of smoke rising up from Frode's hut. Hulda lay in her cot and stared up at nothing, wishing…

Well, in truth, she did not know for what to wish. That Móðir might have taken her part? That Faðir thought more of his own flesh and blood than his reputation?

That she were lying in Quarrie's arms.

Och, by Freya's heart, he did not know. He did not even know that she carried his child. He might never know that she'd given up her place in her home to preserve that child's life.

How could she do aught else? Their child might well be all she'd ever have of him. A little boy with wavy auburn hair. Or a girl with his laughing, hazel-green eyes. And, mayhap, if Hulda were very lucky, his smile.

How could she willingly lose that precious child in a rush of blood? Bad enough that such things happened accidentally. She had lived most of her life in a rough-and-tumble man's world. She had no way to be sure that her body knew how to bear a child.

It had known how to love a man, though. Ach, ja, it had. How to open itself to the one she adored. Give and give to him. Take him in.

Just the memory of it made her dizzy.

She had grown up aboard boats like *Freya*, and lying in her cot, being rocked by the gentle motion of the bay, should be comforting. Instead, it made her feel ill.

She had to rise and run for the rail, where she vomited and vomited, losing what felt like all she'd taken to eat for days.

And what was she to do? How to exist here, on this vessel, when the weather began to turn bitter? When her belly grew. When the *Freya* was hauled in for repairs.

She had gambled for love, and lost the direction of her life.

The night proved a long one. She was up several times dry-heaving over the side, for she had nothing left in her. Limp as a wet sail, she still half hung over the rail when Frode's son, Bjarni, came down to the shore next morning and stood looking at her.

He soon went away, no doubt to tell Frode she was there. Hulda crawled off to her cot and at last fell asleep.

It was afternoon when she woke, and she felt cold. A stiff breeze battered *Freya* at her anchor and the waves felt rough.

Hulda sat up and clutched at her stomach. Yet another trip to the rail brought up nothing. When she raised her head, dripping and miserable, Frode called to her from the shore.

"Hulda! Girl, what are you doing there?"

She lifted her eyes and looked at him, striving mightily not to look as ill as she felt. What could she say?

"Come ashore," he called. "Have something to eat."

At the thought of food, her stomach commenced a slow roll. But if she did not begin to look after herself, she would do old Roskva's job for her.

"Ja, I will come."

Frode lived with his son in the cluttered hut, little more than a kennel, if truth be told. It did not smell good inside, but Hulda was grateful to be in out of the cold wind.

Bjarni sat by the fire and Frode put Hulda there, then began passing her food while scowling.

"Girl, what are you doing there aboard *Freya*?"

"I was trying to sleep."

"You did sleep." He grunted. "I went aboard to see to you." He examined her without much mercy. "Are you ill?"

"I had to leave home." She looked at the bread in her hands. "I have nowhere else."

"*Freya* needs to be hauled ashore for repairs."

"Ja. Give me a few days. I will gather myself soon."

"I suppose I could give you a few days, ja. Why cannot you go home?"

"I am no longer welcome under my faðir's roof."

"Why?"

"That concerns me alone."

"The same as your writhing at the rail of my good boat concerns you?"

"She is our boat now, and ja, like that."

Frode looked at his son. "If you have finished your breakfast, you can go and sort out those planks from yesterday. Ja?"

Bjarni rose and left without question.

"Eat your breakfast," Frode told Hulda, "if you can. It is sometimes difficult for a woman who is expecting, ja?"

Hulda stared at him in dismay. "I—"

"Do not bother lying to me. It insults both of us. Do you think me a fool? I have seen women who behave like you before."

Hulda went silent.

"Has your faðir tossed you out?"

"Ja."

"Can you turn to the faðir of the babe? Perhaps he will marry you."

If only.

"Nei, I cannot."

Frode fixed her with a discerning eye. "Who is the faðir? Is it young Garik?"

"Nei."

"I must say I am surprised, even though I should not be. Send a woman off with a crew of lusty young men, what will happen?"

"It is none of the crew."

That did shock him. "Who, then?"

"I would rather not say."

He grunted again. "Well, if you cannot turn to the faðir and you cannot turn to a friend—"

"I cannot."

"—neither can you continue to stay upon a boat in the winter harbor. You shall have to stay here with me."

"What?"

"Are you deaf as well as stupid?"

"I am not stupid."

"Are you not? Too stupid to know what happens when a girl lies down with a boy."

"Ja, well—"

"There will be more to the story, I am certain."

"My móðir and my faðir want me to get rid of the child." She had to fight back her emotions. "His child."

"I see."

Hulda glanced around. "I cannot stay here." She did not want to. "There is no room."

"We will make room. It is warm. You will help with work on *Freya*. Your child, ja, will be born with skill in his fingers."

"Or hers."

She could not stay here. Not for the whole winter. Mayhap, though, a little while.

"Frode, it is kind of you."

"Is it?"

"I can pay my way."

"I do not want pay. I had a dottir once."

"Did you?" She had not known he had even a wife, though since he had a son…

"She died. But if my dottir had come home to me with a brat in her belly, I would not have thrown her out. Do you know why?"

"Why?"

"That child would still be partly mine."

Hulda found she had tears in her eyes.

"Now eat and drink something, else you will be in far more trouble than you need to be. If you want to keep that babe, you will take care of yourself."

She wanted to keep the babe. Resolute, she choked down her bread and ale.

CHAPTER FIFTY-THREE

WHEN MEMBERS OF the crew began to arrive the next morning, being young men and easily bored once back upon their home shore, Frode told Hulda she would have to be truthful with them.

"It is not a thing that can be hid, girl."

"It is, for a time."

"And how will they feel if they suppose you do not trust them enough to say?"

"Garik knows."

"Tell the others, then."

Hulda dragged her feet on it. She still did not feel well and had spent an uneasy night in the corner of the hut, listening to the old man and his son snore in tandem.

She could not face her crew, from whom she wanted respect. She had commanded them for the season, acting as a man would, and did not want their image of her to change.

As it must, if she began bursting with child. Quarrie's child.

The men decided to help Frode drag *Freya* up on the shore, and then most lingered to help with repairs. She was their boat and they felt possessive.

Many of them had sore heads, having spent much time in the ale hall, talking up their exploits.

Hulda asked Helje, "Has Ivor arrived back yet?"

"Nei, not yet." Did his gaze avoid hers? "But I do not doubt he will be back soon enough. And then…"

And then it would all come out. How Freya had stood between Ivor's boats and the rich prize of the settlement at Murtray.

She had wanted to make explanations to her faðir first. Not that there were any explanations that could truly satisfy him.

"I was thinking," Helje said, "if we claim we have an interest there—a holding or a part in one—then surely the others will understand why we defended it."

"You think so?" She sought his eyes. Helje had never been a friend to her like his brother. But during the voyage, they had come to a steady liking.

He shrugged. "Who can tell? It is a rich prize to have a share in such a holding."

It would be indeed, but what was he saying to her? That he would consider going back?

Going back.

"I also heard," he went on, "back in the settlement, that your faðir has cast you out."

"Who told you that?"

"No one told. Word gets around."

The servants, no doubt.

She turned her gaze away from him and narrowed it on *Freya.* "It is true. He will not have me there because I am carrying a child, one of which I refuse to rid myself."

That did surprise him. She heard his gasp, swiftly muffled. So, Garik had not speculated to his brother.

"I see. But—" Helje's wits were anything but slow. "Not the chief there!"

"What makes you guess that?"

"It wasn't one of us. And—I saw the way he looked at you. The way you looked at him. What will you do?"

"Stay here for now. Keep my child."

"Ja, you are a strong woman. I do not know another who stands on her two feet like you and is willing to fight. But it is not easy with a small child. How to leave it behind when you want to go viking?"

"I do not know."

"Does he know, this chief back in Scotland?"

Hulda shook her head. "I did not realize before I left, to tell him."

"Well, it is a perilous course you set."

It was, and by the end of the day Hulda decided to call together the members of the crew left on the shore and make her announcement.

"I need to tell you all, I am carrying a child. Since my faðir does not want me to shame him, he has asked me to leave his house."

They met her news with sharp stares, as if it had never occurred to most of them that she was a woman.

She did not name the father of her child. If that got out, so be it. Since she saw them with their heads together and whispering after, she figured it might.

Had they been older men, experienced and less biddable, they might not have accepted it so readily. These men did accept it, shrugged it off, and continued to treat her thereafter much the same as always.

And yet things were not the same. Though she was grateful to Frode for a roof, she did not like living with him. The sea beckoned to her, and the far distances.

Quarrie did.

But even if she could go back, *Freya* lay up on the shore. And the season swiftly drew to a hard close.

AFTER A FORTNIGHT, the babe had settled down inside Hulda and decided to thrive. Food went down more easily, and she did not feel quite so tired. The work on *Freya* helped. She hated having idle hands, which allowed her mind too much room to run. Better to feel she accomplished *something*.

She did not venture back to the main settlement, but to be sure, word came from there. Ivor's ships had not yet returned, which made her uneasy. Ja, he had gone to raid in Ireland.

Or so he'd said.

Once the idea was in her mind, she would not let go of it. She and *Freya* had acted the part of the hundr and chased the wolf away. Once the hundr had gone, would the wolf return?

If so, she had to trust in the man she loved. Quarrie was a careful leader of a strong settlement.

Ivor was a monster. At least, he could be when he attacked. The kind of man who showed no mercy in victory, he would *destroy* for the sake of it.

And he wanted, still, revenge for Jute's death. At least, that was the banner under which he flew. In truth, he might kill for the sake of it.

Whenever Hulda thought on that, she grew sick to the heart, so she tried to thrust it away. But nei, it refused to be gone.

One afternoon, when a sky that looked more winter than autumn loomed over Frode's little bay, Garik came to her. *Freya* neared the end of her repairs, but Hulda would not let herself think of that either. To sail, she needed a crew.

Garik took the place at her side where she stood staring out over the sea.

"There is a boat," he said.

"Eh?" That surprised her enough that she stared at him.

"It is poor and small and battered, but Frode insists it is seaworthy, and I think the owner will sell it to us."

"We have a boat." Helda gestured to *Freya*, unnecessarily.

"But the *Fenris* is already in the water. We could leave at once."

Hulda's heart leaped. "We?"

"It is a small boat, as I say. More an overgrown færing than anything else. I think you, me, and Helje could sail."

Hulda gaped at him in astonishment. "What are you saying?"

He turned to face her, his eyes bright. "I am worried. Ivor has still not brought back his fleet. In my bones, I am afraid—"

"He has returned to attack Murtray."

"Ja."

Hulda lifted a brow. "And this worries you so—why?"

"Morag is there. I care for her."

Oh.

"And I seem… I seem to have put down some roots. I do not know if a girl like Morag would consent to marry me—"

"Ach, Garik!"

"—but I am willing to go back and ask her."

"Ja. Ja!"

"Can you sail? Are you too ill?"

"I can sail. But even if Helje agrees to come with us, what good are three swords against Ivor and all his men?"

"I do not know." The words came heavy with regret. "I have wrestled with it in my mind. It comes to me that I need to try. For if Ivor does come home bragging about having sacked the settlement, if I think of that young woman perhaps attacked or killed by Ivor's wolves, and I have done nothing to prevent it—"

"Ja," Hulda said again, softly. "The heart wants what it wants." She studied her friend. "Will your brother agree to go?"

"He is eager to do so. He does not like Ivor Larsson."

"If we buy this wreck of a boat, it will use up most of what we earned."

Garik shrugged. "What are riches for, if not spending?"

They put the matter to Frode soon after, who looked dubious.

"*Freya* is nearly finished," he told them. "If the three of you help us with her, we can have her back in the water in no time."

"We cannot sail *Freya* without a crew," Hulda protested.

"You have a crew, foolish girl."

"Not one willing to return south now."

"You help me, and we shall see."

Frode put them to work, Hulda laboring hard despite her condition. As the day progressed, two miraculous things happened—gifts from Freya herself, they might have been. She began to feel hopeful, the occupation of her hands perhaps lifting the uncertainty from her mind. And slowly, slowly, the members of their crew drifted into the bay. They came one by one, or two together, bored young men with one season's sail behind them. At first Hulda thought they came out of curiosity or just to visit. But Frode assigned them all jobs and they fell to working.

Garik, looking as surprised as Hulda felt, went about speaking to them. He soon gestured to Hulda.

"The crew," he told her, not wasting words, "is reporting to sail."

"What?"

Hulda looked around at the men. They gathered in a ring around her and Garik, looking at her seriously.

"You are all willing to sail—now?"

"Well," Varg quipped, "just as soon as *Freya* is back in the water."

"We figure if we put all hands to it," Brynjar added, "we can get her out on tomorrow's tide."

"Staying in port is boring," Helje added, making an exaggerated face.

"But—" Hulda struggled with her emotions. "We do not go to raid or to gain wealth. This is something far different."

"My sword," said Helje shortly, "thirsts for Ivor's blood."

"You gave us a chance," said Brynjar, "when no one else would. If you need us now, well—then we are here."

"I need you now. And I am grateful."

"By Odin's eye," one of them teased, "do not start weeping. Or how can we follow you?"

"Get to work," Frode ordered them brusquely. And they did.

CHAPTER FIFTY-FOUR

THE NORSE FLEET of four ships—for Quarrie no longer doubted they were the same boats that Hulda and her crew had helped chase away—had decided to play games with him. Late in the season as it was, and vile as the weather looked to turn, they set up a game of hide-and-seek among the offshore islands, allowing the watchers in the settlement to get glimpses of them and then moving off again.

They might show but one sail, or two. The four of them might sail past at a distance and away again, only to circle back around. Like wolves around a wounded hart, or sharks in the water scenting blood.

He was angry, the Norse commander, or so Quarrie decided. At the very least, frustrated at being turned away by Hulda and her crew. He had wanted revenge, had the man called Ivor. Remembering his own encounter with Ivor while being held captive, Quarrie knew him for a man with little mercy. Here at the end of the year, he meant to have the revenge he'd been denied.

Did Ivor know that the *Freya* had gone home to the north? Did the first few passes seek to draw her out, if yet she lingered?

Quarrie did not know. But the presence of the Norse ships out among the islands played havoc with the settlement. Men who watched from the walls and the shore were continually at fever pitch. And the women waited by the day for orders to take their children off and away to the wild hills. Not hospitable places at this time of year.

All Quarrie knew was that if this group of four longboats attacked, it would be a battle for the ages. The kind of which bards would sing in the halls, someday.

If they survived.

The strain began to show on everyone. Men were grim and silent and women wept if anyone looked at them the wrong way. Quarrie barely slept. When he was not on the walls keeping watch, he was organizing weapons or in hastily called, panic-filled meetings with his advisors.

His longing for Hulda became a wound at his heart, and that, even though he could spare less heed to it, refused to heal.

"It would almost be better," Borald said to him once, "if they would just attack and get it over."

"Do no' say that." Quarrie had seen such battles. It sometimes seemed he'd been born with the dread of them. The clash of weapons. Dead strewn upon the shore. The smell of burning in the air. The separate, individual battles on which such an attack could turn.

It could go either way. He could not be sure they would prove victorious.

"Aye, but," Borald told him, "the waiting is killing us all. What *are* they waiting for?"

The weather, mayhap. For aye, it had been wicked with cold winds and snarling rains in which a man would be fortunate to see his opponent. Quarrie figured if they got a bonny day…

Blood would flow.

So, must he be grateful for the bad weather? Not easy to be glad of the things that hurt. Even if they were intended to provide protection.

One morning when the sun refused to rise and clouds raked the sky just as dark combers raked the shore, Quarrie's ma came up on the walls—something she had not done of late, seeming prepared to leave that to her men.

Now she stared out at a world that, if one believed in such

things, looked like end times, and said, "Son, I ha' a bad feeling in my bones."

Borald stood close by—Quarrie had just been speaking with him—as did other members of the guard, the walls always being crowded these days despite the weather.

They all gazed at her.

"Wha' sort o' feeling, Ma?" Quarrie asked. Foolishly, for he knew.

She frowned at the scene before her. Rain danced on the far ocean and the wind blew her hair out in a banner. She looked fey and almost like the girl she must once have been.

"I think I should send the women awa'. And the bairns." For she had been in charge of preparing them. "I think, despite the weather, the attackers will come."

"Tired o' the waiting?" Borald suggested, and all Quarrie's uncertainty hardened to iron.

"Aye, Ma. Send them awa'. Borald, circulate word to the men—"

Quarrie stopped because a sail had appeared out beyond Oileán Iur, black against the deep gray sky.

"Go," he shouted. "Go."

THERE WOULD BE no talking, no negotiating. This, Quarrie knew. No discussion with the men on those four longboats that sailed so inexorably around the island and headed for shore. There would be only raised swords and axes. Death.

He had to trust that Ma would get the women away. Already she ran down the stairs at a pace that terrified him. He had no time to spare a thought for her falling.

"A line on the shore," he told Borald as they also ran, even though they had talked over a defense more times than he could count. "Another at the gate. The last here, on the walls." He turned in flight and engaged his captain's eye. "I want ye at the gate. Do no' let them in."

"But ye—"

"I will be on the shore."

"Aye." Borald reached out and clasped Quarrie's arm. "Promise me ye will fall back to the gate, if hard pressed."

"Aye, so." If that happened, they would be at least half beaten.

Hastily, in the guards' room just inside the main gate, Quarrie donned armor and took up his weapons. A knife in his boot. A long knife in the loop at his belt. His sword.

Men streamed in from everywhere, a fair tide of them, and they gathered on the rocks of the shore in a ragged line to watch the Norse boats come in.

Come in they did. They made a fantastical sight under that lowering sky, like four dragons sailing out from eternity. Almost serene, they looked. And strong, so strong.

Quarrie should have known their commander would have grown tired of waiting. If waiting had been difficult for those in the settlement, only imagine fighting men confined to narrow ships in bad weather. This attack had come born of the impatience that was mankind.

If he died here—

He tried to close his mind to that, though it was a thought that tended to press in at such a time. He could hear the men murmuring all around him.

How many would survive?

The Norse flowed over the sides of the longboats and onto the shore as if they were part of the dark water itself, seething in. Men, and men, and men, more than Quarrie could count. Indeed, his mind stuttered, and he set himself to meet what must come with a single thought.

Let none pass to harm what I love.

With the first sword he met—belonging to a tall warrior in good armor with a sneer on his face—an old knowledge flooded up through him. From whence it came he could not say, but it instantly became part of his bone and sinew, not bidden by any conscious intention.

He was a warrior. Had always been.

They fought. The Norse came in bellowing and the Scots screamed back at them. Wild, indistinguishable cries, they were, that made no sense but nevertheless spoke of courage. Of defiance. Of death.

He had committed the bulk of his men to this stand upon the shore. Though he was aware of little beyond the battle with the man who faced him and the man after him, and the next, he thought others of his defenders had disobeyed him. They—and Borald—had run down from the gate to join this fight.

If they could not win it here…

There were too many attackers. That truth came to him inevitably even as he and his fellows beat back the onslaught. As he killed, wounded, and maimed. His companions fell also—both of those on either side of him did. And as the Norse fell back, others came through the water to replace them.

A few got past the line of defenders. As men fell, there were gaps in the line. Quarrie himself whirled to take a couple of those attackers down. Others were cut down by the men who remained at the gate.

The air vibrated with the crash of metal against metal. With screams and cries. His ears full, Quarrie could not think, only react.

It rained.

But nay, that was not an apt enough word for what came. The dark skies parted and water crashed down. He could scarce see his opponents.

The Norse withdrew. They went much as they had come, pulling back like an evil tide, taking their wounded but not their dead. It came to Quarrie that he might live a while longer.

Someone shouted at him, words he could not hear. He turned to see Borald, wet to the skin. On some level, he was glad to see his man still alive.

"Do ye think they are done?" Borald bellowed at him.

"Nay." Quarrie did not.

Like rats disappearing into a hole in a stone wall, the Norse had gone. The Scots moved about through the rain to gather their own wounded, putting to the dirk what Norse lingerers had been missed.

All but one man, who stared up at Quarrie with fierce blue eyes.

"Bring him," he told his men.

"Are ye hurt?" Borald yelled at Quarrie when they reached the gate.

Quarrie did not know. The rain had washed away any blood.

No doubt, though, that he was.

THEY WERE WOUNDED, all of them. In the great hall where they gathered, the healers scrambled trying to determine the worst of them to be tended first. Two men died under the healers' hands.

Quarrie was dismayed to discover his ma had not gone off with the other women, as planned.

"I sent them," she told him while she herself tended his wounds—numerous cuts to his arms, his knuckles laid open. A slice to one leg that he hoped would not hamper him if they had to fight again. *When* they had to fight again. A long slash to his chest, right through his armor, that hurt when he breathed.

An axe had done that. If not for his chest plate, he would be dead.

Do ye think they will pull off? It was the question on every side. *Do ye think they have had enough?*

Quarrie doubted it. He kept an ear peeled over the rain for a cry from the walls where the men still kept watch.

When he met up with Borald, the hall being filled only with

groans, he said, "Let us ask the prisoner."

The man was being held in a stone shed, well-guarded by some of the older men, and had not had his grievous wounds tended. He sneered up at Quarrie and Borald when they went in, looking more a maddened beast than a man.

"What is your name?" Quarrie asked.

"Loki take you," the man replied in broken Gaelic.

"Wha' is your commander's name?"

The man—large, fair-haired, and covered in blood—spat at him.

Borald bent and laid the blade of his dirk to the prisoner's throat. "Ye will answer the chief."

"Chief?" The man's half-crazed eyes focused on Quarrie. "Are you the one who killed Jute?"

Ah, so Ivor's men *had* returned to avenge Hulda's brother. Och, but he must have been as well liked by the men as by his sister. All at once, Quarrie could almost feel Hulda beside him.

"Is that what this is about?" he asked the man. "Your commander wants vengeance?"

The man bared his teeth. "You do not deserve to live."

"Will the attack resume?"

The man did not answer, but Quarrie already knew.

It would resume. And battered as they were, they would need to stand and defend.

$$\text{\textasciitilde}\diamond\text{\textasciitilde}$$

CHAPTER FIFTY-FIVE

"I WORRY FOR the women and bairns up in the hills," Ma said fretfully, pacing the floor of what had been her husband's private quarters at the rear of the hall, "in this vile weather."

At least the women and bairns were alive—for now. More than could likely be said for the rest of them, when the attack resumed.

Night had fallen, an uneasy night during which few slept. Many were awake nursing their wounds. The rain had let up, and when morning came…

When morning came the Norse would attack, and hard. Quarrie could feel it at the root of his soul.

The warrior in him knew.

He turned to his mother. "Ma, why d'ye no' go and join the women? There is time. Before morning."

"Nay."

"They need your guidance, your leadership."

They would need her strength when they returned after tomorrow's battle to find what they would find. Their men dead, their houses burned—if he, their chief, did not fight hard enough.

She turned and looked him in the eye. "Nay."

"Ma, they look to ye. If—Ye must lead them to Chief Radoch at Dunbeg. He will give ye refuge, and since they are farther inland—"

She gasped. "Ye think we will fall to defeat!"

"I do not. I canna tell what will happen." He had spent half the night totting up numbers in his head. How many wounded. How many dead—people all that he knew and liked. How many warriors he thought the Norse had left.

Ivor wanted revenge. He would not quit.

"You expect me to go off not knowing if ye live or die? Having already lost your da?" To Quarrie's surprise, his ma pulled him into her arms, a fierce embrace. "I canna."

He cradled her tenderly. "Ma, if the keep does fall, ye will no' stand a chance. Ye ken fine what the Norse do to female captives."

"The keep will no' fall."

Quarrie wished he could be so certain.

"Meanwhile, I can tend the wounded. All hands are needed there. Mayhap some o' them might return to fight. Son, let me battle in my own way."

What could he say to that?

Borald came to him soon after first light to report that the Norse prisoner had died, and the longboats were on the move.

They had withdrawn under cover of the rain back to Oileán Iur, but by the time Quarrie reached the walls, they rounded it with that almost otherworldly grace they possessed.

Above them, the sky cleared slowly, dark clouds splitting upon pale blue.

It would all end here, today.

URGENCY CREPT UP through Hulda's body in a steady progression, increasing as they skirted the Scottish coast and slipped through the offshore islands. The weather had been vile and the voyage a difficult one. She wondered if her crew regretted their hasty decision to back her.

But they were young men with more eagerness for adventure than good sense. Moreover, they looked upon most everything as a jaunt. The time spent at home had bored them. Though they cursed the bad weather, their spirits remained high.

The babe inside her—Quarrie's babe—had settled in her belly and no longer caused her such sickness, even aboard ship. She'd been able to eat her breakfast this day that would end…only Faðir Odin knew how.

Would she see her love? Would he welcome her with open arms?

The morning was a gloomy one, heavy with cloud, but at least the vicious rain had stopped. Hulda held a place beside Garik at the tiller, but as they passed Oileán Iur, she started forward, the better to see.

It appeared before her eyes like something unveiled in a dream. The settlement huddled there above the rocks of the shore, looking stark in that ugly morning light. The four longboats—all of which she recognized—ranged in the water, and the mass of men fighting on the shore were engaged in dire struggle.

The men around her began to exclaim. But Hulda, assailed by horror, fell into what she could only call a vision of the past, a waking dream.

She approached the holding from the sea, ja, only she rode in a tiny boat, one propelled by the oars of the man she—

Loved.

Ja, Quarrie was here on this shore, anchored soundly to her heart, and ja, she carried his child. But they were together also in this vision, in this leaf of a boat on the water. The settlement she saw in the vision appeared much different, smaller, but it was the same stretch of coastline. Her lover's place. His home under attack.

Seeing it doubly, then and now, she knew the outcome. They would put ashore. He would go to fight. She risked losing him.

What manner of woman must she be to deserve the risk of losing him again and again?

"Hulda? Hulda!" Someone shouted in her ear, taking her out

of the vision that left her weak with misgiving.

Helje stood beside her, bawling. "It is Ivor! What do you want to do?"

Fight for him. As he had fought for her, life after life.

From the shattered pieces of her past, she reached for sanity. "Put ashore in our old harbor."

She was no longer a helpless girl. If he fought, she would stand to fight beside him.

Helje called the order to Garik, who gave a yell. They turned to the shore.

Hulda faced her men. "I will go to fight with Quarrie Mac-Murtray. For all of you who do not know—he is the faðir of the child I carry. The rest of you, I understand this is not your battle. You may wait in the bay or leave me here and sail off. It is yours to choose."

The deck of *Freya* grew silent so they could hear clearly the clamor of battle, the cries of men dying on the shore.

Then Varg said, "The battle does not look to be going well for the Scots. Ivor and his warriors press them hard."

"Then MacMurtray will possess one more sword. Mine."

Garik called out, "I have never much liked that Ivor, me. He is a snake."

"And his crew," Brynjar added, "forever looking down on us."

"A score of swords," called Varg, "will do more good than but one."

"I am up for a battle," Helje declared. "And mayhap we can earn a berth here for ourselves."

"Then put ashore," Hulda told them, "and we will go."

Surely this too was familiar? Surely the tiny boat had come ashore, long, long ago, at nearly this same place, with the clamor of desperate battle echoing over the rocks, turning her stomach sick with dread. She had crept through bracken and gorse in this same way, on the tracks of her lover.

Who had gone to fight. To die?

Now they went in a silent mob, not just herself, who had been alone but for the gray hound at her side. The ghost of the hound seemed to accompany her now, as it had in the past.

Quarrie might already be dead.

That did not occur to her until their group paused amid the rocks to eye the battle. Ja, and fierce it was.

Most of Ivor's men had come ashore. Hulda could see but a skeleton crew on the four boats, one of which appeared to be afire.

Fighting was intense on the shore and up the rise to the keep. Once again, Hulda's view flickered. The stone keep disappeared, replaced by a sturdy roundhouse where men fought at the very door. Where her love fought.

Was he there now?

Ach, but the roundhouse flickered in turn and stood there no longer. Now there was a gate, one being stormed by Ivor's men. Indeed, she thought she could see Ivor there, his dark hair flying as he struck, and struck.

The old events, the place, the people, all came round again and again as if borne upon the rim of a wheel, until the lessons were learned.

What was she meant to learn?

No time to wonder now. The men around her were muttering.

"Where?"

"Hulda, where do you want us?"

"At the gate. Ivor is there. But we do not want to be cut down as attackers. When you go in, cry *Murtray*. Murtray! Do you understand?"

In a howling mob, they ran.

THE BATTLE HAD not gone well. The four longboats had swooped in soon after dawn, the Norsemen once more pouring over the sides like a dark tide. Quarrie thought his defenders were ready. He had a stand of archers on the rise, and they took out a number of the attackers as they hit the rocks of the shingle. But once the fighting there became hand to hand, it was too risky to shoot.

They fired on the longboats instead.

Aye, at first Quarrie thought they were holding their own. Keeping the battle to the shore, cutting the invaders down. He saw Borald wounded—along with far too many others of his men—but his captain fought on.

It emerged, however, that the Norse commander had not yet brought all of his men ashore.

The second wave, when they came over the sides of the longboats, drove the defenders back from the shore. Up the rise, fighting and dying every step of the way.

Now Quarrie and what was left of his defenders stood at the very gate. Behind him, more Murtray warriors stood ready to keep the Norse out, if he fell. Others occupied the walls, firing down what arrows they could aim with accuracy.

One of the Norse boats was aflame, struck with burning arrows earlier. Quarrie just hoped those ships had no more warriors to vomit up.

His back to the gate, he had his eye on the Norse leader, prominent in the knot of howling men that faced him. Aye, the very man he recognized from the deck of the longboat where he'd been held captive.

Ivor.

The brown-haired Norseman had wanted to kill him before Hulda put him over the side of the longboat. Had wanted revenge for Jute's death.

He did still.

By the way he fixed his half-maddened gaze on Quarrie, he wanted to be the man to kill him.

Mayhap he would.

And if Quarrie died here, if he spent his life with his back pressed against the oaken boards of the gate—it would be well worth it, so long as these savages did not gain admittance. Surely he had been born to defend this place. A warrior's ancient skill flowed through his veins. So long as he killed that bastard who wanted his head before he died.

But that meant he would never see Hulda again.

Borald, bleeding heavily yet still fighting beside him, gasped desperately, "Chief, I donna think the gate will hold."

The Norse came at them with axes. The damage they could do to wood—and to flesh—was prodigious.

Quarrie pushed forward. "Fall back," he told Borald. "Behind me. If I fall, do no' let them in."

That was when he thought he saw Hulda. A vision surely, a gift here before he died.

She appeared like a warrior, all in her armor, pale braids flying. She came with a group of others, attacking the Norse from behind, a single cry tearing from their throats.

Murtray!

There amid the fighting, Quarrie's gaze met hers. And time itself stood still.

CHAPTER FIFTY-SIX

A S SOON AS Hulda saw Quarrie there among the defenders at
the gate, her mind narrowed to a single thought and a single
intention. He was hers. Hers to save. She did not think then of the
past or even the babe inside her, whom she, ja, did risk. Only of
standing at her lover's side. Of fighting with him.

For one glorious moment, their eyes met. Then, with an
unlikely war cry tearing from their throats, her impetuous young
warriors went to the slaughter.

It might never have happened with any other group of warriors, at any other time. But these men—like herself—had stored a
measure of resentment. Had been kicked aside too often. Felt,
mayhap, a measure of belonging to this land upon which they
now stood.

Or perhaps all that was too high flown. Mayhap they just
liked to fight.

It was brisk, bold, and bloody. Half the attacking Norse
turned to face the new peril come upon them. Others ran up
from the shore, and for an instant Hulda feared her men,
intending to pinch the Norse, would themselves be caught.

But Ivor's men were weary, as were the Murtray defenders.
She could see the exhaustion in Ivor's face when he swung away
from the gate to face her.

"Me!" she screamed at him. "Fight me!" *Me, and not Quarrie.*

Ivor recognized her. She saw surprise bloom in his eyes before his gaze narrowed and an ugly sneer twisted his features.

He turned back to Quarrie, his intentions as clear as his disdain for the woman facing him. He would kill Quarrie and have his revenge at any cost.

Hulda thought later—much later, when she could again think at all—that Quarrie could quite likely have taken Ivor. Ja, he was weary, and she had noted the blood that marked him. But he was a fine warrior, the man she loved. Equal to the task.

Her entire spirit cried that he should not fight alone.

She did not consciously raise the sword in her hand. Her arm moved of its own accord even as she screamed Ivor's name so he swung back toward her. The blade took Ivor through the chest where the fabric of his armor was already split, between the ribs and through his lung. He fell like a man going down in pieces, knees buckling, legs failing him, torso crumpling, arms flying out.

Hulda and Quarrie gazed at one another across the fallen man, and for that one instant, the clamor of battle did not exist. The two of them might as well have been alone.

Hulda stumbled forward over Ivor's body and into Quarrie's arms.

No longer a man and a woman. No longer two warriors battling separately or for one another, but one being, riding upon the wheel of time.

And when the immediacy of the battle did return, the clatter and the fury of it, Hulda's young Norsemen took down the last of Ivor's men. On the shore lay only dead and dying. The burning ship made a torch upon the water.

A fitting funeral pyre, mayhap, for what had been and would not be again.

"Hulda," Quarrie yelled, clearly half deafened by the din. "Hulda, how come ye here? Like a miracle."

His voice sounded hoarse, and a terrible wound marked one cheek. He looked wondrous. The most beautiful sight she had ever seen.

"Love brought me," she replied. "Only love."

IT TOOK DAYS to sort out the dead and dying, to treat the wounded and burn or decently bury the rest, to deal with Norse prisoners, the few that survived the Scots' swords.

One of the three remaining Norse ships was sacrificed for the Norse dead, a ceremony attended by only Hulda and her men. The other two—fine ships, they were—were taken as spoils of war, granted to Helje and Garik.

Meetings were held, a certain measure of thanks offered to Hulda and her warriors, after the Scots women came home. Leave granted for the band of Norse to winter at Murtray, if they chose.

Hulda had a glorious glimpse on one chilly afternoon of Garik with his lass in his arms. Enough of what she saw pass between the two convinced her that, ja, Morag was his lass.

The others of her men—well, a curious sort of thing happened there also, one she might never have imagined when this season of raiding began. Her young warriors, who had bloodied their swords on the Scots' behalf, were accepted there in the settlement. At leave to come and go as they would. Hulda saw various members of her crew speaking to Quarrie's clan members, both Norse and Scot doing their best to communicate and understand one another. Laughing together once or twice. Her men eyeing the Scots lasses, and the young clanswomen, some of them, returning the favor.

A few, including Garik, moved into the settlement. The rest returned to their old grounds, where *Freya* remained anchored.

As for Hulda and Quarrie…

Well, she slept in his quarters, in his arms, the night after that great battle at the gate. And from that day forward, she rarely slept anywhere else.

For all that, it took days before they could work separately and together through all the tasks to be done—the women and children coming home and being resettled, the reunions, the grieving, the resumption of anything approaching ordinary life. It took that long for Hulda to tell Quarrie the rest of her news.

She'd barely shared with him how and why she'd returned to Scotland. He'd asked her only whether she meant to stay with him, and she'd promised she would. But not till one morning a sennight after the battle, when they woke together, was there peace enough for her to roll over in his bed and gaze into his eyes.

"Quarrie."

"Hulda."

Only that, to begin. A beginning and an end, the two of them claiming one another.

A smile came to his eyes and then fled, as he became serious. "It fair terrified me, lass, when I saw ye there amid that battle. Terrified me that ye would risk yoursel' for my sake. Promise ye will no' do that again."

"I cannot give you that promise." Slowly she shook her head. He would be more terrified still, if he knew she'd carried his child into that battle. "Ást min, I will fight for you always. For you, and the part of you that rests inside me."

She saw by the widening of his eyes that he took her meaning. His lips parted. "Ye—D'ye say ye carry my child?"

"Ja. An heir for you, mayhap. Or a valiant lass."

"Is that why ye returned?"

"I returned because I find I cannot be happy—can barely draw breath—away from you. Quarrie, promise me something. If it is true we have known each other before in lives gone by, and may so meet again in some future, pledge you will never more return to me as a warrior. You may return—ja, you *must* return—as anything else: a healer, a harper, a fisherman, I do not care what. But promise me it will not be as a warrior. For my heart cannot bear the risk of losing you."

Now it was he who gave her a smile and shook his head. "Can we choose who or what we are?"

"Mayhap we can, if we try."

He caught her hands in his. Dropped kisses into each palm, at both corners of her mouth and on each cheek. He blessed her with a kiss on her brow.

"One promise to ye I will make. That is, I will always, *always* return to ye."

THE GREAT HALL falls silent as Finlay's words rise like the sparks from the fire and fly away upward. A shimmer of notes from his harp follows as his nimble fingers dance, and he tells his listening audience, "So ye see, we are Scot, Norse, we are Pict—we are, more than aught else, our ancestors, whom we carry inside us. We are the very pieces of Scotland brought together by memory—and longing. So do we return again and again. He is here still, our hero, and so is she."

Once more, his gaze searches out but one of his listeners, the young woman who now watches him with bemusement in her eyes.

"Can a love such as Quarrie and Hulda shared endure through the ages?"

A glissando of notes flows from his fingers, as ancient as being. As eternal as the love of which he speaks.

"Aye," he answers his own question, "I believe it can."

THE END

About the Author

Laura Strickland delights in time traveling to the past and weaving deliciously romantic stories for her readers. Her first love has always been Scottish Historical Romance, and her work has garnered her several awards including a RONE. At home in Western New York, she's been privileged to mother a number of very special rescue dogs. Her lifelong interest in Celtic history, magic, and music, along with her mantra of *Lore, Legend, Love* are all reflected in her writing.

Visit Laura at www.laurastricklandbooks.com

www.ingramcontent.com/pod-product-compliance
Lightning Source LLC
Chambersburg PA
CBHW071234300726
48975CB00002B/410